WIND STORM

By
Marlow Kelly

COPYRIGHT

Wind Storm
Published by Viceroy Press

COPYRIGHT 2020 by Marlow Kelly

ISBN 978-1-9991430-2-2

Cover art by Melody Simmons

EBook Indie Covers
https://ebookindiecovers.com

Edited by Corinne Demaagd
From CMD Writing and Editing
https://cmdediting.com

For news of Marlow's next release
sign up for Marlow's Newsletter at:
www.marlowkelly.com

DEDICATION

To
All the essential workers who are caring for
us during the COVID19 outbreak. I cannot
express how much I value and appreciate you.

CHAPTER ONE

"The wind whispered to the warrior,
"You cannot withstand the coming storm."
And the warrior whispered back,
"I am the storm."
Unknown

Sinclair Quinn twisted her hips to the side, trying to absorb the punch with her pelvic bone instead of taking a blow to the stomach. She groaned, doubling over as pain ricocheted through her right hip and down her leg. It hurt, but it wasn't debilitating.

The initial hit to her face had stunned her and allowed the two men to drag her into a nearby alley. The smell of stale urine burned her nostrils. A chewing gum wrapper lay on the ground at her feet. Her heartbeat hard in her ears, and she gasped for breath. Blood dripped from her cut lip; big drops landed on the ground and splattered. She concentrated on them, using them to focus her thoughts and slow her mind. She had her collapsible baton in her jeans pocket. *Don't overthink.* Create an opportunity to escape.

"Tell us where the Indian is." Her assailant grabbed her ponytail and yanked on it, pulling her up and forcing her head back so her throat was exposed.

Michael? What did they want with him?

The thugs had attacked her after she'd left the grocery store. Foolishly, she'd felt secure once she was home in Granite City in northwestern Montana. That was her first mistake. Her Glock 19 handgun was in the glove compartment of her car where it did her no good at all. Mistake number two. Her final error was not noticing she was being tailed. By the time she'd become aware of them following her, it was too late.

The shorter of the two, a man who wore a cheap suit, stood behind her attacker. His hand rested on the pistol in his shoulder holster. "Tell her it'll only get worse for her the longer this goes on. We need to know where she hid Papin."

"She's got ears. She can hear," the larger one snapped. He had the broken nose and muscle-bound physique of a fighter. He let go of her hair and turned to his partner. "You should do some of the work instead of standing back there, yapping. I hit bone with that last punch and hurt my hand."

Sinclair grabbed her telescopic baton and flicked it open. She whacked the big guy's knee, throwing him off balance. Then she struck Cheap Suit's hand so he couldn't go for his

6

weapon.

Big Guy regained his equilibrium and pulled his arm back, ready to punch her.

She took advantage of his wide stance and smashed his ribs. He doubled over. Cheap Suit backed up, holding his injured appendage to his chest, protecting it.

She ran. Her groceries—eggs, flour, sugar, and milk—were scattered over the sidewalk at the entrance to the alley. She jumped over them. She'd just returned from a hellacious trip to Ukraine and had been looking forward to a couple of weeks downtime, starting with a day of baking. That wasn't going to happen now.

She raced for the safety of her apartment on the corner at the end of the block. The fall sunset cast long shadows, setting the west side of the street in darkness. Luckily, there was no need for her to cross the road.

She slid to a halt at the entrance to the red brick building she called home. It wasn't grand or new and it didn't have a fancy security system, just an extra lock on the door to the street that could easily be picked or broken.

For years, she survived by obeying the acronym TLTV or Think-Like-The-Villain. If this was her operation, she would have a man waiting at her apartment in case the first attempt failed. Grateful that sneakers were part of her everyday wardrobe, she changed course and sprinted for her car, which was parked in the lot next to her building.

She slowed as she neared her old battered Volvo SUV and scanned the area, making sure no one was around. Her fingers ached from gripping her baton. She took an extra second to peek through the back window, making sure the trunk was empty, and then did the same with the backseat. Belatedly, she checked to make sure her purse was still attached to her belt. It was a small cheap pouch that hung from her leather gun belt and was just big enough to hold her passport, phone, and a small wallet.

She pushed the end of her baton against the ground, collapsing it. She would've liked to leave it open, ready, but it was the type that doubled as a keyring, and she had to close it to fit the key in the ignition. Maybe she needed a different model. But that was another problem for another day.

She rammed the car into drive. Normally, she didn't access her phone while driving, but this was an emergency. She fished her smartphone from her purse, dialed Michael's number. Up until the moment the thugs mentioned him, she'd assumed this was about her latest trip to Ukraine, but two months ago, she'd hidden him in a safe house.

"Hi." His tone was soft and smooth, and for some reason always made her feel calm.

"You need to get out of there. I was just attacked by two men who wanted to know your location." The words tumbled out. She was acting on instinct and training.

He was silent for a moment and then said, "What about you? Are you hurt?"

Her face throbbed. She took a hand off the wheel and touched her swollen lip, which stung. She had no doubt that once her adrenaline spike wore off, she would hurt all over, and not just her bruised face and hip. "Nothing serious."

"Where will you go?" His tone was flat and devoid of emotion.

"I'm heading to Finn's office. I'll fill out a report. It probably won't do any good, but..." It didn't matter. She needed a safe place to regroup and figure out what was going on, and the federal building in Granite City met that standard.

"I'll meet you there." He hung up.

She'd given him the burner the last time she'd seen him. That was four months ago. He had been limping and in pain. Just walking to her vehicle had been laborious and agonizing, and by the time he lay down on her back seat, he was dripping with sweat.

She slammed on her brakes. She'd been so caught up in her memories she hadn't noticed the stop sign at Hellebore and First Street. She counted to three, making sure she came to a complete stop and then proceeded through the intersection.

They hadn't talked on the long trip to the safehouse. He'd slept or pretended to sleep as she drove him around in circles for hours. She'd told Finn she was taking Michael across the border into Canada, but that was a lie. It wasn't that she didn't trust him, but relying on disinformation was a habit born out of years of hiding the vulnerable.

She pulled up Finn's contact information and called him. He didn't pick up so she left a message telling him she was on her way.

Her grip on the stirring wheel loosened, and then her stomach fluttered as the federal building came into view.

No matter how far she traveled, she'd never met a man who measured up to Michael Papin.

CHAPTER TWO

Michael slipped his backpack off his shoulders as he slowed his pace. The run from his dingy apartment on the east side of Granite City to the federal building had only taken five minutes.

He inhaled, breathing in the cool fall evening. In a few short months, it would be winter.

To most people, Granite City, Montana was a family-friendly town. A large square with a fountain sat at the center of the city. The area, which was used for festivals and concerts, was surrounded by the law courts, the police station, the federal building, and a large granite building that housed the headquarters of Public Domain Energy. But for him it would always be the place where he had begged for food and struggled to survive.

He scoured the area. He didn't like to label his ability to remember everything he saw. Psychologists argued that people didn't actually have eidetic or photographic memories, citing numerous studies, but he'd learned a long time ago that their opinion didn't matter. All that counted was his capacity to recall this moment and recollect license plates, a face, or anything else that might help him in the future.

He tugged the hood of his sweatshirt low over his brow. As far as he knew, he was still being hunted by the Syndicate, a powerful organization with unlimited resources. There were an untold number of cameras watching at any given time. Traffic, weather, and security services all had legitimate reasons for recording the actions of everyday people. Unfortunately, public video surveillance was susceptible to criminal abuse. It would be easy for the Syndicate to obtain the feed and run it through a facial recognition program.

He figured it was only a matter of time before they tracked him down. That reasoning had forced him to commit to a rigorous rehabilitation regime. Losing his mobility had made him feel absolutely powerless. Initially, he hadn't even been able to boil a kettle without help. Even after months of work, he still wasn't as fit as he was before he'd been injured, but he could do fifty push-ups and fifty sit-ups, which wasn't bad. But it took him ten minutes to run a mile, and by the end, he was limping. Before being injured, he'd been able to run two miles in sixteen minutes. Even after all his work and physical therapy, the fractures on the left side of his pelvis sent shooting pains down his leg and caused numbness in his foot. He hadn't had access to a doctor while he'd been lying low, but he had googled his symptoms and discovered sciatic nerve damage was very common with pelvic fractures. Maybe he was trying to do too much too soon.

He slung his bag over one shoulder as he entered the building. It contained his laptop, which had a top of the line processor with a memory cache he had boosted to maximum capacity and a battery that would last fifteen hours. His pack also included all the cash he'd managed to save, his fake ID, and a burner phone with a ghost chip. Just to be on the safe side, he'd destroyed the cell Sinclair had given him after he'd received her call.

Once again, he scoured the area. The place seemed deserted, which wasn't a surprise given the time of day. He flicked his hood down and proceeded to security.

"I'm here to see Supervisory Special Agent Callaghan." Michael placed his backpack on the conveyor belt that led to the X-ray machine.

"Name and ID?" The guard was an older man in his late fifties with a receding hairline and an expanding waistline that flopped over his gun belt.

"Papin." Michael placed his driver's license on the desk. Once the guard was done checking his credentials, Michael walked through the scanner and collected his bag on the other side.

He headed for the elevator. He'd just finished a particularly grueling workout and would've liked time to shower before he saw Sinclair. His heartbeat kicked up a notch, the way it always did whenever he thought of her. He tamped it down. She was his friend and had shown no indication she wanted a relationship. But every time he saw her, she grew more striking.

The elevator door swished open. He stepped inside and pressed the button.

At fifteen, he'd been madly in love with her. Even living on the street, she'd managed to keep clean. Back then, it wasn't unusual for her to cover her long strawberry blond hair with a knit cap. She'd been trying to disguise her beauty so as not to attract the attention of pimps and thugs who preyed on the young and vulnerable. In Michael's opinion, it hadn't worked. It was impossible to hide the exquisiteness of her large green eyes and slim oval face.

He knocked on the door to the office Finn shared with his partner, FBI Special Agent Kennedy Morris.

"Come," he barked.

Michael entered, expecting Finn to immediately give him a sitrep. Instead, the FBI agent glanced at him, gave a slight nod, and then went back to rummaging through the first aid kit, which lay open on his desk.

Sinclair sat in a cheap office chair opposite

him. She turned in his direction. Her hair was disheveled, one eye was swollen, and her bottom lip was split and covered with dried blood.

"What the hell?" The bastards had beat her. He dropped his backpack and rushed to her side and knelt on the ground in front of her. Without thinking, he smoothed her hair away from her face, being careful to avoid her bruises. "Who did this?"

She gave him a weak smile but didn't meet his gaze. "It isn't as bad as it looks. I've been hurt worse."

He wanted to beat the crap out of the son of a bitch who had hurt her. He forced himself to stare at the ground. Losing his temper only served him. It wouldn't help her. Right now, she needed… He had no idea what she needed, but he was certain she didn't want his impotent fury.

"They were after your location," Finn said as he paced around his desk and passed an icepack to Michael.

"Do you think it's the Syndicate?" He squeezed the product until it felt cold. His hands shook, whether from rage or seeing her again, he couldn't say. He held the pack to her black eye, trying not to press too hard.

He'd done a lot of soul-searching since his confinement and had come to realize he'd always been a coward where she was concerned. He'd run out on her when he'd enrolled in Officer Candidate School at eighteen. Which had effectively ended any chance they had at a relationship because she was a private. Enlisted personnel weren't allowed to fraternize with officers. He had justified his decision by telling himself his country needed his intelligence and talents. But in reality, he was just too scared to commit.

Finn cleared his throat, drawing Michael's attention. "Are there other people looking for you? Someone you might have put away when you were CID?"

Michael considered Finn's question. He hadn't thought about his work with Army CID. CID was the acronym for Criminal Investigation Command, which used to be "Division" but when they changed names, they kept the D. "Anything's possible. You know how it is. You close cases and put the bad guys away. Sometimes there are ripple effects that touch people...families, friends, business partners. There are always more threads than you know. But my initial answer would be no."

"Why?"

"I was kicked out at the beginning of the year. That was nine months ago. I didn't go into hiding until four months ago. If someone from my days as a federal agent wanted to get me, they would've done it after I got hit by Portman's car, when I was at my most vulnerable."

Using his index finger, he brushed the bruise on Sinclair's cheek. It was starting to swell and turn purple. "The Syndicate is the only group who have the talent and money to figure out Sinclair hid me."

She pulled away, took the pack from his hand, and pressed it against her hip. "Would someone please tell me what's going on?"

He doubted it would have much effect with her jeans in the way. It was obvious she'd been in a fight for her life. Surprisingly, he was shaking more than she was. He pointed to the kit on Finn's desk. "Do you have another icepack?"

"Never mind the freakin' pack." She jumped out of the chair and threw the cold compress on Finn's desk. It landed with a dull thud. "I want to know what's happening."

Michael stood, facing her. They were the same height, but his muscle mass meant he was heavier. Her clothes weren't fancy, just jeans, a T-shirt, and a leather jacket and, yet, they accentuated her long legs, slim waist, and small bust. The urge to kiss her was almost irresistible, which was stupid because, as angry as she was, she'd probably punch him.

Finn crossed his arms and sat on the front edge of his desk. He was wearing navy cargo pants and a soft cotton shirt with a collar, casual dress for him, but it was eight at night and he'd probably come from home. "It's about a case—"

"Never mind the damn case." She turned on Finn. "I just got off a plane. I was all set for a relaxing few days, but that's not going to happen because I just broke a man's hand and another man's ribs." She swung back to Michael, poking him in the chest. "I hid you, no questions asked. Now I'm telling you I need to know. Who are these people and what do they want? I have women and children who rely on my ability to hide them from the vilest people on the planet. One of the ways we survive and do our jobs is by keeping a low profile. I will not allow these victims to be put at risk, so you'd better tell me what's going on."

Her good eye, the one that wasn't swollen, was wide, her nostrils flared to the point she was almost breathing fire. Damn, she was hot when she was angry.

He paced to the window and looked out over the Granite City Square. Luckily, the office was large with Finn's desk at one end and Agent Morris' workspace on the far side near the window. An old couch was positioned beside the door. Every other inch of wall space was taken up with filing cabinets. He sat in Special Agent Morris' chair at her desk.

In the long months of his convalescence, he'd pictured the moment when he'd finally get to look Sinclair in the eye. But he'd imagined she would be staring back at him with affection. He was wrong. Considering the beating she'd endured, maybe he should focus on her safety instead of his feelings. He sighed. "Remember when David was in trouble and I went undercover at PDE to prove he was innocent?"

She nodded.

"I also discovered an organization that calls themselves the Syndicate. Marshall Portman was scared of them. They're the ones who employed Harper, the gunman who shot up Big Sky News." He paused, wondering how much detail she needed.

"And?"

"And when Tim's neighbor was killed—"

"They killed that old mountain man?" Her voice rose, but she seemed less agitated.

"No. They killed the local police chief."

"Chief Booley, the one that framed Tim?"

"The very same. I think he was trying to blackmail Lance Ackerman. A businessman, who I suspect, was part of the Syndicate."

"Okay, but that doesn't explain why I hid you."

"That's on me." Finn pushed away from the desk and took a step closer, his arms still folded across his chest.

"Explain." Sinclair mirrored his body language and crossed her arms.

Finn pursed his lips, obviously considering how much he could tell her.

"Finn, there are innocents involved. I need to know." Her cheeks flushed, a sure sign she was getting angry again.

Finn sighed. "Okay, but this doesn't leave this room. Got it?"

She nodded.

"In March, my superior, Special Agent in Charge Martin Deluca, asked Michael to join me and my partner, Special Agent Morris, for a meeting at our FBI field office in Salt Lake City. It was in this meeting we discovered that all the evidence Michael had collected was destroyed by someone within the Department of Justice. This mole, or moles, have accessed my personal information and tried to use it to silence me."

Her hand flew to her mouth, but she said nothing.

"The Syndicate has managed to kill two potential witnesses. Brad Harper, who was in prison at the time of his death, and Paul Harris, the former mayor of Hopefalls. He was in witness protection when they put a bullet in his head. There is an ongoing investigation into his death, but I'm not holding my breath."

Her gaze slanted to Michael. "You got hit by a car helping David, and it was all for nothing."

Michael grinned. "It wasn't for nothing. David isn't rotting in jail for a crime he didn't commit. I'd say it was a successful op."

Except he had lost his job as a civilian agent with Army CID, and as much as he'd worked to recover from his injuries, he knew he would never get his old body back. The broken bones had knitted, but he didn't move in the same way, and constant pain had become a new way of life.

Sinclair strode to the door and then turned to the two men and smiled. It was the kind of smile that caused fear to cramp his insides, like the moment of silence before a bomb exploded. "Here's a question that's burning in my mind... Did it occur to either of you to warn me that I might be in danger? What if they'd attacked when I was helping a group of children?"

She stepped closer. "What are we talking about here, rich businessmen who hire gunmen? That's just lovely. They sound like upright members of society and not at all like the kind of men who would leave a child in slavery. Why would you have to warn me? I don't travel to dangerous countries and help the vulnerable." She punctuated the air with her index finger as she made each point. There was a tightness to her expression. Her cold, hard gaze settled on him and then Finn.

Finn backed up a step.

Michael held up his hand in an expression of surrender. He should've warned her, and he liked to think he was big enough to admit his mistake. "You're right. To be honest, I was too tired and sick to consider all the consequences."

The night she'd stashed him at the safe house, he'd been exhausted from forcing his fractured body to move. Something they never mentioned in the movies was how pain drained a person's energy reserves.

Finn cleared his throat. "Sinclair, can you give me a description of the men who beat you?"

She dragged the chair closer to his desk, making an ear-splitting screeching sound. Then she grabbed the ice pack, sat in her seat, and held it across her face so it covered her eye and her lip.

She was detailed and concise in recounting her evening. She tucked a strand of dark blond hair behind her ear as she talked. The action drew him in and made him notice her features. Her small earlobes, the delicate slope of her jawline, and her dainty neck. His gaze dipped lower. He knew he shouldn't stare, but he was a man with all the normal male urges. He remembered her breasts as being small and tight with perfect pink nipples.

She shifted, easing the ice to her hip. The movement drew his gaze to a small pouch attached to her belt. The purse, he realized, wasn't just a testament to her practicality. It was a choice to leave her hands unencumbered for combat and spoke of her commitment to her work.

She stretched out her right leg, so the compress fit more snugly against her bone. That reminded him of the second ice pack. He stood and strode to Finn's desk where he rifled through the first aid kit. "Here." And held the ice to her black eye, without adding pressure.

"I'll hold it." She placed her palm over his.

He kept his hand in place for a moment longer than was necessary, stunned by her touch. It was as though she had sent a charge of electricity through him.

Get a grip. He stepped away and went to sit, once again, at Agent Morris' desk on the other side of the room, leaving her to answer Finn's questions uninterrupted.

He stared out of the window, looking out over the Granite City square. In his quest to figure out who the Syndicate were and what they were up to, he never once considered they might come after his friends. Which was stupid on his account because this had all started with an attack on David. Sinclair had paid the price for his lapse in judgment.

Once she had finished with her account of the evening's events, Michael swiveled in his chair to face them and rested his elbow on the desk. "I've been thinking... They obviously know my real name, but how did they know that Sinclair knew my location? Why not Tim or David?" He pointed to Finn. "I can see them not wanting to tussle with an FBI agent, but how did they know I wasn't in witness protection?"

Finn stood and faced Michael. "It's like I already said. They have someone in the DOJ. You can stay in my apartment until we can figure this out."

Sinclair fished her phone from her purse. Using a paperclip she'd snagged from Finn's desk, she flicked open the compartment that held the sim card and removed the tiny piece of plastic. "Finn, that makes no sense. No one at the Department of Justice knew I'd hidden him unless you told them. Figuring out that I knew where Michael was has nothing to do with you. There's something else…" She stopped talking while she concentrated on prying open the back and taking out the battery. She dumped it all into her purse. "Michael, what about your mom and sister? Are they still in Canada?"

"Shit. No, they're here in Montana at my stepdad's house, just outside of town." The bottom dropped out of his stomach. He should've thought of them months ago. "I have to warn them."

Finn pointed to Agent Morris' desk. "Use Kennedy's landline to call them. I'll call David and Tim."

He dialed the number to his parent's home, silently begging them to pick up. He'd tell them to take off and head to his mom's family in Alberta or to his cousin's cabin on the reservation in the Cabinet Mountains. The area, which bordered Idaho, was considered one of the wildest locations in Montana.

The phone kept ringing, eventually going to voice mail. He hung up and dialed his mom's cell phone. It went to voice mail, too. He got the same result when he tried his sister's and stepdad's. Maybe they were out. There was cell service at his stepdad's house but if they weren't home, they could be in a dead zone. There were lots of places in the state where there was no cell signal.

He slammed down the receiver. "I need a vehicle."

"We can use mine." Sinclair waved goodbye to Finn who was talking on the phone.

As they reached the door, Finn said, "David's good. Call me as soon as you know something."

They sprinted across the street, heading for her rusted Volvo. He wasn't a religious man, but as he climbed into the car, he started praying, hoping his family would be okay.

CHAPTER THREE

Sinclair complied with Michael's directions and headed west toward the mountains.

He was staring out of the window. "Do you have a spare weapon I can use?"

She couldn't see his expression and his tone was flat and emotionless, making it impossible to read his thoughts.

In all the years she'd known him, she'd never met his family. At fifteen, he'd run away because he hadn't liked his mom's new husband. Michael had become part of their group when David had saved him from being snagged by one of the pedophile rings that roamed the bus terminal, looking for runaways. The four of them had been close, but David and Tim were tough guys who didn't understand that sometimes she needed to talk about her feelings. Looking back, she wasn't entirely sure that Michael understood, but he had listened and made her feel special.

"You can use the one in the glove compartment. It's a Glock 19. I have a spare in the trunk."

She preferred the Glock 43 anyway.

He nodded and smiled at her, just the way he had all those years ago.

One day, she'd woken in the grim alley where they lived to find he'd left her a note, telling her he'd gone home. She'd been sick at the time and had been devastated by his departure. A week later, she, along with David and Tim, were taken in by Marshall House, a charity for street kids run by Marshall Portman.

He leaned forward and retrieved her handgun.

"There's a round in the chamber," she said. Given his law enforcement experience, he would probably check the handgun anyway, but firearm safety was second nature to her.

In the efficient manner of an ex-CID agent, he ejected and checked the magazine and then slid it back into position. "Thanks."

Even if he wasn't an ex-federal agent, his proficiency around weaponry was to be expected considering the four of them had reconnected when they were in boot camp at Fort Leonard Wood in Missouri. He'd appeared as if he'd known they would be there, and maybe considering his computer skills, he had. She'd fallen madly in love with him all over again. They'd spent a passionate weekend together. She hadn't been a virgin—her stepfather had seen to that— but in every way that counted, Michael had been her first love. The next day he'd transferred to

Officer Candidate School and was gone. It was as though he'd been conjured away. In that long weekend, when they'd laid in each other's arms, he hadn't once mentioned his plans for the future. He must have known about the transfer. She'd trusted him and believed they shared a unique bond. But he had left without even saying goodbye.

She'd tried over the years to get over him. She used to socialize and go on dates. But after a while, dating seemed like a waste of time, and she gave up on men and focused on her work. Maybe it would've been easier to forget him if he wasn't so damned attractive. His intelligent eyes and chiseled good looks were always a punch in the gut.

When he'd knelt in front of her in Finn's office, she'd been unable to move or breathe. It was as if she'd been waiting to drink him in. His almost-black eyes were more alert than the last time she'd seen him. His hair was now military short, and she could see by the muscle definition under his black sweatshirt that he was fit once again.

They turned off the highway onto a plot of land that was surrounded by forest. A black Chevy Suburban was parked on the road by the entrance. The sound of gunshots rang out in the cool night air.

She killed the lights and drove down the driveway. Eventually, they slowed to a stop in front of the house. Sinclair extracted her Glock

43 from its hiding place in the trunk.

"What's that doing in there? Montana's an open carry state." Michael climbed out of the SUV.

She caught up with him on the pathway to the front door of a small log cabin. Why he was criticizing her decisions at this moment in time was a mystery. "Relax, I have a concealed carry permit."

"Why?" He ducked behind a large lilac. The front door was off its hinges. A small black battering ram lay on the porch. It had obviously been used to gain entry. These guys were prepared and organized.

"I don't want to pack my weapon with me everywhere I go, and I can't take it with me when I travel," she whispered.

"Considering everything that's happened tonight, you might want to rethink that," he replied in equally hushed tones.

She was about to give him a smart answer but stopped herself. Gunfire still sounded from inside the house. Picking on her was probably his way of dealing with tension.

He retrieved a small flip-phone from his pocket and dialed. "Finn, there are armed intruders at my family's house."

"Stay in the car. Do not engage," Finn shouted loud enough that she heard him even though she wasn't on the call.

Michael slipped the phone into his pocket.

Without a word, he climbed the porch steps.

He hadn't signaled to her or given her any indication of his intent. They needed to operate as a team, but telling him that would be a waste of energy. She could tell by his clenched jaw and the way he wouldn't look her in the eye that he was fighting to keep his emotions under control. She suspected he was feeling a combination of rage, coupled with terror and guilt. For all that, he was focused and deadly, his Army CID training coming to the fore.

Michael peeked around the broken door jam. She went to the other side of the opening and did the same. The foyer appeared to be empty. The house was small. Two men stood in the hallway straight ahead. They fired down a flight of steps, which presumably led to the basement. Neither looked up, and the noise of the gunfire drowned out any sound they might have made.

With two rapid head shots, Michael took out the two gunmen. Both fell to the ground. He moved closer, keeping his Glock 19 trained on them, and then aimed his handgun down the stairs. Once he was satisfied there was no one at the bottom of the steps, he kicked their weapons away.

Sinclair covered his back while he searched the two assailants. Describing Michael as smart would be an understatement, but this was something else altogether. This showed he had abilities she hadn't considered. His shots had been accurate and deadly. No one could shoot like that without weeks, if not years, of practice. It exhibited a commitment she hadn't known he possessed. She'd always imagined his position in the cybercrimes unit of Army CID to be a desk job even though David had told her he worked undercover. He couldn't have done that without intensive training, which would have included weapons. She'd allowed her own bias to color her opinion.

"It's Michael. Who's all down there?"

"The three of us, your mom, your sister and me," answered a disembodied male voice before the sound of something scraping against a concrete floor echoed through the now quiet house.

"How many men were there?" Michael knelt on the ground and checked the pockets of the dead men.

"Three."

He stood, instantly alert. "We only have two. Don't come out until I give the all-clear." He nodded in her direction. "How good are you?"

"I was trained by the US Army and my Special Forces brother. What do you think? You should've asked me that before instead of nitpicking about where I keep my weapon," she snapped, unable to stop herself. She wasn't anyone's punching bag, physically or emotionally.

One corner of his mouth turned up in a half-smile. "That's my girl. Let's scour the house. If he's not in here, we'll check outside. That'll be a bitch in the dark."

She nodded. They moved at a measured pace. First, they searched the ground floor, checking behind the doors and in closets, being sure to investigate every possible hiding place. Once they were certain no one was there, they climbed the stairs. Michael took the lead while she covered his back just in case their third man was outside and planned to rush them from behind.

They had finished searching all three bedrooms and two bathrooms and were standing on the landing. The log cabin interior was stylish, yet cozy at the same time. She was tempted to ask him if this was the home he'd grown up in but decided against it. This wasn't the time to indulge in idle chit-chat.

"What do you think, is he outside? Her lip and cheek throbbed, as did her hip. She was tired and had a headache forming behind her eyes. She'd slept on the flight from Ukraine, but not much. Since arriving back in Montana, she'd gone from one emergency to another, and her aching body was telling her to rest.

He marched to a bedroom at the front of the house and nudged the edge of the curtain to peep outside. "Finn's here, and I see our bad guys' vehicle is still by the road, so either he took off on foot—"

"Or he's outside."

Finn announced his presence, "Michael, it's me." It sounded as though he had just entered the building.

Some of the tension eased from her shoulders. Backup had arrived.

Michael rushed downstairs where he met Finn on the bottom step. "There were three of them. We only found two." He pointed in the general direction of the corpses.

"Your family?" Finn asked.

"Safe. They're still in the basement." Michael kept his weapon pointed toward the ground. "I told them to stay put until we find the last one. Their vehicle is still here—"

"He hasn't gone anywhere," Finn finished for him.

Sinclair eased around Michael, who was still standing on the bottom steps, and nearly bumped into Special Agent Morris. The attractive agent was dressed in a pair of cargo pants and a collared FBI issue T-shirt, and wore her long brown hair in a ponytail. If she was upset about being called out late at night, it didn't show. She seemed to be trying to squeeze past Finn as she snapped on a pair of latex gloves. She probably wanted to inspect the bodies. The stairs to the basement ran parallel to the steps to the upper floor, which meant Michael and Finn were essentially in her way.

"Move this to the kitchen," Special Agent Morris barked, her patience obviously spent.

The three of them scrambled out of the way but still stood in the hallway.

"Could he have escaped into the forest?" Sinclair wanted to examine all the possibilities before exposing Michael's family to any danger.

Michael paced to the entrance and then turned to face Finn. "There's ten acres of land back there with forests, a small lake, and fields —"

Plaster splintered beside his head. He ducked and slammed into her, forcing her down and away from the shooter.

More wood splintered. This time along the floor.

He put his arms around her waist and rolled, taking her with him into the relative safety of the Kitchen.

Several loud cracks sounded, and then there was silence.

They lay there listening, waiting.

Special Agent Morris moved to the entrance, followed by Finn. Both had their weapons aimed and were focused on their target.

Sinclair heard a clattering sound, which she imagined was a gun being kicked out of the third guy's hand.

"Clear," Finn called.

Michael lay on top of her. Somehow, they'd landed so he was nestled between her legs. Her breath caught in her throat. He covered her with his body. His weight pressing down on her made her feel as if they'd been thrown back in time. The urge to rotate her pelvis was overwhelming.

As though reacting to him was the most natural thing in the world. She shook away the notion. It was just muscle memory from their weekend together all those years ago, when she was young and stupid enough to believe in happy endings.

His gaze connected with hers. He inhaled sharply and said, "I think I should move."

He pushed to his feet and held out a hand to help her up. Then he turned on his heel and sprinted downstairs, presumably to free his family from the basement.

She sat on an oak chair in the large open kitchen and watched as Finn and Special Agent Morris talked on their phones. She assumed there were people who had to be called into a crime scene but, at the moment, she didn't care who they were or what they did.

Her legs felt wobbly. The swelling on her eye, lip, and hip hurt. She missed the loss of Michael's touch, but she was also angry with herself for being so weak. Some arbitrary chemical reaction had determined she should be attracted to him. It wasn't fair. They'd been friends for nearly twenty years, but there was nothing in their history that suggested they could make a relationship work. She was too independent, which meant she tended to shut people out. Whereas he was obsessive when it came to his work, to the point he was closed off. The fact that both she and his family had been attacked was a case in point. He should have told them months ago they were in danger, but he hadn't thought of it because he'd been focused on what he was doing to the exclusion of everything else. There was no way two people who were so isolated could form a lasting bond.

For her peace of mind, she needed to get out of here and put some distance between her and... everyone. Most of all, she had to get away from Michael. There was a sexual undercurrent between them that neither of them wanted, but for some reason wouldn't stay buried. Plus, she needed an end to this God-awful night. Once she was alone, she'd be able to process her emotions and gain some peace of mind. Suiting thoughts to actions, she stood and headed for the door.

"Sinclair, where are you going?" Finn shouted.

"Out." She used the same tone he'd used on her.

"Wait," he ordered.

She ignored him and kept on walking.

Finn caught up with her on the porch and grabbed her elbow, which forced her to turn and face him. "I need you to hide them."

"I thought you were going to put them up at your apartment."

"I have a one-bedroom. It would've been tight with Michael, but—"

"I can't." She shrugged his hand off and faced him, meeting his gaze. "I get that the Department of Justice is compromised, but I can't put the women and children I've rescued in danger, and I won't. They've been abused enough. Maybe protecting them isn't important to you, but I've dedicated ten years of my life to them. Hiding Michael when he was injured was one thing, but now I know the risks, I realize it was a mistake. I should've asked more questions."

Finn gave her a quizzical look. "Where are the victims now?"

"It's an ongoing process. Child Seekers searches for missing children and fights sex-trafficking, not just abroad but here in the States, too. Some can safely return to their families, but others are considered property by the larger cartels. We hide them in various places around the country until we can get them a new identity.

"Is that legal?" Finn asked.

She poked him in the arm. "This is one of the reasons I don't want you near our operation."

He tilted his head to the side. "And the other reason?"

She inhaled. "The way you talk about the Syndicate…it scares me. What if they find out where our safehouses are and come after them?"

"She's right. I know a place in the mountains where we can hide," a calm female voice said.

Sinclair turned to face an older woman with long graying dark hair.

"Are you talking about the cabin on the reserve in the Cabinet Mountains?" Michael stood in the doorway, looking relaxed and at ease, which was just wrong. How could he be so centered when she was a mess?

The older woman nodded.

"I'm Sinclair." She held out a hand to the woman, who she assumed to be Michael's mother.

"I'm Nadie, Nadie O'Connell, Michael's mom." She shook Sinclair's outstretched hand and then pointed toward a tall, clean-shaven, handsome white man with silver hair who stepped forward and greeted her. "This is my husband, Milo."

Sinclair guessed him to be in his fifties. He didn't try to squash her hand when he shook it, which was a good sign. He gave her an easy smile. "Thanks for everything."

"Sinclair has to come with us," Michael said, his gaze connecting with hers. The set of his jaw and the way he ground his teeth suggested he didn't want her to argue.

Tough shit. "No." She crossed her arms in a defensive stance.

"How will I get in touch with you?" Finn asked Michael. He was either oblivious to her attitude or had decided to ignore it.

Michael continued to scowl at her. Most people backed down under his laser focus, but she wasn't most people. She glared back, refusing to look away. Finally, realizing their staring contest was childish, she switched her gaze to Finn. "They'll have to pick up a burner. How much cash do you have on you?"

Michael shrugged. "Don't worry. I'm prepared. I have cash and a burner."

Anger flashed through her like a bolt of lightning. She poked him in the chest. "Good for you. It's easy to be prepared when you know what's coming. Some of us"—she pointed to Nadie and Milo who stood silently watching—"had no idea what to expect. I'd just arrived on a flight from Ukraine this evening. I was jumped getting groceries on the way to my apartment. Do you know what that means?" She poked him harder but didn't give him time to answer. "It means all I have is a carry-on with dirty clothing and a toothbrush." She held her hands wide. "What you see is what I've got."

"You have a car and a gun." Michael glanced at the weapon in her hand. Not only had she forgotten it was there, which was dangerous enough, but it was also in her left hand. She was right-handed and didn't remember switching hands. She tucked her handgun into her belt. *Dear God.* She needed to get her act together.

"About the Volvo." Finn winced.

She groaned. This wasn't going to be good.

"It would be better if you take a different vehicle. First, they must know your car. And I was thinking about what you said in the office."

She narrowed her eyes. "What I said?"

"How did they know you were the one to hide Michael? They must've acquired the street cam footage of that night, gone through it until they saw him leaving the federal building with you. Unless you two have met in the last few months?"

"No." She didn't like where this was going.

"Which means they know your vehicle. You can't continue to drive it. I should have thought of that. My bad." Finn had gentled his voice, obviously thinking that would ease the message.

"Seriously, who are these guys?" She scrubbed her face.

Nadie put an arm around her. "I'm sure you can collect it once this is all sorted out."

Sinclair gave her a weak smile. She appreciated the older woman's attempt to comfort her, even though it made her feel a little awkward. She wasn't used to being consoled. The last person to be motherly to her was...well, her mother, and she'd died over twenty years ago.

"It's just a car. It's not as important as being safe." That was a lie. Her car was her backup in case she ever found herself homeless again. It was a roof over her head and a safe place to sleep. Even though, logically, she knew that, as long as she could work, the chance of her ever living on the street again was slim, but she liked having a safety net.

"We have an old truck we use on our land. It's unregistered and will work well enough to get us where we need to go." Milo pointed to a barn on the north side of the house. "We'll tuck your SUV in the barn, out of sight."

Sinclair stepped sideways out of Nadie's embrace, hoping to make her escape. She had no idea where she was going but desperately needed some space to decompress.

Michael smiled at her. "You're coming with us."

She shook her head, pacing to the end of the porch. "That's not a good idea."

He followed, crowding her. "Why?"

"Because..." *Think.* She didn't want to be in close contact with him for any length of time. Whenever he was near, she lost a piece of herself. Instead of being the confident woman who worked to find missing kids and stop human trafficking, she became an infatuated teen who had the sense of a gnat.

She knew he cared about her but not in the way she needed. That was one of the reasons she'd avoided him for sixteen years. They'd only met on holidays, always in the company of others, and never for longer than a few hours. "I don't want to put you out. There are places I can go to ground. If your bad guys find me, then I won't be able to tell them where you are."

"Are you kidding me?" Michael gripped her shoulders. He was gentle despite his anger. "You've just gone through hell. You're covered in bruises. Do you honestly think I'd just let you go off on your own and hope you survive?"

"'Hope I survive.' Who the hell do you think I am? I have resources. You came to me when you needed a safe place. I'm not some helpless bimbo."

Michael's eyes widened, and he let go but said nothing.

She stared out at the night, focusing on Special Agent Morris who was now searching the gunmen's SUV.

Finn cleared his throat. "It would help me, personally, if you were all together."

She opened her mouth to argue, but Finn held up his hand. "I know you're more than capable of taking care of yourself, but you're also very good at protecting others. I would feel better knowing everyone was under your protection."

Put like that, how could she say no? She nodded her agreement, admitting defeat. "This cabin we're going to, does it have an oven? Can I bake?" Occupational therapy wasn't the same as alone time, but she didn't have the luxury of unraveling. She would do what she could to refocus her mind.

Michael and Finn stared at her like they were seeing an alien.

"You bake?" Michael's question suggested he didn't believe her.

She ignored him.

Nadie smiled. "Baking sounds like a wonderful idea. Let's see what ingredients we have in the kitchen." She waved a hand as she turned and walked into the house. "Come."

As she eased by, Michael brushed his fingers against hers. "You okay?" It was a small caress, probably meant to console her, but his touch burned through her like a wildfire. The memory of him lying between her legs on the kitchen floor appeared in her mind. She suppressed a groan. It would be wonderful to curl up in his arms, have wild passionate sex, and let him hold back the world. But reality would still be there, waiting, and she was nothing if not a realist.

Summoning all her willpower, she nodded and carried on walking. The next few days were going to be torture. Once they were safe and everything was settled, she would get her alone time and come up with a strategy to deal with her emotions. Until then, she would bury her feelings just like she had for the last sixteen years.

CHAPTER FOUR

Ethan Moore stood just inside the door of Lucy Portman's office at the PDE building in Granite City, watching her give instructions to a computer geek.

Surprisingly, she hadn't appropriated her late husband's office next door. Maybe it didn't matter. Her space was just as big, taking up a quarter of the floor. An ornamental wood desk sat at one end of the room opposite a large picture window that overlooked the Granite City square. A door on her right opened to an opulent private bathroom. He had no doubt she'd made the room her own. Everyone knew she called the shots, so maybe moving was inconsequential.

Until yesterday, he'd been employed to protect the Syndicate's oil and gas interests in Russia. The executive in charge of the operation, Yuri Ivanov, appeared to be a cheerful, friendly, and benevolent host. He provided his employees with good food and excellent living quarters. Normally, Ethan's assignments involved the removal of rivals, journalists, and the occasional activist, anyone who got in the way of the Syndicate's interests. Ivanov had needed him to do away with a business partner named Petroff. For some reason, the Russians seemed to prefer the use of poison over other methods. Ethan would've chosen to use his blade and make it look like a mugging, but he had followed orders and slipped sarin into Petroff's contact lens solution.

Unfortunately, Ivanov was also known for his indiscriminate killing of innocents.

Ethan had never considered himself a man with a conscience, but he was having a hard time coming to terms with being employed by someone who gunned down children. His skills were subtle, like a surgeon's blade carving out a brain tumor. He had honed his expertise over the last twenty years and considered himself a craftsman. The murder of juveniles was like smashing a head with a hammer. If the Syndicate expected him to waste his talents on mass exterminations, then he would have to rethink his work with them.

He leaned with his back against the door in an attempt to seem disinterested as he waited for Lucy to notice him. It didn't matter how he felt about Ivanov or his actions. He had a symbiotic relationship with the Syndicate. They paid him to do what he loved—killing people—and in return, he would rid them of anyone who interfered with their plans. It was a match made in Hell.

His skin tingled as sweat dribbled down his back. He hadn't knifed anyone in a month, and it was making him antsy, like an addict's withdrawal. It was getting harder to stay focused, which was unfortunate because he had to be on guard when dealing with Lucy Portman.

She was a ruthless woman who liked to use her body to manipulate men into doing her bidding. Luckily, he was immune to her charms. That distance helped him appreciate the brutal determination with which she conducted her business. If she saw something she wanted or decided a rival needed to be dealt with, she took steps to accomplish her goals.

As a member of the Syndicate, she was powerful and deadly. She was also a stone-cold psychopath, which meant that in no way whatsoever was she trustworthy. *It takes one to know one.*

She smirked at Ethan and curled her finger, beckoning him closer.

He took two steps into the room.

She turned her attention to the gangly nerd with the shaggy hair who sat in the chair opposite her desk. "Ethan, you've been assigned to me because, yesterday, Michael Papin instigated a cyberattack."

Ethan had read the Syndicate's files on Papin, and while it was true he was a skilled hacker who had worked for the feds, something about Lucy's revelation felt off. "How do you know it was Papin?"

Tyler twisted in his seat to address Ethan. "I spent two years in prison because an Army CID hacker, with the alias Spider, wrote a piece of malware that back-traced me. I've been studying his code. I'd recognize it anywhere."

That all sounded a little too personal for Ethan, as though Tyler might have his own reasons for wanting to get Papin.

Using her left hand, Lucy flicked her dyed blond hair over her shoulder. "And we know through our contacts at the Department of Justice that Michael Papin and Spider are one and the same." She arched her back. The motion pressed her nipples against the thin fabric of her blouse. She wasn't wearing a bra.

Sweat formed on Tyler's forehead. "Y-y-yes. There are markers in the code that are as obvious as fingerprints. He wrote the virus that attacked the Syndicate."

Ethan had only met the Native American, known as Michael Papin, once. He'd been sitting at the kitchen table in a rundown ranch house owned by Timothy Morgan. Ethan had been there to plant evidence. It should have been easy. The home was supposed to be empty, but Papin had been waiting. Instead of walking in and planting a bloody knife in the freezer, Ethan had found himself with a Glock 19 aimed at his chest. It was only later he had discovered that

Papin was a genius programmer who was a direct threat to the Syndicate. He'd expected to receive an order to take him out months ago, but it hadn't happened.

Lucy toyed with a gold chain that lay between her breasts. "Tyler, who has been assessing the damage, was about to give me a report."

Tyler swallowed. "It took me a while to go through all the code and figure out what was stolen. He got key logs and passwords. With that information, our secret server is an open book."

Lucy stood and walked around her desk before stopping in front of Tyler. "There's been no trace of him for months. Why would he go after us now?"

"He could have planted the code when he was undercover and triggered it remotely." The nerd sounded appalled by Papin's audacity, which was a surprise considering he was a hacker himself.

"And you suspect his family is hiding him," Ethan stated, realizing it was the obvious answer. The last time he'd seen Papin he was recovering from extensive injuries.

She sat on the edge of her desk. Her skirt rose, revealing her stocking tops. "Yes. I've scanned through his list of acquaintances. Most of them are ex-military, hard targets, so I've dispatched men to bring in his mother, sister, and the woman who hid him, Sinclair Quinn. Unfortunately, Quinn proved harder to subdue than we anticipated."

"What happened?" The Syndicate had extensive files on Papin's friends. Ethan wouldn't have described any of them as "soft," including his family and the woman.

"Ludlow and Kemp were supposed to get her, but she got away." Finally, she made eye contact with Ethan. By the way she clenched her jaw, he suspected she was livid about the failure.

"What makes you think they know where he is? He could be in witness protection." After Ackerman's death in the spring, he'd done some digging, looking for Papin, but he'd gone to ground.

"My contact at the DOJ says he's not. They have no idea where he is. Tyler here"—she nodded her head toward the runt—"says he was last seen in the company of the Quinn woman on the same night Ackerman died."

Tyler didn't add to the discussion. Ethan suspected he was mesmerized by Lucy's attempts to seduce him.

Ethan had only ever been physically attracted to men, and his sexual appetite was inconsequential compared to the delirium he felt when he sliced someone. He was addicted to the moment when his blade split the skin, the cries of agony and the smell of the blood. They all coalesced to give him an orgasmic high. "So, the attempt on the woman failed... What about the mother and sister?"

"I've sent out a team to collect them. I'm still waiting to hear."

"What's my role in all of this?" Ethan flexed his fingers. He'd killed Petroff, and although he'd taken pleasure from watching the light dim in his victim's eyes, it wasn't the same as using his knife. He really wanted to slice that bastard, Papin. Ethan's contact within the Syndicate, a computerized voice who called himself "The Trainer," had been very clear: he was here to assist Lucy and follow her orders. Once the job was done, he would be reassigned.

Lucy smiled down at Tyler. "When I have his women, I will coax Papin out of hiding. It'll be your job to ensure that he tells us everything he knows."

Tension eased from Ethan's spine. Finally, he would have an opportunity to use his blade. "You know torture's not my specialty. I kill."

Lucy kicked off her high heels and placed her foot on Tyler's crotch. "I've heard you like to take your time."

"I do when it doesn't interfere with the job." Ethan would never let his need get in the way of his professionalism.

"It won't. I want him dead. You can play with him and find out how much he knows about our organization."

Ethan nodded, resisting the urge to jump up and down with joy. Instead, he headed for the door, not caring that he hadn't been dismissed.

"You know how to get in touch with me."

Lucy didn't answer. She was busy unzipping Tyler's pants.

CHAPTER FIVE

Michael eyed Sinclair as she bounced in the passenger seat, her right hand hanging on to the strap that was attached to the roof of the truck. The back road into the reservation was nothing more than a rough dirt track that was pitted with potholes and rocks.

They'd spent hours talking to Detective Ramirez of the Granite City-Elkhead County Police Department about everything that had gone down tonight. The detective had confiscated Michael's Glock so he could confirm his side of the story, but Milo had provided him with a Barretta so he was still able to defend himself.

Sinclair had done a double round of interrogation because she also had to answer questions about being attacked in the alley. The cop had referred to that crime as a mugging, which was ridiculous. But he doubted Finn had told the Granite City Elkhead County Police Department about the Syndicate, so they probably had no idea what they were dealing with. To local law enforcement, tonight's events were a mugging and a home invasion, and they had no reason to think differently.

Michael's stepdad, Milo, Michael's mom, and his teenage sister, Ava, sat on the bench seat behind them. They were headed to a cabin that belonged to his cousin's husband. The kinships held by his mother's Cree family ran deep. There was no way they would tell an outsider they were here, not even the police.

Sinclair had been way too quiet on the trip up here. Every muscle in her body seemed to be wound tight. She'd made no attempt at chitchat, which wasn't surprising because she wasn't really a small talk type of person. If she had something to say, she said it.

Her silence could be a sign she was still pissed with him. He had to admit she had a point. He should have warned her and his family. But saying he hadn't been thinking straight because of the pain sounded like he was making excuses. Instead of involving her, he should've hidden on the reservation.

To make matters worse, Finn had taken him aside while Sinclair and his mom were in the kitchen. Michael thought he'd wanted to talk about the Syndicate, but his concern had been for Sinclair. *Whatever is between the two of you, sort it out. I don't want to see her get hurt.* That order had been given in a curt, menacing tone.

Finn was the second person in their friend

group to notice his connection to Sinclair, or maybe it was the awkwardness between them that gave them away. Her brother, David, had also mentioned it.

It was interesting that Finn thought Michael could hurt her. She wasn't a fragile butterfly who needed delicate handling. In every way that mattered, she was a warrior who protected the weak. But Finn was a trained FBI agent. He saw things that others missed. Although Michael had also been a federal agent, his specialty had required a different skillset.

The only time they'd ever worked as a couple was the weekend they'd spent together when they were in boot camp. They'd had three wonderful nights and two whole days lying in each other's arms. They'd returned to their outfit on Sunday. He'd told her he loved her, knowing he was due to leave that Monday for Officer Candidate School. He'd completed boot camp and had degrees in computer engineering and computer science and wanted to use his abilities to serve his country. He'd thought she would understand. But he'd never discussed his decision with her, not when he applied and not when they spent their weekend together. One day he was with them and the next day he was gone. He'd done what was right for himself, and that was all that mattered. Looking back, he realized he'd behaved like a selfish child who was scared of commitment.

That was sixteen years ago. David was right. It was too long to yearn for someone and do nothing about it. When David had given Michael the okay to get involved with his sister, Michael had been lying in a hospital bed, unable to sit up, walk or use his left arm. He hadn't been in any position to act, and if he was being honest, he was terrified she would reject him. He also wasn't sure what would happen if they actually did reunite and it didn't work out. Would it mean the end of his relationship with Finn, David and Tim?

What if he never tried and spent the rest of his life not knowing what it was like to hold her or wake up next to her every day? That last question terrified him more than the idea of losing his friends. Not taking the chance was worse than being rejected. If she turned him away, he would deal with it, but he didn't want to live with the regret of not trying, or the knowledge that he was too much of a coward to try. At this moment, she was here with him. It was now or never.

He gripped the steering wheel tighter as the truck hit a rock and bumped sideways. This was the first time his two worlds, his street family and his home family, had met. He had never allowed their paths to cross because he'd broken his mom's heart when he ran away and lived with Sinclair and the others on the street. His mom had been gracious and kind to Sinclair, but that wouldn't last once she figured out their history. Nadie had a sixth sense where her son was concerned. Nothing got past her. She'd known the reason he'd stayed on the street for months, instead of days, was because of a girl. What would she say when she discovered the girl he'd lived with was Sinclair? It could get ugly.

Although, to be fair, Sinclair wasn't the only reason he'd remained. As a child prodigy, he hadn't shared classes with kids his own age and had never fit in. When he was with his "street" family, he belonged. They accepted him. They didn't care that he was smart. When it came down to it, he knew they would always be there to protect him, and he would do the same for them.

He braked within sight of the darkened cabin, but left the engine running and the lights on so they illuminated the isolated property. He hadn't visited the place since he was twelve and remembered it as being off-grid and rundown.

Sinclair reached under her seat, retrieving her handgun. "We're gonna check this place out, aren't we?

Milo loaded his shotgun. "We'd better."

Michael scanned the area. "There's only so much we can do. There's no way we can comb the forest. We'll check the two outbuildings and main cabin. Let's go."

The three of them climbed out of the vehicle. Michael withdrew his weapon and a flashlight from his pack.

After they'd searched the perimeter and ascertained the coast was clear, he entered the main cabin first with Sinclair following close behind and Milo bringing up the rear.

It had been renovated since his last visit. It was now a simple yet surprisingly stylish open-plan home. The spacious kitchen was to the right of the front door. The living area was straight ahead. A bedroom with a double bed was at the rear of the structure, and a small clean bathroom was located in an addition off the left side of the living room.

"Indoor plumbing. Nice," Michael said once they'd made sure the place was clear.

"Your mom's family did this place up a couple of years ago. They dug a well and put in a septic tank. There's also a generator and a propane-powered fridge and stove. They did a good job," Milo agreed.

"Let's get the outbuildings checked, then we can get settled." Sinclair sounded tired. Her jet-lag, the thumping she'd endured, and the horrendous encounter at his parent's place had to be catching up with her.

The garage was as derelict as Michael remembered and, unlike the main house, hadn't been restored. It was a miracle it was still standing. The logs that made up the walls were rotten and reeked of mold.

The third structure was new. It was a simple log construction with just a main room and a bathroom. There were no closets, just a large couch with two end tables. The interior walls were plastered and covered with exquisite pencil sketches of people and animals. The images were in black and white, and yet they displayed a beauty and knowledge of their subject matter that was stunning.

Sinclair gasped as she stopped and stared at the artwork. Her reaction told him that she, too, was affected.

Milo entered, filling the small space. "Your cousin, Daniel, is very talented."

"Where is he now? Won't he need this place to work?" Sinclair ran a finger on the edge of a half-finished drawing of an older woman. With just a few strokes of the pencil, Daniel had displayed her wrinkles, her age, the sparkle in her eyes, and her wisdom.

"He's in rehab so..." Milo shrugged his big shoulders, not finishing his explanation.

"Sinclair can sleep here." The sofa bed was large enough for two people. There was a distance between them, and if he was going to get closer to her, they needed time alone.

She stared at him, wide eyed. "I don't want to put anyone out. Whatever works best. I'll sleep wherever."

He turned and met Milo's gaze. His stepfather was a man of the world. He would've noticed the undercurrents between them.

Michael hadn't always had a positive relationship with his stepfather. He'd run away at fifteen because Milo had committed the sin of falling in love with, and marrying, his mom. But over the years, he had proven himself to be a good husband and father. Plus, he'd supported Michael's decision to join the Army and later to become a federal agent.

Milo nodded. "That's settled. Your mom and I will take the bedroom in the main building, and Ava can have the couch. Then he turned and exited the small cabin.

Sinclair was still staring at the sketches on the walls and failed to notice that Michael hadn't been assigned a place to sleep. He followed Milo out. She would figure it out soon enough.

He waved to his mom and sister who were climbing out of the truck. Milo hauled a large rubber container of food past him, heading for the house.

Michael smiled as he grabbed Sinclair's small carry-on case out of the bed of the vehicle. The term *carpe diem* sprang to mind. *Seize the day.*

****

Sinclair stood near the front door of the main cabin as Michael's family made themselves comfortable. They seemed to know what had to be done without being told, but she didn't. That lack of familiarity made her feel like an outsider, someone who had been forced upon them. Milo had turned on the propane and started the generator. The gas motor hummed in the distance. Then he headed outside to chop wood. Nadie filled a kettle and set it on the stove to boil.

"Can I help?" Sinclair took a step closer, hoping that if she had something to do, she wouldn't feel so awkward. The kitchen filled one corner of the cabin. The counter stretched from the front door to the far wall where the stove and fridge were hooked up.

"I'm making tea. I have to admit I'm a little unsettled." Nadie's hand shook as she removed a china mug from a cupboard and set it on the small white table. Then she stopped and stared straight ahead. "I didn't bring milk. I can't drink tea without milk." Her lower lip quivered as she picked up another mug. "I thought we were going to die."

Sinclair put an arm around her shoulders, comforting her in the same way the older woman had consoled her earlier.

Nadie had been strong throughout their ordeal, but now things were catching up to her. She picked up the mug, her trembling making it shake violently.

"You handled yourself well. Do you want to talk about it?" Sinclair took the cup from her before it hit the edge of the table and broke and placed it out of reach.

Nadie shook her head. "Do you mind if I sit with my daughter for a while?"

"I think that's a wonderful idea."

Nadie shuffled to the living room, her shoulders slumped. She had probably been in fear for, not only her life, but her daughter's and husband's, too. She made herself comfortable on the couch in the living room and watched as Ava sorted through a pile of DVDs. Without a word, the teen picked a movie and slid it into the player. Then returned to the sofa and snuggled with her mother.

In many ways, Ava looked like her brother. She had the same dark hair, high cheekbones, and good looks. But that was where the resemblance ended. Unlike Michael, Ava seemed sullen. She rolled her eyes every time Sinclair talked, which was just downright disrespectful. Sinclair hadn't said anything because she was a guest, and everyone had been through enough tonight. If she was honest, she just didn't have the energy to argue with a teen.

Sinclair exhaled. This would be a good time for her to focus on her own healing regime. With that in mind, she hoisted the rubber tote from the floor onto the counter. "Do you mind if I do some baking?"

Nadie waved from the couch. "Help yourself."

She would've liked to give Nadie and Ava some alone-time, and she could've done with a few hours by herself, too, but hiding in her cabin didn't feel right. Everything was too fresh, too raw. She was still on guard. She needed to make sure everyone was okay before she could stand down.

A dull thud followed by the sound of splintering wood caught her attention. She glanced through the kitchen window to see Milo splitting logs. She wouldn't be surprised if he was keeping busy in an attempt to grapple with his own feelings of shock.

She searched the cupboards, looking for utensils and pans and found a flat tray and a muffin pan. There was no food processor or whisk, which wasn't a problem. She wasn't a high-tech, fancy baker. The act of measuring the ingredients, combining them until they were the right consistency, and then placing them in the oven grounded her in a way that nothing else did.

The tote held flour, sugar, salt, eggs, butter, cooking oil, blueberries, and chocolate chips. She wasn't sure what Michael's family liked. Maybe they didn't have a sweet tooth. Maybe they didn't like baked goods.

She was second-guessing herself, which was out of character for her. Normally, she decided on an action and took it. But this wasn't business as usual. Her job was to get victims out, whether it was a group of women who were held in bondage or a teen tricked into sex slavery. She rescued them. Their emotional recovery was taken care of by experts who were far smarter than her.

She stared at the chocolate chips. All these

ingredients had come from Nadie's kitchen, so someone in the family liked them. She would just focus on cooking and not care whether they liked the results. This wasn't about them; it was about regaining her equilibrium.

Michael entered. She wasn't sure what he'd been doing and decided not to ask. She didn't have the strength to deal with him right now. He grabbed his mom's purse, which sat at the far end of the counter, and rummaged through it. "Aha." He held up her smartphone with a look of triumph. Using a tool that looked like a straightened paperclip, he slipped out the sim card. Then he pried off the back and took out the battery. He threw the pieces into an empty fruit bowl, which sat on the white laminate table.

He'd watched her disable her phone back in Finn's office. He had complete recall; he would remember. That was one of the more infuriating things about him. With most men, if they didn't send you a birthday card or notice your new haircut, you could believe they'd simply forgotten all about it and cut them some slack, but with Michael, if he didn't react to something, it was because he'd decided it wasn't important. Of course, an argument could be made that if a man didn't notice your haircut, it was because you weren't important to him, which meant all men were jerks. She had to smile at that bit of absurd logic.

She concentrated on her recipe, which she

knew by heart, hoping for the Zen-like moment. There weren't any measuring cups in the cupboards. None that she could find, anyway. She guesstimated the ingredients. Her muffins would work out fine as long as she got the consistency right.

She froze when Michael stood next to her and stared out the window. An image of him standing behind her and slipping his arms around her waist, so her back aligned with his front, appeared in her mind, unbidden. The memory of him nestled between her legs when he'd rolled her away from the gunfire was fresh in her mind. Her pulse raced.

God, it had been years since she'd lain with a man. She liked men well enough, but she didn't like to get involved. Her work got in the way of relationships. She never knew if she would be called away. Come to think of it, she didn't know from one day to the next which country she would be in. But the memory of lying in Michael's arms after a mind-blowing organism was a siren's song that called to her. She shook the idea away, forcing her mind back to her baking. Michael was a friend, and using him for sex would be wrong, and she didn't want anything more than that.

"What do you think, is it safe to go out there while he's swinging an ax?" Michael raised his eyebrows.

"You have to get his phone, whether you want

to or not." It was standard for her to dismantle her phone when she didn't want to be tracked. "We should've taken care of this before at your parent's house."

"I wasn't thinking."

"You, *Michael the Brain,* wasn't thinking," she teased, calling him by the childhood nickname she knew he hated.

"It may surprise you to know that I get distracted just like anyone else."

"How can that be when you remember everything?"

"I can only recall what I *see.* Sounds and smells, not so much." He smiled. "Although, I do remember every detail of a wild weekend we had when we were eighteen."

Her heart hit a steady beat as her nerve endings sprang to life. He was flirting with her. She had no idea how to flirt. It usually wasn't necessary. Men were easy. Whenever she wanted sex, she made sure her target male was single and straight, and then she invited him to her place. It had been over two years since her last erotic stress release, and she knew Michael would be good. She glanced at Nadie and Ava cuddled up on the couch. No, this wasn't the time or place.

She schooled her features, giving him her best *I'm-bored* expression. "It's ancient history. Stop procrastinating and get on with your job. You need to dismantle those phones. Face the man with the ax and hope he doesn't take your head off by accident."

"Milo was a helicopter pilot for the US Air Force. He'll get it."

"I thought you didn't get along with him."

He gave her a rueful smile. "When I was fifteen maybe, but I've grown up a lot since then. Milo always uses work as therapy. He's not the problem." He nodded his head in Ava's direction. "She is."

His sister turned the volume up on the TV. It was now high enough to cause hearing damage.

Michael marched to the living area. "Ava, turn that down. We need to talk."

She straightened away from her mom's embrace, flicked a strand of long black hair over her shoulder, and then focused her dark eyes on her brother.

Sinclair turned her back and concentrated on adding her wet ingredients into the flour mixture. She substituted water for milk, seeing as they'd forgotten to bring some. Hopefully, no one would notice, and if they did, she didn't care.

"Why do you want my phone?" Ava shrieked. The alarm in the teen's voice caught Sinclair's attention. Michael was right. This would be unpleasant.

"They can track us. I should've taken this off you before we left."

"Don't be ridiculous. We're out of range. They can't track us when there's no signal." Ava's confidence rang out, loud and clear.

Michael sighed. "You know as well as I do there are times when we catch a stray signal."

"I'll give it to you after I call Caleb."

"Who the hell is Caleb?" Michael shouted.

Sinclair kept mixing, wishing she wasn't here, listening to this family moment. She argued with her brother, David, but not like this.

"He's my boyfriend." Ava's voice grew louder, and Sinclair wondered if the teen was now standing.

"Are you serious?" Michael yelled. "You want to endanger everyone just so you can call your boyfriend?"

"I knew you wouldn't understand. He might think I've dumped him. He might—"

"Do you want the men with guns to find you? Do you want to watch Mom and Dad get shot?" He was playing hard ball now.

Sinclair couldn't blame him. Ava's plan would put everyone in danger, but she also understood the need to contact friends and assure them everything was okay.

She spun around, coughed loudly, and then waited until he acknowledged her. "Actually, I have to call the office. If I don't make contact, they'll try and track my phone. Once they discover there's no signal, they might think I've been killed or taken. I don't want them to waste resources looking for me." The administrator for the Granite City branch of Child Seekers International was Amy Tupperman. Her sweet grand-motherly demeanor disguised a woman who was a pit bull when it came to protecting the operatives in her charge.

"That's not a good idea."

Sinclair's anger flared. "I said it before, I'll say it again, and this time you will listen." She cast her arm wide to include everyone present. "We were not prepared for this. We had plans. We have other people who care about us. People who will look for us. Not all of us have been in hiding for months."

He rolled his eyes.

It must be a family trait. A sea of red burning anger flooded her mind. She pounded the table with her fist "You shit. Don't you dare roll your eyes at me."

He stared at her for a moment. Finally, he said, "I apologize."

"For what? Not warning us or for being a giant asshat?"

He gave her a weak smile. "Both."

She wasn't ready to let him off the hook. "You must have a ghost chip in that burner phone of yours so we can all make a call."

He pulled his smartphone from his pocket and stared at it. "A ghost chip isn't a guarantee. There's new software on the market that makes it traceable."

"Then we won't call from here. There must be a pay phone we can drive to." She switched her gaze to Ava who sat with her mouth open, staring at Sinclair. She pointed to the teen. "Hand over your phone, now."

The young woman slipped her device out of the pocket of her hoodie and gave it to Michael.

"Thank you." Michael flipped off the back, dismantling it.

Sinclair turned back to her baking. Her hands shook after her outburst. Losing her temper was out of character for her, but he had managed to push her to her limit. A clinking noise echoed in the now silent room. She assumed it was the sound of the disassembled phone hitting the china bowl.

Michael marched out of the house without a word and slammed the door behind him. So much for her using him for sex relief.

CHAPTER SIX

Sinclair stood in the kitchen and picked at a blueberry muffin. Her baking therapy hadn't been as relaxing as usual, which wasn't surprising considering she was in a strange place with people she didn't know.

Plus, she had lost her temper with Michael. It had been foolish of her to think she could banish everything that had happened on this awful evening. It was just too overwhelming.

She was used to leaving home at a moment's notice and having her life in disarray. Her work abroad, which had slowed in the last year, required flexibility. But this was different. There were things waiting on her desk that she needed to get to. An informant had called her just as she was boarding her flight from Ukraine. The woman, a street worker in Kyiv, had called and told her Child Seekers had a leak and she would no longer be sharing information with them. Sinclair had tried to convince her to talk, but she'd hung up without saying more.

She took another bite. Normally, the taste of the sugar-covered muffin top comforted her. But it just turned to sawdust in her mouth. She blamed Michael. Their argument over the phones had only served to drive her stress level higher. In fairness, it wasn't all his fault. Just being in close proximity to him put her on edge. When it came to him, her emotional state shifted from physical attraction to anger. There seemed to be no balance, no middle ground.

As far as she knew, Michael hadn't seen his family in at least four months, and yet they seemed to be at ease with each other. She hadn't experienced that kind of affinity with anyone since Carla, her best friend and partner at Child Seekers, had died on assignment.

It made her feel inadequate, as though she was merely existing. She should be sharing her life with at least one other person. There was David, her brother, but he was starting a new life with Marie, and she didn't want to intrude. Besides, talking to him wasn't the same as gossiping with a girlfriend. She'd had close friends when she was in the army, but once she was out, they'd drifted apart.

She'd lost Carla a year ago. *God*. She would give anything to be able to chat with her again. Sinclair was currently coupled with Jake, a fine co-worker, but there was a distance between them that she couldn't span. He was in his fifties, divorced with two grownup children, but he never talked about them. As far as she could tell, his downtime consisted of watching sports while he drank beer.

The front door slammed open, and Michael marched past her and headed for a storage closet next to the bathroom. He grabbed an armful of blankets and sheets. "I'll put these in your cabin," he said as he headed out again.

"I'll help," Ava offered.

He smiled at his sister. "That's great, munchkin."

Ava grabbed some pillows and followed him out.

Sinclair peered at them through the kitchen window. The pair laughed as they entered the small outbuilding. Ava now seemed like a different person. Gone was the insolent teen. Now she seemed like a smiling, easy-going, happy girl. Sinclair took another bite of her muffin. The way they had put their argument aside was impressive. They hadn't talked about their differences and hadn't made a big deal about it. They'd simply moved on.

Her stomach cramped. Food wasn't what she wanted right now. She needed some space, a place to be alone. She put the plated muffins and scones on the kitchen table and headed for the door.

The moment she stepped into the cool night air, she felt better. She could sense the change of seasons, from summer to fall. She wasn't sure why. Maybe it was the cool night air or the scent of the leaves changing. An owl hooted somewhere in the distance as if it were laughing at her. Insects chirped in the forest. She inhaled, breathing in the calming sounds of the wilderness.

She stepped down from the porch. When she looked up, she gasped. She'd seen the Milky Way before, but now that they were away from the light pollution of the city, she could see a thousand points of light sparkling in the sky. It always filled her with a sense of wonder.

Michael and Ava walked out of the little cottage. They're voices were low as they talked in hushed tones. Once again, she felt like an interloper, someone who had been thrust upon them.

Ava broke away from her brother, smiled at Sinclair, and said, "Good night." Then headed into the main house.

Sinclair smiled back but couldn't form any words. She was suddenly beyond exhausted, every muscle in her body hurt, and her bruised face was aching.

Michael met her in the middle of the yard. "When I want to be alone, I climb on the roof."

Was it that obvious she needed time to herself? She swung around to stare at it but couldn't make out any details. The only light came from the kitchen window. "Is it corrugated? How do you get up there?"

"There's a trellis at the far end of the porch.

It probably won't support my weight now and, yes, it's corrugated and uncomfortable as hell, but on a night like this, when the breeze is keeping the mosquitos at bay, there's no better view."

"I'm not going up there."

He stood close, invading her space, but she didn't back away. She enjoyed his nearness and his warmth that seemed to caress her without touching. His scent, a combination of soap and musk, surrounded her. He must've taken a shower in her room because she would've known if he'd used the bathroom in the main house.

He nudged her shoulder with his. "Are you scared of heights?"

If she'd had the energy, she would've laughed. "You know I'm not. I did rope climbing in boot camp. I'm just too tired."

His gaze roamed her body. What he saw she couldn't say, and with her exhaustion, she was beyond caring.

"If you don't want to go up on the roof, you can sit on the deck. You'll be out of the breeze so there'll be more mosquitos, and you won't be able to see the stars—"

"Of course, I can see the stars."

He frowned. "You'll be under the porch roof."

"I can turn my head; the porch isn't completely closed in."

One corner of his mouth curled in a lopsided smile. "Good point."

"How are you a genius?"

"I never said I was a genius."

She snorted. It wasn't very ladylike, but sometimes a well-placed grunt got her message across better than words.

He toed a loose stone in the driveway and then stopped and stared at the house. Finally, his gaze settled on her. "I'm sorry. I should have thought of your safety. I should have thought—"

"You were injured...hurt. You probably weren't thinking about much else." Maybe she was letting him off easy, but four months ago, he'd been in so much pain it had been torturous to watch him try to move.

He acknowledged her words with a curt nod. "I'm also sorry I brought Marshall Portman and the Syndicate into our lives."

"We met Marshall when we were Sixteen. You'd already gone home. You never even knew him. How does he have anything to do with you?

"Didn't David tell you?"

"Tell me what?"

He rubbed his jaw. His dark eyes focused on her for a moment and then he looked away. "You were sick when I left. You'd given up. I was scared you were going to die. I came home so I could look for a place for you. I found Marshall House, a charity that took in street kids and helped them get an education. I emailed Portman and told him about you and where to find you. I'm sorry, I should've—"

"Should've what? Not saved us?" She stepped back and stared at him and then opened her mouth to speak but no words came out. All these years, she thought he'd abandoned her... them. She'd forgiven him because, if she'd had a safe home, she would've gone in an instant. But there'd been nothing to forgive. He hadn't deserted them at all.

He shrugged, staring at the ground. "I wouldn't have said anything, but I thought David told you."

She shook her head as her eyes filled with tears. She pressed her lips together. This was the end of a long, stressful day, but she'd be damned if she would cry. She wasn't the weepy type. "Thank you for not leaving me on the street to die." She placed her hand on his elbow. "You saved us. Marshall House gave us food, a secure place to sleep, an education, and a future. You should be proud of that."

"But all the trouble—

She kissed him on the lips lightly, a peck, and then withdrew, shocked by her own actions.

He stared at her with the same sense of amazement.

She retreated, walking backward toward the small cabin. "Sorry, I never meant...you looked so...like you'd done something wrong. You didn't."

She turned and ran. What the hell was she thinking? That was the problem; she hadn't been thinking. She'd allowed her emotions to override her commonsense. This was exactly why she hadn't wanted to come here. Michael was too good to resist.

CHAPTER SEVEN

Sinclair could've soaked in the shower for hours. Unfortunately, she ran out of hot water after fifteen minutes. Her teeth were chattering by the time she was clean. The bathroom was small with just a shower stall, a sink, and toilet.

She dried her hair, as best she could, feeling almost fit. That is, as well as she could expect when she had a fat lip, ached all over, and her right eye was almost swollen shut. The bruise on her hip wasn't a concern. It might hurt for a day or two, but it was nothing an icepack couldn't cure.

She hung the towel on the rack and opened the door to find Michael making up the sofa bed.

He stopped tucking in the sheet and stared at her, open mouthed.

"What are you doing here?" she demanded.

He grinned. "I see you weren't expecting me."

She looked down. "Shit." She was naked. She slammed shut the bathroom door. "What the hell, Michael? I can figure out the bed. I don't need you to do it for me."

"I'm not doing it for you. I'm doing it for us."

"Us?" she squeaked. Unfortunately, the towel wasn't big enough to cover her completely.

"Did you say you'd just got back from Ukraine?" he called.

"Yes." Where was he going with this?

"Are all your clothes dirty?"

"Yes." She'd been planning to sleep in the nude rather than wear dirty clothing to bed. That wasn't going to happen now.

He knocked on the bathroom door. "I have a clean shirt you can use. There's a washer and dryer in the main cabin. If you give me your clothes, I'll put them in the wash for you."

That was a kind offer, but she didn't feel comfortable with the idea of him laundering her underwear. She checked to make sure she was decent and then opened the door a crack. "I'll do it myself."

He shoved his top through the gap. "You're going to traipse through the main house in nothing but a T-shirt? Interesting, I never pegged you as an exhibitionist."

She could hear the laughter in his voice. "Bastard."

That triggered a belly laugh.

He was still grinning when she opened the door. Luckily, his T-shirt came down to her thighs. Her wet hair was slicked back over her shoulders and, although her breasts were small, she knew it was chilly enough in the room to make her nipples pucker.

His Adam's apple bobbed as his gaze traveled down her body. "I-I brought you two aspirin and a glass of water. I figured you'd be achy." He pointed to an end table next to the sofa bed, all the while staring at her chest.

She couldn't help but smile when she saw the bulge in his pants. She'd spent most of her professional life trying not to be a sexual creature. Attracting that kind of unwanted attention was dangerous in her line of work. But it felt good to know she could excite him, at least physically. For years, she'd wondered what it was about her that had driven him away. She'd buried her insecurities once she'd come to the realization that it didn't matter why he'd left. If he considered her lacking, then to hell with him. Plus, she needed to find her own balance and live the life she wanted instead of waiting for someone else's validation. The girl who'd been in love with him was gone, but the woman she'd become didn't mind indulging in a little payback.

"Thanks." She skirted past him, grabbed the pills, and downed them with the water. She did hurt, and hoped they would work quickly.

She opened her small case and tugged out a plastic bag full of her dirty clothes. She then added the jeans and T-shirt she'd been wearing and thrust them toward him. "Here, you may do my laundry." She felt like a snotty princess ordering an underling around, but he deserved it.

He stared at her, then at the bag. Finally, his gaze switched to her breasts. "Err-err."

He seemed to be struggling to talk so she helped him out. "You were right. I can't walk through the main cabin dressed like this." She waved him away. "Goodnight."

He took the bag and left without saying a word. It was very satisfying to put him in his place. Maybe she should be bossy, or overtly sexual, more often.

She took a deep breath and released it, blowing away tension that had built up in her muscles. She shook one leg and then the other, then followed the same procedure with her arms and hands, loosening all her joints. Finally, she rolled her neck. A few ligaments popped.

It might be the end of a horrendous day, but she was still in one piece. She needed sleep, even if it was only for a few hours. But she couldn't relax unless she was armed. She sat on the edge of the bed and grabbed her backpack off the floor. First, she retrieved her pistol and placed it on the nightstand. Then she fished out her collapsible baton and unhooked her car keys. She'd have to rethink the combination; it had been a little awkward in action. Although, this was the first time she'd had to dive into her car with it extended, and maybe she'd overreacted when she'd headed for her car instead of her apartment.

Urgh. She was too tired to think of all the things she should, or should not, have done. Experience had taught her that her emotions stayed under control when she was in the thick of a situation, but once the danger was over, then the second-guessing, nightmares, and insomnia would follow. She rubbed her face. All these issues could wait. Right now, she was in survival mode and needed to rest while she could.

She placed the baton under her pillow then turned off the light and climbed into bed. A groan escaped her lips at the pleasure of being horizontal. Thankfully, Michael had laid two sleeping bags side-by-side so they wouldn't be sharing a blanket. It was one thing to tease him and know he was attracted by the sight of her; it was quite another to lie under the same cover and share their body heat. That would be too intimate, and there was no way she could handle it. She zipped up the side of her bag and shifted until she was comfortable.

Starting with her feet and working her way up her body, she contracted and relaxed her muscles while she ran through the day's events. The routine always helped her decompress.

The cabin door opened, and Michael entered. She could tell it was him by the sound of his footfalls and his scent.

The mattress sagged as he sat on the edge and

then he laid down next to her. He rolled on his side, facing away from her. It had been sixteen years since they'd been in the same bed, a lifetime ago, and yet something inside her wanted him to turn her way and wrap his arms around her. An old saying ran through her mind. *The more things change, the more they stay the same.*

****

Michael tried not to move, but the metal bar that ran underneath the mattress poked him in the back, making it impossible to sleep. An errant mosquito buzzed near his ear. He waved it away.

The day had caught up with Sinclair. That much was obvious. Working for Child Seekers International had to be hard on her emotionally. He'd done some cyber-sleuthing when she'd joined them, just to make sure they were on the up and up. What he'd found was a team of dedicated individuals who worked tirelessly with law enforcement across the globe in an effort to track down missing children and bring an end to modern slavery by preventing exploitation, rescuing victims, and educating society.

It wasn't a surprise that Sinclair, who had been sexually assaulted as a minor, would be drawn to save others, especially as she was a gifted linguist.

She sighed and rolled over. The bed sagged in the middle, which made him feel as though he was sliding toward her.

She whimpered and then rolled back to the other side.

She must be dead to the world because there was no way she would have shown any kind of weakness if she was awake. He liked that she was a force to be reckoned with, even when he was on the receiving end of it, like this evening in Finn's office or when she had lashed out over Ava's phone.

He groaned and rolled away from her. She'd been right to blame him. He hadn't warned her about the Syndicate, but he had kept tabs on them while he was recovering. There'd been nothing invasive about his research, at least nothing that would make them come after his family and friends. Lance Ackerman's heirs were busy fighting over his estate. In fact, they were so wrapped up in their petty squabbling they posed no threat whatsoever. He'd also checked on Lucy Portman's activities to make sure she wasn't making trouble and found nothing.

He shifted again so he wasn't lying on his left side, which tended to go numb if he rested on it for too long.

"Can't sleep?" Sinclair whispered.

"Sorry, did I wake you?" he answered in the same hushed tones. Although why he was talking so quietly, he couldn't say.

"No, bad dream."

"You just fell asleep. How did you have time to dream?"

"Really? I was hoping I'd gotten an hour at least."

"I think it's been about five minutes, maybe ten."

She was silent for a long time. He thought she might have drifted off again when she said, "He was aiming for you."

He knew, without explanation, she was talking about the third gunman at his parent's house. There was no denying her observation. The moment the wood had splintered by his head, he'd known he was the target. The Syndicate had come for the people he loved because they wanted to know his location. Everything that had happened on this God-awful night was because of him. "I'm sorry you got drawn into this."

"I was always in this...whatever 'this' is. The four of us always stood together. And if a bunch of greedy corporate CEOs need taking down, then we're the ex-street bums to do it."

He smiled. "Thank you for hiding me."

"Anytime. It's what I do."

"That and baking. Which is awesome, by the way. When did you learn to bake?"

"My mom taught me when I was a little girl. I miss her."

He was surprised by her openness. "You've never talked about your life before you ended up on the street."

"I'm an adult now, and I decided to face my past."

"Why?"

"I figured there'd always be a piece of me missing if I didn't learn to deal with what happened. I don't know if that makes sense."

"It makes perfect sense. You don't want the past to define you, but how can you move on if you pretend it didn't happen? That would be like lying to yourself. Is that it?"

"Yes. Exactly." The smile in her voice made everything seem brighter.

"Actually," she continued, "it worked out great. I tracked down my aunt. She inherited my parents' house after my stepdad, Russel, died and David and I ran away."

"Why didn't you go live with them? Why'd you end up on the street?"

"We killed Russel, remember?"

"David said he killed Russel."

"I had a part in it, too."

"That's not the way your brother tells it."

He could almost hear the cogs turning in her brain.

"I'll have to talk to him."

He snorted. "Good luck with that. David's as closed off as they come."

"Marie's changed him." Her voice softened. "He's happier now, easier somehow."

"You like her."

"You make that sound like a bad thing and, no, I don't like her. I love her. Without her, David would still be a shell, living a life of self-imposed isolation. Besides, she gave me one of her solar panels."

"She what?"

"She gave—"

"You have a solar panel that can be folded into a backpack and create enough electricity to power an apartment building?"

"Not on me. I use it to power my she-shed."

"Your what?" He felt like he was repeating himself.

"My she-shed. It's a—"

"I know what a she-shed is. You live in an apartment. Where the hell did you put it? On the roof?"

She laughed. It was a musical sound and one he realized he hadn't heard since they were teens. Back then, their amusement had been born out of a desperate need to escape their situation. This was different. It wasn't forced. It was as though he was meeting a new version of Sinclair—Sinclair 2.0.

"It's on my cousin's brother-in-law's land near the Beaverhead-Deerlodge National Forest."

"Hold on. You have a cousin? I thought it was just you and David."

She sighed, clearly exasperated with him. "I told you I got in touch with my aunt who inherited the house."

"Yeah, so?"

"Seriously, how are you considered smart? My aunt had children. They felt terrible about the house. I mean, it wasn't really theirs. I assured them I wasn't after the money—"

"What did you want?

She sighed. "I'm getting to that. Stop interrupting."

"Sorry."

"I wanted photos. I didn't have any pictures of my mom and dad."

"Did they have any?"

"Yeah." She rolled to face him. "And they're good people."

"Did David go with you to meet them?" Even though his eyes had adjusted to the darkness, he still couldn't make out her features.

"No, he's my brother. I don't need his permission to find my family."

"But they're his family, too."

The bed moved as she shrugged. She fidgeted for a while, getting comfortable, and then said, "I asked him at the outset. He didn't want to know. He thought we should leave the past in the past."

"But you couldn't." It was a statement of fact more than a question, but she answered him anyway.

"Like I said, part of me was missing. For a long time, I buried the memory of my parents because I couldn't deal with everything I had lost."

"When we were on the street, you always longed to be part of a family. You used to tell us stories about how one day we would live in a big house and we'd always be warm and have food." They'd sat in their plastic bag shelter on cold winter's nights and listened to her tales. She'd described everything in wonderful detail. The house would be surrounded by trees because Tim loved the wilderness. She included computer games in her stories because Michael loved them. The twin's needs were much more practical—a warm bed and full bellies. Looking back, he realized how much it said about them that their big dream was not to be hungry.

"Anyway." She drew out the word, a reminder he was getting off topic. "My elderly aunt and her children felt bad they'd sold the house and used the money for medical bills."

"Even though you told them you didn't want it."

"Like I said, they're good people. My cousin's brother-in-law owns a massive property. His place stretches for miles. It's larger than Tim's ranch, and he offered me use of his land. I asked if I could put a she-shed on a small corner. I need a bolt hole, a place to unwind, and now I have a cabin I built myself."

"And powered by your sister-in-law's solar panel."

"Of course," she said and then gave a jaw-popping yawn.

"You should get some sleep."

"Why are they after us? And why now?"

He couldn't blame her for sounding baffled; he was confused, too.

"I've been trying to figure that out." He lay on his back and massaged his temples "I have a gap in my memory. I can't remember what happened before Portman hit me with his car. I recall being in the fifth-floor conference room of the PDE building, but everything after that is a blank."

"What's the last thing you do remember?"

"I emailed a video clip to Finn that exonerated David. After that—nothing. The doctor said it was caused by the concussion."

She shivered. "I saw you fly up and onto the hood of the car. I swear you bounced when you landed on the sidewalk. It makes me feel sick to think about. I was always grateful you were unconscious because, otherwise, you would've been screaming in agony."

"I always thought that was a good thing, too, but now I'm not so sure."

"I don't understand."

"What if I implanted a piece of malware that was set to go off in the future?"

"How likely is that? I mean, it's been over nine months since you helped David."

She had a point. "I could have written a code that I meant to trigger remotely and someone else accidently set it off, or I could've put a timer on it...like a failsafe."

"Say you did write a virus that would infect their computers at a later date...what would you get out of it?"

"Information on the other members of the

Syndicate, but that's a guess. I don't know for certain. You need to get some rest. We'll talk in the morning."

She didn't answer. Within moments, her breathing became deep and even.

He lay in the darkness, waiting for sleep. Images from the day poured through his mind: Sinclair's bruised face, his family barricaded in the basement, rolling with Sinclair across the floor, scared she'd get hit by stray gunfire, the argument with Ava, and Sinclair baking.

That final thought filled him with peace. He didn't know why, and he didn't care. He held onto it until he drifted off.

CHAPTER EIGHT

Finn Callaghan sipped his coffee and sighed. Appreciating the stale, day-old, microwaved java meant he had no standards. He'd caught a few hours' sleep in his chair with his feet up on the desk, which hadn't been comfortable.

Kennedy smiled as she marched into their shared office. She held out a large disposable cup and then frowned. "You already have one."

He met her in the middle of the room and took the offered drink from her hand. "Yeah, but it tastes like shit."

She eyed him, her frown deepening. She obviously didn't like what she saw. "I thought you were going back to your apartment after the home invasion."

He swallowed a mouthful of coffee. It was hot and smooth. He resisted the urge to drain every last drop. "Army CID released Michael's old cases, at least the ones that aren't classified."

"And you stayed to go through them. Did you turn up any suspects?" With her free hand, she straightened the papers on her desk.

He shook his head. "No. Most are either dead or still in jail. The ones that are out are more likely to commit identity theft and screw with his credit rating. I can't see they'd have the means to carry out a coordinated attack on Sinclair and his family."

"We had to check it out. Papin didn't sit behind a desk, decoding computer viruses when he was with Army CID. He had an undercover identity that he used without permission when he went into PDE. We wouldn't be doing our jobs if we didn't look into his background."

"You do realize that, technically, these cases don't fall under FBI jurisdiction."

"I don't know about that. Papin is a former federal agent."

"I like how you think." He took another mouthful, enjoying the invigorating feeling of caffeine flowing through his veins.

She stopped what she was doing and scrutinized him over the rim of her mug. "You think it's them, don't you?"

"Who?" He didn't want to drag her down into what was almost certainly a career-killing case.

"What do you mean 'who'?" She slammed her cup down on the table, causing a small amount of liquid to slosh through the sip hole. "The Syndicate. The group that set up David Quinn for kidnapping, tried to steal an old man's land using Eminent Domain laws, engineered a bank robbery to expose an arson-for-profit ring, and who have someone in the Department of Justice who has access to our personnel files." By the time she was done they were nose to nose.

"Oh, the Syndicate." He stepped back, putting some distance between them. Damn it. Not only was she too smart, she was also the only person he could trust. If he lied to her, he would destroy any faith she might have in him, and he wasn't prepared to go there. He had to be upfront. "It has to be them. Who else could it be?"

Kennedy never let him get away with anything. Behind her upper-class background, expensive clothes, and good looks was an ex-US Marine and a patriot who believed in doing the right thing regardless of the cost.

She nodded. "Do we have enough surveillance on Lucy Portman?"

"No, and Deluca was warned by the assistant director of the FBI to stay away from her. She's well-connected. Our orders are not to go near her unless we have something concrete." Finn had no doubt that his superior, FBI Special Agent in Charge Martin Deluca had nothing to do with the Syndicate. But he was a man who understood, and obeyed, the chain of command.

Kennedy whistled. "You never told me it went as high as the assistant director. Do you think he's the one who sent your personnel files to Ackerman? The Syndicate will share them publicly if we get too close."

He paced to the window, staring out over the Granite City Square. The sun rose, streaking vibrant shades of orange and pink across the sky. It was going to be a warm fall day. He suddenly wished he and Kennedy were having breakfast at a restaurant with a patio, talking about anything but work. The PDE building stood at the opposite end of the square, tall and forbidding in the stark morning light, a reminder there would be no time for intimate meals. "I wonder why they haven't revealed my past yet. I expected it to be splashed across social media months ago."

"Maybe they thought they could blackmail you with it, but apart from a human-interest story, there's nothing about the son of a prostitute making good that's notable. It's not like you doctored evidence, took bribes, or sent an innocent man to jail. You had no control over where you were born or who your parents were. None of us do."

Her comment reminded him she had her own family issues with which she grappled. He faced her and gave her a curt nod.

She folded her arms across her chest and leaned against his desk. "How are we going to get anything on Lucy if we can't go near her?"

He understood her frustration. "We'll start at the beginning, and if the evidence points to her, we will follow it, just like any other case. If we have proof, then the higher-ups can't tell us to back off."

She nodded then pressed her lips into a thin line. Which meant despite her agreement, she had her doubts about his plan. "What do you want me to do?"

He plucked a report off his desk and gave it to her. "Sinclair Quinn was attacked on the west side. Why don't you see if there's any footage from street cams? Let's identify her attackers. The medical examiner won't have the reports on the three men from the home invasion until this afternoon. I'll call the Granite City-Elkhead County crime scene guys and see if they have anything yet. But first, I'll call Deluca and fill him in on everything that's happened."

She raised her eyebrows. "You haven't called him yet?"

"No." Deluca was as troubled by the discovery of the Syndicate mole as Finn. He had no idea if his superior was taking steps to discover the culprit. He was out of the loop, which wasn't unusual. Investigators only shared the details of a case with those directly involved in the enquiry.

Despite the early hour, Special Agent in Charge Martin Deluca picked up on the first ring. "Callaghan, if you're calling at this time of the morning, it can't be good."

"No, sir." Finn explained the situation, ending with the fact that since Michael had been a federal agent, it would justify FBI involvement.

"It's better if you let the locals take care of it."

"Sir?" Finn couldn't believe what he was hearing. "Michael Papin got us evidence. Evidence that was stolen by someone with access, and now they're hunting him. There's no proof, but I would put money on this being the Syndicate. They are going through his family and friends to get to him."

There was a long pause. "I agree. That's why we're better off letting the locals take this one, with our assist. The two crimes are essentially a mugging and a home invasion. They come under local jurisdiction."

Deluca wanted the Granite City-Elkhead County Police Department to lead, which must mean the FBI was still suspect. No, not the FBI. Paul Harris, the former mayor of Hopefalls and a witness in the Molly's Mountain case, had been killed while under the protection of the U.S. Marshals. That meant the problem was within the Department of Justice, which oversaw both agencies. If the file was handled by local law enforcement, there would be no paperwork leading directly back to the DOJ. Finn knew the FBI had launched an investigation into all three security breaches; Harris's murder, the stolen evidence that proved a connection between Marshall Portman and the Syndicate, which Michael had collected, and the release of Finn's personal information.

Given Deluca's instruction to hand the cases over to local law enforcement, Finn had to assume the FBI were no closer to plugging the leak.

"I understand. I'll contact Captain Tate and share what we know."

"Sounds good."

"Sir?" Finn said before his superior could hang up.

"What?"

"Just to clarify. You want me to tell them everything we know or suspect...about the Syndicate, too?"

There was a long pause. "In confidence, yes, but make it unofficial. We have no proof they exist and..." He paused again.

"Yes?" Finn prompted.

"This should go without saying, but use your commonsense and don't make us look bad. Be vague on the details."

"Understood."

"And, Callaghan, watch your back. That goes for Morris, too." Deluca disconnected.

As far as Finn could tell, the Syndicate was a multinational criminal organization. There was no way the Granite City-Elkhead County Police Department were equipped to deal with the case, but this wasn't an investigation—this was damage control.

CHAPTER NINE

Sinclair kept her eyes closed, pretending to be asleep as Michael crept around the small cabin. Hopefully, he would leave, and she could have some time to get her act together before she had to face him and the rest of his family.

She'd woken in the middle of the night to find herself curled against him, his breath warming her neck. She'd lain there for a moment to enjoy their closeness and the feel of his strong body alongside hers. His deep and even breathing had told her he was asleep and unaware of their physical contact. The intimacy of them sharing a bed, if not a blanket, brought back all the sensual memories of their wild weekend. For that short time, they had lain together, hot and sweaty with their legs entwined.

Finally, she'd summoned all her willpower and turned away from him. Unfortunately, the mattress drooped in the middle, so she was forced to cling on to the edge to prevent herself from rolling back to the center.

After that, she had napped, waking at every unfamiliar noise. She was haunted by disjointed dreams in which she replayed the day's events over and over. Finally, when the gray light of dawn leeched through the flimsy curtains, she had sunk into a deep sleep.

The bed sagged as Michael sat on the edge, mug in hand. "I wasn't sure how you take your coffee. I figured black would be good."

She opened her eyes, yawned, and then glared at him. "Go away." She rolled to the middle of the bed, happy to have the space to herself. Her head still ached, probably from a mild concussion, and the swelling around her bruised eye meant it would only open a crack. She patted her fat lip and then ran her tongue along the inside of her mouth. There was a split where the punch had landed, but it wasn't bad, and luckily her teeth weren't damaged.

"My family enjoyed your baking. Ava, especially, liked the muffins. It's nearly nine. I'm not going away."

She sighed and sat up. "You do know I have jet-lag, don't you?"

When he smiled, she was captivated by the lines around his mouth. Deep creases formed a dimple on one side, making him look young, cheeky, and charismatic. His face was fuller now than it had been when they were teens. There were crow's-feet at the corners of his dark eyes and a smattering of gray at his temples. His high cheekbones, thick pelt of short-cropped hair, and tanned complexion spoke to his Native American heritage.

Funnily enough, it'd been years since she'd noticed his appearance. Not because he wasn't a handsome man, but because the way he looked really didn't matter. His intelligence, integrity, and the way he'd always been there for her were way more important. She had an overwhelming urge to reach out and trace the contours of his features. She fisted her hands, resisting the temptation. At eighteen, she'd imagined he was as in love with her as she'd been with him. That had been a mistake. She took the coffee from him and sniffed. It smelled great, not too strong.

"Thanks," she mumbled and took a sip.

"I thought we could go for a hike after breakfast." He leaned across her legs and rested his elbow on the bed so his head was supported by his hand. He was essentially lying over her so she couldn't move. She hadn't expected him to be so familiar and wasn't sure how to deal with it.

She attempted to comb her hair away from her face. What should have been a soothing move became a tug of war with her fingers getting stuck in a giant knot. Finally, she managed to disentangle herself and calmly took another sip of her coffee as if nothing had happened.

He lay before her, looking like a cover model for a men's fitness magazine, whereas she probably had the appearance of a woman who'd just survived a blender. That thought brought her back to reality. She pointed to a neatly folded pile of clothes on his side of the bed. "Are those mine."

He gave a mock salute. "Yes ma'am. Clean, fluffed and folded."

She placed her coffee cup on the end table. "You need to leave so I can get dressed."

"Really? I saw you naked yesterday."

"That was a mistake, as you well know. I want some alone time to get my act together, and you are going to give it to me." Was he trying to aggravate her on purpose or was he just an idiot? If she was a betting woman, she would put her money on him being an idiot.

"If I don't go, you'll probably kick my butt." He levered himself into a sitting position.

"I am armed." She pulled her baton from under her pillow but didn't flick it open.

He grinned, stood, and walked to the door.

"Let's set some ground rules," she said, stopping him as he reached for the handle.

"Such as?"

"I let you sleep here last night because I was too tired and sore to argue, but do not take that as a sign of weakness. You will not push my buttons. You will not crowd me or try to goad me. Do you understand?" She wasn't a woman who played games. The fact that she had feelings for him didn't mean she would put up with any crap. In fact, it meant the opposite. He was important to her, and she should matter enough for him to treat her with respect.

He gave her a small smile. "It's good to see you're feeling better." And then he left, closing the door gently behind him.

She stared after him, unsure of what had just happened. Was he testing her resilience? She thought he might be. She'd recently finished reading a biography of the British wartime leader, Winston Churchill. He was credited with coining the phrase, "It is a riddle, wrapped in a mystery, inside an enigma." Churchill hadn't been talking about Michael when he'd uttered those words, but the description fit him to a T all the same.

****

Michael stood with his back against the kitchen counter, watching Sinclair interact with his family. They liked her, which shouldn't come as a surprise. She was a good person, with a kind heart, who could kick butt with the best of them.

His mom had given him a knowing look as she made breakfast. He'd shrugged it off. He was a grown man, and if he wanted to spend his time in the company of a beautiful woman, he would. Especially when that woman was Sinclair Quinn, warrior woman and savior to the victimized.

Ava and Milo had stayed for a while, but as the conversation drifted to his mom's job as a victim's advocate, they said their goodbyes and went outside, planning on trying their hand at carving a dugout canoe. The process required them to find a large tree, chop it down, and shape the trunk into a boat. It was a lot of work and didn't interest him in the slightest.

He took another gulp of coffee. It was cold and stale. He hadn't slept well. Being in the same bed as Sinclair had reminded him of their weekend together. Those memories had led to a raging hard-on. Thank God, they'd been in separate sleeping bags, so she was in no danger of being poked by his erection. But when she'd curled up against him in her sleep, he thought he might explode.

He'd always been physically attracted to her, and that hadn't diminished after all this time. But he was surprised by how much she'd changed. She wasn't the lost teen who needed rescuing. She'd saved herself. This woman was confident, centered, and capable.

Her laughter brought him back to their conversation.

She'd showered and left her hair to air dry and wore no makeup. It was as though she was saying to the world, "I am who I am. Take it or leave it."

His mom refilled her coffee cup and sat next to Sinclair. "You knew Michael when he ran away, didn't you?

Shit, shit, shit.

"Yes. We met the first night he arrived. There

were a group of pimps who worked the bus station. They're specialty was convincing runaway boys they would care for them, and then they would force them into prostitution as repayment."

"And you got him away from them?" His mom tilted her head to one side, questioning Sinclair's version of events.

Sinclair Smiled. "The way my brother tells it, he was trying to get away. He just needed a little help. After that, he joined us."

"Who's us?"

"Me, my brother, David, and Tim."

"And you were all living on the street?"

Sinclair nodded as she fingered the top edge of her coffee cup, her nervousness evident. "Then we met Finn when we were in boot camp, and he…I don't know really. He just became a friend, someone we could trust."

"And now you help find missing children?" His mom's eyes narrowed. She was assessing Sinclair.

"Child Seekers investigators work on a variety of cases. Depending on the skillset required for the case. We can deal with runaways, lost or stolen children, or sex trafficking," Sinclair explained. Her green eyes met his mother's gaze, revealing her confidence. "Because I speak several languages, my work often involves rescuing women and children from human trafficking. Most slavery is domestic, although there are occasions when it crosses international borders."

Nadie patted Sinclair's arm. "That sounds... intense."

"It is. I just got back yesterday evening from Ukraine." Sinclair took another sip.

"And then you came to save us. You must be exhausted."

Sinclair gave a sheepish grin. "That's why I slept so late."

"I'm so pleased Michael has you in his life." His mom stood and scanned the cabin. "If we're going to live here, I need to get organized. We have no food or cleaning supplies."

Her abrupt change of subject surprised him. It was as though she had found out what she needed to know and was now ready to move on.

"I'll help." Sinclair pushed her chair away from the table.

Michael cleared his throat. "Actually, there are things you and I need to discuss. I thought we could go for a hike."

Her brow crinkled. "Sure, I'm ready. I just need a water bottle."

He reached into the cupboard above the fridge and took out a canister. "And bear spray."

CHAPTER TEN

She'd been armed at breakfast. Her Glock was secured in a thigh holster. Michael had been so worried about his mom's reaction to Sinclair, he hadn't noticed. She led the way through the yard toward a dirt track. She wore skintight black leggings, a white T-shirt, and her water bottle, and baton hung from her gun belt, which was wrapped around her middle. Her outfit accentuated her slim waist and her curves. His mouth went dry, and he suddenly felt light-headed. He needed to get his act together and not allow himself to get distracted by her long legs, great butt, or the powerful way she moved.

He pushed ahead of her. "I'll lead the way. I know the area."

What a load of bullshit. He hadn't been here since he was a kid. He knew there was a narrow trail that ran around a small lake. The path had probably changed over the past twenty years, but staring at her behind for the whole trek was not going to do him any good.

They reached the water's edge and stopped. The snow-capped Rockies were no longer obscured by the dense forest.

The western larch trees were bright yellow, a stark contrast to the green pine and the bright blue sky. The whole panorama was reflected in the still water of the lake, creating a breathtaking mirrored effect.

She stared at the view. "You wanted to talk to me?"

He nodded, picked up a flat stone, and threw it, trying to skim it across the water. It bounced twice and then sank. "When I went undercover at PDE, I noticed some accounting irregularities."

"What kind of irregularities?"

"They were funneling a lot of money to other companies, ones held by Lucy Portman." He turned to face her.

Her gaze darted from his butt to the water as her cheeks reddened. "I don't understand the significance."

A fission of excitement shot through him. She'd been checking him out. "Before she was Mrs. Portman, she was Lucy Holstein."

"Like the cow?"

His brow crinkled. "What cow?"

"There's a breed..." She waved away the thought. "It doesn't matter, continue."

"Her family ran a brokerage firm. They were hit hard by the last recession and were bailed out by the sale of five properties. That, in itself, doesn't seem too strange. You'd expect rich people to have more than one real estate holding —"

"But you dug a little deeper." She started walking, following the footpath that circled the lake.

He joined her, matching her stride. "They purchased all five homes only six months before they sold—"

"Money laundering." She tilted her head to one side.

"How much do you know about it?"

"The basics. A human trafficker will take their ill-gotten gains and pay cash for a property. Then six months to a year later, they sell the place. They can then declare the money they made from the sale. That's how they make their illegal money look legal. Although, I think it's more complicated than that, but I'm not someone who understands accounting."

"You've got the essentials. I did some cyber-investigating while I was recuperating. Nothing that could be tracked back to me. I just peeked at the company's business and personal bank accounts and social media, but I kept hitting a wall. I know she has money coming in from somewhere, but I can't find it. Although, they have an air-gapped computer—"

She stopped in the shade of a Ponderosa pine. A bead of sweat formed on her neck. "Is it an isolated system? Like the police?"

"Yes, which means I can't hack it because it's not on the internet. Although a truly air-gapped computer isn't even part of a network. You can only download data to it physically, but this one was part of a secure system."

"Could you have planted a virus to access this network when you were helping David?"

He stopped to consider the ramifications and then kicked a clump of weeds. "I can't remember, but I had to have caused this. I could have infiltrated their grid. You, my mom, Ava, Milo, you're all in danger because I probably planted some malware and then forgot about it. I've never forgotten anything, ever. I'm actually incapable of forgetting."

She held up her hand. "Hold on, do you know for sure you planted this virus or whatever it is?"

"No, but I've written a piece of code that would seek out a link to the nearest internet signal and connect an isolated grid to the web. From there, I would be able to hack in and trace all their transactions. I used it when I was Army CID. All I had to do was upload it."

"How would you know if you planted it or not?"

"If I had access to their computer, I'd know within seconds."

"Can we figure it out without walking into the PDE building?" There was something in the way she looked at him, her eyes soft and tender, that made him ache to touch her. Her tongue darted out to lick her lips.

He brushed a silky strand of hair away from her face and then leaned close. "You smell like cake."

He lay small kisses beneath her ear. She lifted her head, allowing him better access. It was a small gesture on her part, but his heart slammed against his ribcage.

Then she stiffened and stepped back, staring at him wide-eyed.

Her reaction was like having a lump of ice shoved down his shorts. He'd acted before he could think. He'd fantasized about caressing her for years. "I'm sorry. I didn't mean to force myself on you. I just—"

"Shut up." She wrapped her arms around his neck, tugging him closer. Her mouth slanted over his. His senses seemed to go into overdrive. He could feel the chill in the breeze that told him winter was coming, hear the rustle of the leaves and smell the pine needles underfoot.

Then he inhaled her scent, vanilla cake mixed with sex, and he was lost. Blood raced through his veins. He caressed her lips with his, trying to be gentle, not wanting to hurt her bruises. It was as though he'd been thirsty for years and was finally able to drink.

When her tongue slipped into his mouth, he forgot about everything else. He was lost in a mind-blowing combination of heat and sensuality.

Her hands moved down the front of his shirt and strummed his nipples. He shivered, which was an unexpected reaction because he was burning up. He'd been semi-erect when they'd left the cabin, and now his dick was as hard as fuck.

His hands grasped her hips, aligning her body with his. He danced her backward until she rested against the trunk of a pine. He rotated his hips, rubbing his erection against her sensitive folds. She groaned into his mouth. When he slipped a hand inside the waistband of her leggings and cupped her butt, she cried out at his touch.

He wanted to go all the way and take her here and now, but she had to be with him for every step. He needed to hear the words. He broke the kiss, gasping for air. "How far do you want to go?"

She stepped to the side, out of their embrace, her eyes wide and blinking, like someone who'd suffered a shock. "Thanks for stopping."

He groaned as he scrubbed his face with his hands. "What's going on?"

She adjusted her clothing, which didn't do much good because her puckered nipples could be seen through her shirt. "You started it. You kissed me, and then you were playing a game with this whole sexy hip thing." She pointed to his groin.

He didn't try to hide the bulge in his jeans.

"Why would you think I'm playing?"

She turned toward the lake so he couldn't see her face. "I shouldn't have kissed you back. That's on me. I'm sorry. It was a mistake."

"How is it a mistake?" He hated how angry he sounded.

"Oh, come on, Michael. We're stuck here together. It would be easy for us to get carried away. I'm attracted to you. That much is obvious, and I won't lie about it, but this is about more than just the two of us. I would love some easy sex, but once we're done and this is over, how would we be around the others? Would we be able to go back to how we are now, or would it be awkward?" She turned and smiled at him, but it didn't reach her eyes.

"Who says it has to be over?"

She pressed her lips into a thin line and placed her hands on her hips. "I do. I don't do serious relationships."

"Since when?"

She laughed and then said, "Since forever. Have you ever seen me with a boyfriend?"

"Is this because I ran away sixteen years ago?" He wanted to close the gap between them mentally, emotionally, and physically, but he couldn't move because he couldn't feel his feet. "Signing up for officer training wasn't about you. It was about—"

"I get it." She nodded as if she understood, but he could see the hurt in her luminous green eyes.

113

"You didn't want to take orders from some idiot when you're the smartest man in the room. But it would've been nice if you'd told me. Finding out from David sucked."

He swallowed the lump in his throat that seemed to be choking him. He didn't want to admit the real reason he'd run, but if he didn't come clean, they would never be able to put the past behind them. "As a kid, there were all these expectations. I had to become somebody, help my people, and make their lives better. I felt like I was responsible for the whole reservation, and they had my whole life planned out for me. Then I met you guys, and for the first time, I had friends who didn't want anything from me."

"What does all that have to do with me? I didn't expect anything."

"No, but I could see our future. Babies, house payments, car payments, a steady job. I wasn't ready for that, not then. I was just a kid myself."

She blew out a long breath through pursed lips. "Wow. I really can't believe people think you're smart. Did it ever occur to you to discuss this with me? Maybe I didn't want to settle down either."

"I assumed you wanted a home and a family because that was all you talked about when we were on the street."

She poked him in the chest. "Of course, I wanted a home. I was homeless. When you became an officer, I lost my best friend. That hurt.

Whatever you *imagined* our future would be wasn't even on my radar." She glared at him, but the longer she stared, the more he could see her pain.

Prepared to defend himself, he opened his mouth but then closed it and focused on the white-tipped mountains. He'd deserted her without explanation. How could he justify that? He couldn't. "I can write code. I can work a computer the way other people can play a musical instrument, but when it comes to people... you...I'm a moron."

She grunted. "You got that right."

"There's a reason I'm not married, or in a serious relationship, and that reason is you."

Once again, she turned to look at the water. He thought she might walk away, but she straightened her spine and said, "And I suppose you're ready for commitment, a mortgage, and a family?"

He nodded.

She sighed. "Then I should be honest, too. It's like I said, I don't do relationships and I don't want kids."

He blinked, trying not to show any reaction. He'd imagined if she accepted him and wanted to be with him, a family would be part of their future.

She obviously saw through his attempt to hide his surprise because she moved to stand in front of him. "What did you think? You'd declare your feelings for me, and my life would stop? That might have worked sixteen years ago, but not now. I won't walk away from Child Seekers. The work I do is too important."

Put like that, what could he say? She rescued children and made the world a better place, whereas he was currently unemployed and in hiding. "I'll take you any way I can get you."

She didn't meet his gaze. Instead, she started walking again.

"I blew it with you, didn't I?" He thought he might throw up. He'd been a fool and chucked away the best chance he'd had at happiness.

She stopped, tilted her head back, and stared at the sky. Blinking, she said, "No...maybe. I just..."

"Give me another chance. I'm not a kid anymore." He knew he was begging, but he didn't care. He'd wasted so much of his life running away from commitment, and he had no idea why. Being with Sinclair would never be a burden. She was fiercely independent, loyal, and brave, but more surprisingly, she didn't need him; she never had and probably never would. Maybe that was the way it was supposed to be. He wanted her to spend time with him simply because she enjoyed his company. What a fool he'd been. He'd thought she would be a burden, an unwanted commitment, when in reality, he had denied himself her presence, her laughter, her counsel, and most of all her companionship.

She smiled as she scrubbed her face with her hands, her frustration with him evident. "But nothing's changed. You're still a moron."

He chuckled, a response that had more to do with stress than anything else. His knees felt like jelly. There was still hope, a chance they could make it work.

"Let me think about it." She continued on the trail.

He hurried after her. "What is there to think about?"

She swung around and poked him in the chest again. "How would it work? Are you down for being the guy I call when I need to get laid?"

He held up his hands in a show of surrender. "Absolutely." He would need to spend time with her if he was going to worm his way into her affections. And it wasn't unheard of for physical intimacy to lead to emotional attachment. Plus, the idea of her calling someone else to satisfy her needs made him feel like he'd been struck in the chest with a hammer.

Months ago, when he was in hospital recovering from his injuries, David had advised Michael to deal with his feelings for Sinclair. This was his chance. At eighteen, he'd run away, and he'd kept on running. He was thirty-three years old now; it was past time he grew up.

She started walking again. "Besides, you couldn't deal with a real relationship because that requires communication."

He grabbed her elbow and spun her around. "You're talking about me not telling you about the Syndicate."

She nodded.

"You're right. My only defense is that I handed everything over to Finn. As a federal agent, you learn to compartmentalize. You never discuss a case with anyone who isn't directly involved, not your colleagues, not your friends. You only talk to officers on the same investigation."

"You're saying, after being in Army Intelligence for eight years and Army CID for ten, you got used to not saying anything."

"Yes, but you're right. I should've warned you about the danger." If he could go back in time and do things differently, he would.

"Look, I get it. You're not used to talking about your work, and you were injured and focused on your recovery. It's a lifetime habit that would be hard to break. That's why I think we should only use each other for sex."

He rubbed his jaw. "That would be tough. I don't know if I could commit to that kind of pleasure."

She tossed her head back and laughed. It was an uninhibited gesture. He was captivated by her lack of restraint in the moment. It reminded him of how she'd cried out during orgasm all those years ago.

"Why are you looking at me like that?" She stood with her arms crossed.

"Do you want the truth?"

She rolled her eyes in answer. Which he understood to mean he'd asked a dumb question.

"Every time you get angry or laugh or breathe, I get aroused. It's like my dick is a compass and you're the north. It keeps pointing to you. I can't seem to control it."

Her arms dropped to her side, her mouth fell open, and she gaped at his crotch. "Even now?"

He smiled and waggled his eyebrows "Oh, yeah."

She laughed again.

It was the most heart-stoppingly beautiful sound he had ever heard. He wrapped a hand around her waist and pulled her closer. His lips crushed hers. He wanted to be gentle, to take his time, but he couldn't. His heart, soul, and body belonged to her and had for a long time. She groaned and deepened the kiss. Her tongue dueled with his, and he was lost. He pressed his hips to hers, aligning their bodies. He slowly moved his pelvis so his erection rubbed against her sensitive nub. One hand spread across the soft skin of her lower back while the other reached under her shirt, searching for her breast, feeling the fabric of her bra.

"This tree will work," Ava called to Milo. The sound of his sister's voice was alarmingly close.

Sinclair pushed him away. "Not here."

He blew out a long breath and looked down.

There was no way he could let his sister see him in this state. He didn't care so much about Milo. His stepfather would just laugh at him, but Ava was only fifteen. "You should go ahead. I need a minute."

She grinned, obviously relishing in his discomfort.

"You don't have to enjoy it so much," he complained, but couldn't help but smile.

She shrugged and walked away. "I don't have to, but I do," she called over her shoulder.

He found a boulder and sat, squinting up at the clear, blue sky. He couldn't wait until tonight when they'd be alone again.

CHAPTER
ELEVEN

Captain Tate's office wasn't as cramped as Finn had expected, but that could be because Tate was a minimalist. There was nothing in the space that didn't have a practical function. There were no bowling trophies or family photographs, just a clear desk and comfy office chairs for Tate and his visitors. Finn liked to think the seats were meant for colleagues, but despite the luxurious furniture, this felt more like an interrogation room.

Tate, whose official title was Captain of the Investigative Bureau, had joined the Granite City-Elkhead County Police Department after Finn had uncovered evidence that the former Police Chief, Dan Notley, had turned a blind eye in order to aid Marshall Portman. If Tate felt any animosity toward Finn over his actions, he didn't show it.

Finn sat. "I'm here about the home invasion

west of town." Granite City and the surrounding Elkhead County had combined their law enforcement departments in order to save costs and cut some of the jurisdictional red tape. It meant that a home invasion in the county fell squarely in their lap.

Tate's brow creased, and he pointed to Finn. "You left me with three corpses who have no identification. Tell me you're planning to take over the case."

The pointing, along with the brow wrinkle, indicated Tate had negative feelings for them. Finn glanced at Kennedy who pressed her lips into a thin line. She was probably noticing the same non-verbal body language and knew that Tate's animosity was, in all likelihood, going to get worse.

Finn tried to smile, hoping it would soften the blow. "No, and I need to tell you about a situation that has come up."

Tate held up a hand. "One minute." He stood and walked to the door. "Ramirez, get in here and bring the files on the mugging and the home invasion from last night."

Kennedy stood and paced to the back of the room, leaving her seat free for Detective Ramirez. She would observe their conversation. Afterward, they would compare notes and figure out what action, if any, needed to be taken.

Ramirez strode in. He had two manila folders tucked under one arm and a notebook and pen in his hand. He nodded at Kennedy to take the empty chair. She shook her head, refusing the offer. He shrugged and made himself comfortable.

Tate rested his hands on his desk, interlacing his fingers, which was a sign that he had serious concerns about this interview. "What situation?"

"How much do you know about Marshall Portman?" Finn asked.

"He ran a charity, took in street kids, and once they were older, he manipulated them into working for him. One of them, who just happens to be a friend of yours"—Tate pointed at Finn again, his facial muscles tight and tense—"refused to play ball, and Portman tried to have him killed."

Finn cleared his throat. He was used to collaborating with local law enforcement, but this was different. They were dumping a problem on the police. "We suspect—"

"And by 'we,' you mean the FBI?" Tate clarified.

"Yes." Finn started over. "The FBI suspects that Portman was a member of a group who call themselves the Syndicate. We had a man on the inside while Portman was still alive, and he managed to get evidence of the Syndicate's existence."

"But?" Tate growled.

"But what?"

"You wouldn't be here if there wasn't a 'but.'"
Tate relaxed his hands and leaned back in his
chair, puffing his chest, confident in his assessment.

"We believe the home invasion was instigated by the Syndicate."

"And you'd like to take over the case. Sure, it's
yours." Tate smiled.

"No." Finn shook his head. "We'll leave it in
your capable hands. And the mugging—"

"The victim is a Sinclair Quinn." Ramirez
checked the file, which was open in his lap. "Is
the attack on her also linked to this...this...Syn-
dicate?"

"We can't say definitively," Finn hedged.

Tate crossed his arms and surveyed Finn. The
captain was uncomfortable with this conversation. "Why are you leaving this with the Granite
City-Elkhead County Police Department? Why
not just take over yourself?"

Finn didn't have an answer except maybe a
half-truth. "We have our suspicions, but that's
not the same as proof. My superiors have told
me that, without any evidence, I can't pursue it,
so it has to go through the proper channels, and
that's you."

Tate narrowed his eyes. "Is there anything
else?"

Finn shook his head, knowing that Tate
wouldn't believe him if he said the Syndicate
were part of an international conspiracy and

was comprised of billionaires who were manipulating events in their favor. He rose to leave and then stopped. "Oh, wait. Yes, there is. Ramirez, do you remember that guy from the bank robbery when they torched the place with you inside?"

The detective gave a long, low whistle. "Don't tell me they were behind it."

"I'm not sure, but there was a man named Ethan in the Molly's Mountain case who killed the Hopefalls Police Chief. They have the same name, and it could be him. The descriptions are similar, but not a perfect match. We thought he was dead but…"

"You're not sure," Tate parroted. He stood and walked across the room, opening his office door. He was throwing them out. "You have a big bunch of nothing, and you're dumping it with us."

"That's about it." Finn smiled. "Keep us in the loop."

"You're an asshole, Callaghan." Tate smiled. He seemed relaxed and forthright.

Finn had no doubt this was his honest opinion. He grinned in response. "It's always a pleasure working with you, Captain."

CHAPTER TWELVE

Sinclair had tidied the cabin and finished doing the dishes. She was now sitting on the couch, wondering how to occupy her time. She couldn't really do more baking since they were short on supplies. As it was, they'd had pancakes for lunch since they didn't have the makings for anything else.

The sound of an ax chipping away at wood told her that Milo and Ava were still working on their dugout canoe. They'd set up a long tree trunk on supports near the old garage and seemed to be content to work on their project. Michael had driven Nadie to the general store on the reserve to buy groceries. He had assured Sinclair the risk was minimal and they'd be protected by the small, tight community. That could be true, but it was a gamble, in Sinclair's experience. Luck was a fickle bitch, and the human factor would always screw you in the end. The less people who knew about them the better, but she'd conceded in the end. They needed food, and therefore they had to take the chance.

With Nadie and Michael out of the house and Milo and Ava occupied, she was alone for the first time since she'd been jumped near her apartment. Going over the pros and cons of having sex with Michael would be a waste. For nearly twenty years, they'd pretended they were just friends, but they weren't and never had been. She remembered how it felt to lie naked beside him. He'd made her feel cherished, although she couldn't say exactly why. He hadn't whispered any words of love, which was good because it would've made her uncomfortable.

And the sex... Even now, after all these years, her nerve endings hummed at the memory. He was the best she'd ever had. She couldn't remember the last time she'd been intimate. She'd given up on men about a year before Carla died. August had marked the anniversary of her death, so it was at least two years since she'd had sex. That was quite a drought. It was past time she dipped her feet in the water.

She stood and paced the room. Did she even need a man in her life? Absolutely not. Plus, Michael was problematic. How would their relationship, or whatever it was, affect those in their group? It probably wouldn't matter to them. David, Tim, and Finn were adults with lives of their own, and as much as she loved them, she understood their friendship wasn't as important to their makeshift family as it once had been. David had Marie, and Tim was now living with Dana.

If she wanted, she could enjoy Michael physically. But she questioned her ability to remain detached. She knew him, knew his smile, knew he hated eggs, and knew he didn't like to be pressured into making decisions. At the same time, they had not only grown apart over the years, they had both changed.

"Oh, for God's sake." She would have sex with him. They both wanted it, and it had been way too long for her. End of story. Thinking it to death wasn't going to change a thing. She had to stop obsessing.

Her choices for entertainment were limited. Computers and smartphones were out. When she spent time alone in her she-shed, she always brought a couple of books, her sketch pad, and her camera to photograph wildlife. It helped her unwind and deal with her emotional fatigue, especially after a tough case. She didn't have access to any of those things, and this wasn't downtime. They were in hiding because they were being hunted.

That brought her back to reality. She would workout.

There wasn't enough room for her to practice inside, so she went outside in search of a private location, which was also in proximity to the house.

Ava stopped hacking at the tree trunk and waved to her. "Do you want to help us?"

She had the same high cheekbones as her brother and was already very pretty. Sinclair had no doubt she would grow into a stunning woman. "Thanks, but I'm going to get some exercise."

She did a few practice swings with her baton and then walked a hundred feet along the trail until she came to a tree strong enough to take her blows.

She'd been practicing for about five minutes when a movement to her left caught her attention. Ava waved at her. The teen was far enough away so as not to be accidently hit.

Sinclair stopped. "Am I making too much noise?"

"No." She shook her head. "I was wondering if you could show me how to fight."

"Hasn't Michael taught you?" David had tutored her in all sorts of moves he'd learned in his Special Forces training.

Ava stepped forward. "He showed me how to get out of a bearhug, how to elbow someone in the head, and kick an attacker in the groin, you know, stuff like that."

Sinclair eyed the teen. She had been confrontational with Michael last night but then they had made up as if nothing had happened. Being in Ava's company was like riding a bull. Sinclair never knew if she would be thrown to the ground and trampled on. But she believed that every woman should be able to protect herself, and Michael had obviously given Ava the fundamentals of self-defense. "When did he coach you?"

"A year before I went to kindergarten." She shrugged, her long dark hair bouncing as she moved. "But I beat up a boy who tried to kiss me, so I didn't get any lessons again until I was ten."

Sinclair laughed and then said, "I can demonstrate the basics of stick fighting, but you have to promise me you will only use it for self-defense."

Ava solemnly put a hand over her heart. "I promise."

Sinclair handed Ava the baton and showed her how to collapse it and how it hooked inside the pocket of her jeans like a pen. "Don't strike for the throat or head. You could kill someone and could be charged with using a weapon with lethal force.

"Did you hit the men who attacked you?"

She thought about lying but decided to turn it into a teachable moment. "Yes. I was lucky to escape. There were two of them. I broke one guy's hand because he had a gun, and I hit the other one in the knee and the ribs."

"What did you do then?"

"I ran, and that's exactly what I want you to

do. You just need to create the opportunity to escape. Now, watch how I flick it open."

She demonstrated the action, pulling it from her imaginary pocket and flicking it so it extended to its full length. Then she showed Ava how to strike the muscles of the arms and legs, how to jab and how to use it to block an attack.

After Ava had practiced a few moves, she stopped and said, "Do you think Mike will let us make our phone calls today?"

Sinclair shrugged. With everything that had happened, not just the trauma of the attacks, but also being so close to Michael, she had completely forgotten about calling work. "I don't know. I'm not expected back at work for a few days, so I have some time."

A vehicle, which sounded like it needed a new muffler, rumbled up the dirt driveway.

Sinclair grabbed the baton from Ava's hand and hauled her behind a bush, forcing her to duck and hide. "Stay here," she hissed, her hand on her Glock.

"It's okay. It's just your mom and Michael," Milo called, giving them the all clear.

Michael parked the old, battered truck near the main cabin. His mom climbed out of the passenger side, followed by an old, stooped woman with long white hair.

Sinclair and Ava joined the others.

Nadie led the Elder inside while Michael surveyed the compound. He seemed calm, controlled, and way too sexy for her piece of mind. He grabbed some grocery bags from the back seat.

"Hey Sprog, whatcha been up to?" Michael smiled at his sister.

Ava pointed at Sinclair as she stood toe-to-toe with her brother. "She made me hide when you drove up. Overreact much?" She flicked her hair over her shoulder and turned to follow the others.

Sinclair wasn't used to the attitude. The people she rescued were normally grateful for her protection.

"That's enough." Michael grabbed Ava's arm. "Sinclair's protecting you."

"There was no need. It was just you." High color rose in the teen's cheeks.

"Next time it might not be."

Ava tore her arm out of his grasp. "I hate this. You promised I could make a call." Then she stomped off, taking the path to the lake.

Sinclair turned to go after the teen.

Michael stepped in front of her, stopping her. "Sorry about that. Fifteen's a tough age."

"Shouldn't one of us go after her?" She wasn't sure if it was a good idea to leave Ava alone.

"Some quiet time will do her good, and there's really nowhere for her to go. The path just trails the lake shore and will lead her back here. She won't venture into the forest. It's too dense."

They joined the others at the kitchen table.

"Sinclair, I'd like you to meet Grandma Pelle," Nadie said as she set a kettle on the stove.

Sinclair smiled, bowed her head. She'd met Grandma Pelle before at a conference on missing women organized by Child Seekers International but doubted the Elder would remember her.

Milo searched the cupboards. "Aha." He retrieved a pouch of tobacco and handed it to Nadie.

Nadie placed the pack in her left hand and presented it to Grandma Pelle. "We ask you to pray for our safety."

To Native Americans, tobacco was considered the first medicine and represented their spiritual connection to the Creator. It was used as an offering to Mother Earth in exchange for the gifts she provided.

Unexpectantly, the door jerked open and Ava stood there. She left her hand on the handle as though she were deciding whether to stay.

Nadie glanced at her daughter and then nodded toward a chair at the table, silently ordering her to sit.

Grandma Pelle smiled at the teen and then opened her bag and retrieved a ball of dried herbs.

Sinclair assumed, from her previous experience, that it was sage, and the Elder was about to conduct a smudging ceremony.

Nadie set a small cast-iron dish on the table.

Grandma Pelle placed the smudge in the dish. Using a match, she set it alight and then she waved it to flame with an eagle feather. Traditionally, they never blew on the spark to get it going; it was always fanned, either with a hand or a feather.

The Elder scooped up the smoke, very much like cupping water and cleansed her hands with the vapor. She did the same with her face, and lastly her heart. Then she passed the bowl to Nadie who repeated the purification process. Everyone at the table took their turn.

Once they were finished, Nadie poured tea into a mug and set it in front of Grandma Pelle.

The Elder took a polite sip and then said, "The Blackfoot have a story about the Chinook Wind. Chinook Wind was a girl who married Chinook Glacier. He took her to his home of ice and cold, but she didn't want to stay there. She wanted to return to her warm family near the sea. But Glacier wouldn't let her go. Her people heard she was unhappy, and they came and fought with Glacier. After a great battle, they took her home." Grandma Pelle turned and spoke to Michael. "All of our young people have a foot in two worlds, one in the white man's world and one in ours. But you have forgotten where you came from. It's time for you to return. You will bring our women home. It is time for you to help your people. This is how it is." She took another sip of her tea, obviously finished with her announcement.

Michael said nothing. He rose and silently walked out.

Nadie's face flushed. Her reaction could have been caused by embarrassment or anger at Michael's behavior. Both were a possibility. He hadn't been overtly disrespectful to Grandma Pelle, but he hadn't shown her the esteem that was normally reserved for Elders, and it reflected poorly on his family.

Sinclair was tempted to go after him but stayed in her seat. One person being rude to an Elder was enough.

Grandma Pelle smiled at her. "Go talk to him. Tell him he needs to follow your path."

Grandma Pelle obviously remembered her. She left the cabin and went in search of Michael. She found him pacing on the trail.

"Do you see how it is?" His neck was corded, and every muscle in his body seemed tense and jerky.

"How what is?" She put her hands on her hips.

"The expectations." His jaw was clenched so tight she thought he might break his teeth.

"Get over yourself. The statistics of violence, abuse, and human trafficking for Native American women are horrific. She's an Elder. Aren't they supposed to look out for the young?"

He turned to face her. "What's your point?" He didn't seem impressed by her lack of sympathy.

"Not everything is about you. Maybe this is about her getting an ex-federal agent to help her people."

"And how am I supposed to do that? We're in hiding." He gave a long, drawn out sigh. He seemed calmer, less frustrated. "I can't do anything about the women until we stop the Syndicate, and I'll be honest with you, I don't know if that's possible."

The enormity of his statement sucked the air out of her lungs. She hesitated, needing some time to catch her breath. "What makes you say that?"

He shrugged, suggesting the answer was obvious. "Think about their resources and what they've done already. They have someone who's probably high on the food chain working in the DOJ. Do you honestly think Marie's solar panel was the first project they've stopped? Or that they haven't used eminent domain to steal land before, like they did with Tim's neighbor? They have money, technology, connections, and we know they won't hesitate to use lethal force."

She hadn't thought about this as a long-term situation. She'd been too busy dealing with... everything. "If that's the case, we need a better plan. We have to change our appearance, get new IDs, and make a clean break. Leave Montana and go to a different state where no one will recognize us. Do you have the means for that?"

"I'm not sure I can run away. Finn, David, and

Tim would still be at risk. Sooner or later, the Syndicate are bound to come after them. If I hide, I'll put all of you in danger again. But you, my mom, Milo, and Ava will need to go away for a while."

"No."

"What do you mean, 'no'?" He stared at her as if she'd lost her mind.

"I mean, yes, it makes sense to hide your family, but I'm going to stay with you and watch your back."

"Tim and David—"

"Have other responsibilities. Finn has Agent Morris to cover his ass. I'll cover yours."

He muttered something unintelligible and shook his head, but he didn't argue with her.

"Are you going to tell your mom they have to disappear?" Even though she had no intention of going into hiding, there was a good chance she wouldn't be able to return to her apartment or use her car for the foreseeable future. How would Nadie, Milo, and Ava handle not being able to go back to their lives? "Ava's going to have a fit."

"I know." He pressed his lips into a grim line. "I'm going to put off telling them until tomorrow." He grinned at her. "Unless you want to do it?"

It was an impish smile that made butterflies dance in her stomach. "Not a chance."

"We'll deal with it together, and if we ever

get out of this, I'll do what Grandma Pelle tells me." He grabbed her hand and led her back to the cabin. "Come on. Milo's making burgers for dinner."

CHAPTER THIRTEEN

Ethan stood behind the two gorillas, not wanting to have any part in this job. Three operatives, including him, had been summoned to Lucy Portman's office on the fifth floor of the PDE building in Granite City. One of them had a broken hand, the other covered his ribs with his arm. He tucked the knowledge of their injuries away in case he needed it in the future. He wasn't planning to hurt them, but he never knew when it would be necessary to sacrifice a colleague, and the weakest link was always the first to go.

Lucy paced to the large window overlooking the square, her steps slow and deliberate. "I have techs tracking the family's phones and watching all highway cameras looking for the Volvo. I also have someone checking their financials for any hotel, restaurant, or rental service. If they stop for a fucking pee, we'll know about it."

"What do you want us to do?" asked the goon

with the broken hand. Ethan thought his name was Ludlow but didn't care enough to check.

She wheeled around to face him, her gaze cold and hard. "Be ready. The minute they ping on the radar, you will be called in to apprehend them."

"All four?" asked the thug with the bad ribs.

She rolled her eyes before she shouted, "No, I want you to leave them to roam around the state! Keep the women and kill Papin and the father."

Ethan didn't like interrupting her when she was in a rage, but he needed clarification. "I thought you wanted me to play with Papin and figure out what he knows."

Her cheeks flushed, but she didn't scream. "Change of plan. Kill him. If you want to slice Papin, that's fine with me, but don't touch the mother and sister. They'll go in my stable."

The hair on the back of Ethan's neck prickled.

"Stable?" Ludlow asked.

For the first time, Ethan was grateful for the presence of the two idiots. He'd wanted to ask the question, but self-preservation had stopped him.

Lucy shrugged. "I have a hotel on the east side where I keep a small group of women for business purposes. Two attractive native American women will make a nice addition. If you're really good and don't screw it up, I might let you spend an hour there as a bonus."

Ethan had no intention of taking Lucy up on

her offer. Killing Papin and indulging in his need to see skin split wasn't a problem, but he had never raped anyone. He was a killer, pure and simple. Now he had a problem because he had no intention of handing over the mom and sister to be raped every day for years. No one deserved that. He'd kill them before he'd allow that to happen. He wouldn't play with them. He'd simply slip his blade between their ribs and into their heart. They'd be dead in seconds. It would be kinder than Lucy's plan.

"You may go." Lucy waved them away.

He'd missed her instructions but figured they were in a holding pattern, waiting for Papin's family to ping some geek's radar.

CHAPTER FOURTEEN

Nadie tried to keep the conversation going around the dinner table but eventually gave up. Sinclair was grateful when they fell into silence. They weren't on some family get-together where they could celebrate and plan activities for the following day. They were being hunted.

They'd eaten in silence for five minutes when Nadie started up again. "Have you thought about what Grandma Pelle said?"

This wouldn't be good. Michael hated being pressured into doing...anything. And talking about Grandma Pelle meant he would have to talk about their situation.

Sinclair rose and started to clear the dishes, not wanting to get involved in the conversation. Milo and Ava shared a here-we-go-again look and went outside, presumably to work on the dugout.

"You're unemployed. Finding those women

would make a difference to our community." Nadie thumped the table.

Michael leaned forward. "I agree, but I'm not in a position to do anything. None of us are. We need to lay low and figure out what our next step should be."

"You have a plan." Sinclair dumped the dirty plates in the sink to soak and sat beside him. "What do you have in mind?"

Sinclair hadn't wanted to eavesdrop on their discussion, but she could tell by the determination in his voice that he'd made a decision.

He scrunched up his face. "You're not going to like it."

"Tell us anyway." With the flat of her hand, Nadie brushed at imaginary crumbs on the table.

"When I was working undercover at PDE, I came across a group called the Syndicate that—"

"Are trying to kill us. Yes, I gathered," Nadie said. "Cut to the chase."

"I think I may have planted malware that started all this, but I can't be sure. I need to go back inside. First, I have to find out why they came after us now, and I also need to be able to track how much they know about us. That way we can stay ahead of them and make informed decisions about what to do next."

Nadie sprang to her feet. "No, as your mother, I forbid it."

"Forbid it?" Michael stood, matching her posture. "Mom, I'm in my thirties. I get that—"

"No, you don't get anything. You ran away, then you joined the army, and after that you were a federal agent, always putting yourself in harm's way. Did you ever once think about anyone but yourself?"

"He is thinking about you." As soon as the words were out of her mouth, Sinclair regretted it. While Nadie and Michael faced each other like prize fighters in the ring, she was still sitting and had no intention of taking sides.

Nadie scowled down at her. "What do you know about it?"

"You're right, I can't begin to imagine what it's like to be a mother—always wondering if your son is going to come home safe. But remember what happened last night." She couldn't believe it had only been twenty-four hours since she'd been attacked. "They will come again, and the next time we might not be that lucky."

"But I thought we were safe here." Nadie slumped into her seat.

"No, we're not." Michael gentled his tone as he dragged his chair closer and sat. "We can't stay. People know we're here. It's only a matter of time before word gets out."

Sinclair cleared her throat. "Are you sure you have to go back to PDE? Isn't there a way you could do this remotely?"

He shook his head. "No, as I said before, they have an independent system. The only way to access it is from a unit on the fifth floor."

Sinclair groaned. "I should come with you."

"That's not a good idea. We'd be too conspicuous. I'm a native and you have a bruised face. Trust me, a woman with a black eye stands out."

"Ava's very good with makeup. She can fix it so no one will notice." Nadie stared her son down. "And if you care for me at all, you'll bring her along as backup," Nadie decreed.

Michael sighed. "Okay. If it'll make you happy."

Nadie's ability to guilt her son into agreeing to her demands was impressive.

Despite the seriousness of their situation, Sinclair couldn't help but smile. "So, what's the plan?"

"I was thinking we could go in as janitorial staff. When I was undercover, I paid a couple of guys to lose their IDs. That should get us into the building and past any security guards we encounter. After that, we'll be winging it."

Sinclair gave him a look which, hopefully, suggested he was out of his mind. "Winging it? I don't think so."

He placed his elbow on the table and rested his chin on his hand. He looked shockingly gorgeous. It wasn't fair that a man could be so handsome and so smart at the same time. Someone with his looks should have the brains of a rabbit. And the same could be said about his mind. Anyone as intelligent as him should have warts on his face or some other affliction to make him hideous.

"It's been nine months," he said, bringing her thoughts back to the subject at hand. "I have no idea if they've upgraded their computer system, or they might have updated their security. Everything could have changed since Marshall's death."

"In that case, you'd better talk me through all the details you remember, and we need to come up with a step-by-step plan of what you want to do once we get in."

****

Sinclair stepped out of the shower, and after brushing her hair and applying a cheap moisturizer, she slipped Michael's T-shirt over her head. The inflammation on her lip had subsided. A small nick was the only evidence she'd been punched. The swelling around her eye had gone down a bit, but the bruise was now purple in the center with green edges. "Very attractive," she said aloud to her reflection.

It was the end of another grueling day. Although it hadn't been as hellacious as yesterday, it had still been fraught with emotion and uncertainty.

They had gone over their scheme to enter PDE until the specifics were burned into her brain. They had no idea if they would acquire the information they needed or if they would even get away unscathed. As far as she was concerned, in the dictionary, under the definition of *risky*, there should be a picture of the pair of them walking into PDE.

After tomorrow, one way or another, everything would change. Even if they managed to access the secret server and figure out what Lucy Portman had planned, they would probably have to change their identity and move.

Which meant she would be living in close quarters with Michael's family for the foreseeable future. That thought scared her more than the idea of going into PDE. They were nice people, but she was used to having her own space and wasn't sure how well she would adapt.

"What are you thinking about?" Michael stood at the door to the bathroom, looking as stunning as ever. He was wearing a pair of jeans and no shirt. Her fingers ached with the need to touch his chest.

"I was wondering if your family like me." Great, now she sounded needy. "I mean, we're going to be together for God knows how long. I've lived alone for years. And Ava can be..."

"Difficult?" He raised an eyebrow.

"Sometimes she's nice and then—"

"She has a hissy fit out of nowhere and you have no idea what you did wrong."

She stared at him. "She's like that with you, too?"

He met her gaze. "It's not you. She's like that with everyone. It's a family trait. I was difficult at that age. In fact, I ran away because my mom met Milo. I mean, he's a good guy, and I was a selfish shit."

She felt burned under his laser-focus, as though her skin was too tight. "You get along now, though?"

He stepped closer, invading her personal space. He took the towel from her hands and rubbed the ends of her wet hair. His unique scent surrounded her, the same combination of soap and musk. He must've showered in the main cabin. "Oh, yeah, we're good and have been for years. Give her time. She'll grow out of it. You don't have to worry. My family love you because you stand up to me."

"Doesn't everyone?"

He gave her a lopsided grin that warmed her insides. "I'm good at getting my own way."

"Since when?" She stared at their reflection in the mirror. It was getting hard to concentrate, especially when he smiled like that. There was something predatory about him. It wasn't anything overt. But every single inch of her was aware of him, waiting and ready. It was as if her body had already decided her next course of action. Her nipples were puckered, rubbing against the soft cotton fabric of his T-shirt.

He leaned in close so his breath warmed her neck. "Since forever. I'm smart, remember?"

Her whole body responded, as if she had been dormant on a molecular level and was now coming out of hibernation. "I thought we both agreed you're a moron when it comes to people."

Dear God, she had no idea how she managed to form the words, and she wasn't sure she could do it again.

He laughed, and her resistance vanished.

She ripped the towel out of his hands and threw it aside. Then she wrapped her arms around his neck and drew him into her embrace.

He reciprocated. His bare chest rubbed against her tender breasts. She caressed his arms, relishing in the sensation of his warm skin under her fingertips. Her exploration continued, but when she reached his shoulders, she stopped. There was a dip in his left shoulder. It marked the spot where he had broken the bone. She remembered him flying over the car and hitting the pavement. He could have died. She'd almost lost him. She kissed the dent. "Does it hurt?"

He smiled, aligning their hips and backing her up to the bathroom counter. It was the most wanton move she'd ever experienced. He pressed against her, his erection nudging her in a silent promise of things to come. "There are other places that hurt more."

She laughed, but was silenced when his lips slanted over hers and she was lost in a world where nothing existed except her physical need to be held by him. She slipped her tongue inside his mouth so it wound around his. He groaned and rubbed his hand over her bare behind.

He pulled back. "There's something I should tell you."

This couldn't be good. She stepped out of his embrace and pushed past him, walking into the other room, preparing herself for an emotional blow. "What?"

"I'm not sure how good I'll be. I haven't... It's just..."

"What are you trying to say?"

"I broke my pelvis."

She spun around and pointed at his groin. "Are you saying you can't...?" Then realized she was being rude and lowered her hand.

"No." He closed the gap between them. "It all works. I'm just not sure..."

Controlling her exasperation required a superhuman effort. "Not sure about what?"

Color rose high in his cheeks. "Endurance might be a factor. I'm not sure how strong my hip muscles are and if they can..." His fisted hand pumped the air. "Go for the necessary length of time."

She smiled, more out of relief than anything else. "You don't have to worry about that. I like to be on top."

He swallowed and gave her another of those slow, sexy smiles.

She reached out and ran the tip of her finger over his nipple and was gratified to see it respond. Then she leaned forward and licked it.

He shivered. "Fuck."

She unzipped his jeans and pushed them down, taking his underwear with them. His erection sprang free. She wrapped her right hand around it, enjoying the smooth feel of his length. He stood with his arms clamped by his sides and his jaw clenched, allowing her scrutiny. She ran her free hand over his form, caressing his round, firm buttocks, his flat abdomen and, lastly, his testicles.

He bent and nibbled her neck below her ear, sending quivers of need cascading through her. "I can't keep this up. If we're going to—"

She kissed him, ending his talk with her tongue. There was no need for conversation. She broke the kiss and put a hand to his chest, moving him backward until he hit the bed and lay down. She was hot, ready, and could feel the moisture gathering at the apex of her thighs. She straddled him and grinned.

He smiled back. "I don't understand you."

She rested her hands on his shoulders and leaned closer. "Do you understand this? Her mouth slanted over his again. Each time she kissed him, every tiny part of her came alive, as though they were being shot with electricity. She drew back and yanked her T-shirt over her head.

She lowered herself down onto his penis, taking the tip in and then easing up and off. Then she sunk down onto him again, teasing him. She repeated the motion, taking him a little deeper each time until she was impaled by him, filled by his engorged cock.

She set a steady rhythm, leaning back, pinching her areolas with her fingertips.

He jack-knifed into a sitting position and sucked her nipple into his mouth. A cascade of sensations invaded her, as though there was an imaginary conduit running from her nipple to her sex.

She bounced harder, increasing her speed as every cell in her body cried out for more. She was close to the edge. There was no way she could slow down. She pushed him down. The distance allowed her to play with her clitoris.

He brushed her hand aside and took over. He found the exact spot for maximum satisfaction. Using his thumb, he traced small circles, applying just the right pressure and tempo.

Oh, God. She leaned forward, placed her hands on the mattress for support, and increased the speed.

He held her hips as she raced to the edge of the abyss, pumping him, demanding fulfillment. There was a flash of white light behind her eyes, and she was lost as she was overtaken by throbbing waves of pleasure.

As the effects of her orgasm slowed, he grabbed her hips and flipped them so she was beneath him. She hooked her legs around his lower back, ensuring him access as he pounded into her.

Her sex was too sensitive, her nerve endings too raw. Her vagina clamped around him as she came for the second time. This was too much, too intense. She thought she might fly apart. She heard someone screaming his name, and then there was nothing except the light and the throbbing waves of pleasure as they rolled over her again.

She lay in the darkness. His body covered her as his cock softened inside her. How could she be so stupid to think that she could have sex with him and not be affected? He had always been important to her, and making love had only deepened her feelings toward him. They shared a bond, but just because she believed that, it didn't mean he experienced the same connection. He was a good, but flawed, man whose rational mind controlled his actions whereas she operated out of love and allegiance. Hers was an emotional response to an irrational world. And she had to wonder if he could ever love her the way she needed.

CHAPTER
FIFTEEN

Michael traced Sinclair's spine, enjoying her smooth, satiny skin. She lay with her head resting on his shoulder, so she was tucked into his side. The light from the bathroom illuminated the room. Strands of her hair were strung across her face, the ends moist from their exertion. Her eyes were closed. He didn't know if she was genuinely resting or if she was faking to avoid talking to him. That thought bothered him. He hadn't planned on having sex with her. Yes, he'd wanted it, but she'd instigated it. He didn't want her to have any regrets. "I'm gonna go on record and say this was a good idea."

"Did I hurt you? Is your hip okay?" She leaned up on her elbow and searched his face.

He tucked a lock of hair behind her ear. "Never better. Tell me about Child Seekers. What's your job like? Do you have a title?"

She snuggled closer and stared at the ceiling.

"I'm an investigator. It's like I said this morning, I can't give it up. It's a calling. Although, it hasn't been the same since Carla died."

"Who's she?" He wanted to turn off the light but was scared if he moved, she might clam up and they would lose this moment.

"She was my old partner."

"What happened to her?" The tip of her finger traced his abdomen and was driving him crazy.

"She was killed by an IED in Afghanistan."

"I'm sorry. Do you have a new partner?"

"Yes, his name's Jake. He's okay. But there's something about him. It's like there's a wall between us. Maybe it's just me because I loved Carla so much. She was like a sister and Jake is…well… he's an old ex-police officer who's rude and smokes a pack a day. Perhaps I expect too much from him. It's just…I don't know. I can't put my finger on it."

"You don't trust him."

"Why do you say that?"

"I've had partners. I've also worked undercover and had to rely on my Army CID contact. You have to be one hundred percent certain they have your back. If you get into trouble, they are the first person you call. With everything that's happened, you haven't once mentioned calling him."

"If you had that kind of backup with CID, why did you go into PDE? It was unsanctioned. You lost your job."

He allowed her to change the subject. "I was unhappy there. It wasn't anything they did. It was me. I soured. It felt like every time I put one of the bad guys away, another two would crawl out of the woodwork. I just couldn't do it anymore. Helping David was a no-brainer."

"Do you miss it?"

He gave a harsh laugh and then said, "I haven't had a chance to miss it, what with being injured and all." He hadn't said the words "the Syndicate," but they hung in the air anyway, like a ghost floating over them.

Her body heat sank into him, and her soft hands were doodling loops over his stomach, gradually moving lower.

"You're driving me nuts." He grabbed her hand and placed it on his erect penis. "Do you see what you've done to me?"

"Good." She licked his nipple while she pumped his dick. "Do you think you can manage doggy style?"

"Fuck. You're hot." He sat up as she rolled over and then lifted herself up onto all fours. He positioned himself behind her.

PDE, the Syndicate, hiding his family—none of it mattered because he was going to die satisfying Sinclair. He couldn't think of a better way to go.

CHAPTER SIXTEEN

It was a beautiful autumn evening. There wasn't a cloud in the sky. The way the sunlight hit the golden fall leaves in the surrounding forest made Sinclair wish they were a couple on a road trip and not two people heading to the PDE building in Granite city in order to commit what could only be described as a data heist. She pointed to a gas station. "That seems like a good spot."

Michael had decided she should use a payphone to call her work instead of his burner phone. There were some *ifs* and *buts* to his decision. *If* the Syndicate had tracked his movements, they might have his cell number and be able to track it and listen in on their conversation. *But* making a call from a landline meant they could trace the exact location where the call was made. *But* that would take longer, and they would be gone by then.

They'd spent most of the morning in bed, which probably wasn't the best thing to do when they were in hiding, but it was an indulgence. There was a good chance that after today, they would be living in cramped quarters with his family, and there would be no time, or space, for intimacy.

Surprisingly, she didn't regret going to bed with him, even though everything seemed to have happened so fast. Or maybe it was a relationship years in the making. He felt like home, which was both comforting and terrifying at the same time. Perhaps she had absolved him of his crimes too easily. He had, after all, dumped her and left without saying goodbye. That was a double whammy. But she was also forgiving herself. For years, she had wondered what she'd done wrong. Had she been too clingy? Was it the way she looked? In the end, she told herself to get over him and move on, but there was always a question at the back of her mind, a small seed of doubt that said she wasn't good enough.

Besides, she had been way too young when they were in bootcamp. At eighteen, she'd lacked confidence and had no conception of her true potential. But now she knew whatever happened, she would survive. If Michael changed his mind about her tomorrow and decided she was a mistake, then she would be fine...hurt, but fine. She would face the world and carry on—that is, after she punched him out.

They had spent the afternoon packing up their gear and preparing to leave. If they didn't return, Milo, Nadie, and Ava would trek into the mountains and make their way to Tim's. It was a long hike, but Milo and Nadie had a lot of experience roughing it in the bush. With the right preparation, they should be able to make it. From there, Tim would be able to contact Finn.

They had also gone over their plan for accessing PDE again. They would enter the building by the back entrance, which was normal procedure for janitorial staff. Then they would make their way, via the stairwell, to the fifth floor where they could log on to the secure network. Her biggest concern was that someone would recognize Michael. His good looks were too striking not to be noticed. He was planning on wearing a ball cap and a pair of glasses. Milo had knocked the lenses out of his sunglasses. It wasn't much of a disguise, but it would have to do.

Michael parked next to the phonebooth. "Despite what you see on cop shows, calls from a landline can't be traced instantly, but you still want to keep it short. That way we can be long gone by the time the guys with guns show up."

Calling her Administrator, Amy, was dicey, but sooner or later she would have to make contact with Child Seekers. She didn't want them wasting their valuable resources looking for her. She opened the passenger door.

He grabbed her elbow. "Watch what you say."

She gave him her you're-an-idiot look and said, "I'm not a civilian." Then jumped out of the truck before he could reply.

Luckily, she'd committed Amy's work, home, and cell numbers to memory. It was one of the little things she did that made her feel in control, and this time her need to be prepared had paid off. She tried Amy's home number first, figuring a landline to landline call was the safest bet.

She picked up on the first ring. "Hello."

"Amy, it's Sinclair."

"What's up?" Amy, a childless widow, had volunteered at Child Seekers after being trafficked by a relative as a young woman.

"I was jumped by a couple of thugs yesterday."

"Did you call Jake?" Their normal operating procedure would be for her to contact her partner for backup, but this wasn't about her, or her work for Child Seekers, and she was reluctant to involve him. Maybe Michael was right, and she didn't trust him.

"No." She sighed. "I'm not about to bother Jake..." She wasn't sure how to explain politely that Jake would probably tell her to F-off.

"I hear you, honey. He's not the cream of the crop. There's a reason that man retired early from the LAPD."

"I thought it was because he has a bum knee." Sinclair pictured her partner limping around Kiev on their recent trip.

"I have my doubts." Which translated to mean she didn't know anything definite, but she had her suspicions.

Michael tapped on the driver's side window and then pointed to his watch, a reminder for her to hurry it up.

"Listen, I need to take some personal time." She ran through the bare details, leaving out what she'd learned about Michael and the Syndicate and the fact they had come after Michael's family. She loved her job, but at this point, it didn't matter if Child Seekers fired her because she had no idea if she would be able to go back to her old life.

"Honey, you have another problem." She could almost see Amy pointing a perfectly manicured finger at her.

"What is it?"

"Our office had a break-in."

The hairs on the back of her neck stood up. She gasped but didn't interrupt.

"They trashed the place. Nothing was taken. As far as the police can tell, they only accessed the payroll files. Actually, one payroll file—yours."

"Why would anyone want that?"

"Because it has all your personal details including your address, your bank accounts, your social security number, and all the flights I'd booked for you. I called you and left a message, but I guess you dumped your phone."

"When did it happen?"

"I reckon it was just after you landed."

"Shit." She was silent for a moment. She should hang up and walk away, but she had to warn her just in case. "Listen, these people are bad. You need to watch your back. And I know Jake's not your favorite person but warn him, too. I'll try and call him when things get settled."

"Don't you worry about me. I have a few tricks up my sleeve." She disconnected, and Sinclair could almost see the middle-aged woman unlocking her gun safe and loading her weapons.

Sinclair climbed into the truck and snapped her seatbelt into place.

"What's up?" Michael started the truck and pulled onto the back road. He didn't harass her into talking. He simply sat there, silently waiting.

She took a deep breath and blurted out everything Amy had told her.

"They're trying to track you, and they needed that info to do it."

"There's something about the break-in that doesn't feel right."

"None of this *feels* right."

"That's true, but this is...more. I don't know exactly."

"We'll get the information we need from PDE, and then we can form a plan." He turned right onto a secondary highway, heading east toward Granite City.

Michael glanced at Sinclair. She seemed pensive and tense. Every muscle in her body was wound tight as she fingered the pocket that held her baton. She also wore a gun belt, which looked like a regular belt, fit through the loops of her jeans and was strong enough to hold her Glock and a spare magazine. Ava had produced a makeup bag and had done an amazing job covering Sinclair's bruises. For the first time since he'd seen her two days ago, she reminded him of the girl she used to be. Maybe it was the way her strawberry blond hair was covered with a bandana or the softness in her gaze when she looked at him. Last night had been fantastic. Now all he had to do was convince her to stay for the long haul. Although that could be out of her hands because, unless they figured out a solution to their problem with the Syndicate, she might be forced to stay with him. On a personal level, that worked, but in every other way, it sucked.

"Talk to me," he demanded, knowing full well if she didn't want to speak, she wouldn't.

"I'm really worried about the robbery at work. What did they think they would find? Did they think I'd be fool enough to use my accounts? I work in a sensitive area. I have procedures to follow. No phone. Cash only. Carla drummed it into me."

He was so relieved she had shared her thoughts he almost smiled, but managed to contain himself.

She was intelligent, strong, and capable. With all her strength, there was something fragile about her. It was as though she stood alone, her against the world.

"You know you can count on me. No matter what happens, I'll stand by your side." He slipped his hand in hers and was gratified when she held on tight, but she didn't acknowledge his words. Instead, she stared out the passenger window, making him wonder if she was too emotional to speak.

She cleared her throat. "In my world, actions speak louder than words."

It sounded like a rebuke, but she squeezed his hand. The way she gripped him told him she wasn't used to having someone watch her back. Whoever this Jake was, she didn't trust him. When all this was over, he would check Jake out and if there was anything, even a parking ticket, he would make sure the bastard lost his job with Child Seekers.

CHAPTER SEVENTEEN

A knot formed in Sinclair's stomach as she stared up at the five-story PDE building. It was constructed of gray granite blocks and must be nearly a hundred years old. She seemed to remember that it used to be a hotel before Public Domain Energy purchased it and converted it into their headquarters.

Michael maneuvered the old Ford pickup into a parking spot at the rear of the building. The square was well known to both of them. It had been their "home" when they were on the streets. She remembered every doorway where they'd slept, the good places to beg, and the best dumpsters to find food.

She wore her jeans and one of Michael's plaid shirts. It was long enough to hang over her waistband and conceal her weapon. They didn't have access to any fancy disguises. The best she could do was cover her hair with a scarf Nadie had found. She would've also preferred to dress in something that more closely resembled a custodian's uniform, but they didn't have access to those clothes so they would have to wing it. When her stomach cramped again, she reminded herself that the PDE staff weren't hunting them, just Lucy and her thugs.

Michael wore a pair of sweats and a ragged shirt, which somehow accentuated his muscular arms. He pulled his baseball cap low over his brow and then grabbed his backpack. After rummaging through, he passed her a lanyard with a security card attached. PDE was printed in bold blue letters next to a photograph of a short, dark-haired man.

"There's a back door that requires me—"

"This guy looks nothing like me. There is no way I'll get past security with this." She held up the ID.

He opened the truck door. "It doesn't have to look like you." His tone implied he was explaining quantum physics to a child. "There's no security checkpoint. Everyone in that building wears one. You'll stand out if you don't have it on. Besides, security guards hardly ever look at the picture."

"The words 'hardly ever' implies that sometimes they do." She joined him as they headed toward the back door. "Did you recon this building when you were here before?"

He nodded. "Once I realized this went a lot

deeper than the head of a power company, I decided I would come back and take a look. It never occurred to me Portman would hit me with his car. I need you to block me from the camera."

She glanced at the half-globe security monitor up high on the wall by the entrance and positioned herself so she stood in front of Michael.

He produced a computer and a small power screwdriver from his bag and removed the front of the panel. "While I'm doing this, you could flirt a bit."

"Flirt? I don't know how to flirt, and even if I did, this wouldn't be the time."

"I would've thought you'd be good at it, seeing as you only do casual relationships." Using another tool that looked like a screwdriver but with a different tip, he attached three wires to the chip.

"Is that criticism I hear in your voice?"

"Not at all. It's just a skill all women seem to have." He produced a computer chip and inserted it into the circuit board.

"I never learned. What do you think, they take girls aside in high school and teach them how to flick their hair? Not that it matters because I didn't go to high school. Why are you trying to distract me, and why can't we just slide our cards through the scanner?"

"The original owners would've reported them lost, codes would've been changed. If we use them, we'd be in handcuffs within a minute. I'm rewriting the commands so anyone can access it." He reattached the front of the panel, placed his computer and tools in his backpack, and flashed his card. The door unlocked, and he pulled it open. "Come on."

He led the way through a maze of corridors until they reached a door with the word *Maintenance* inscribed in plain letters. He shoved her inside and turned on the overhead light.

They were cramped into a small windowless room with cleaning supplies on shelfs at the back. Used clothing hung on a hook by the door.

She grabbed a yellow apron and handed him a blue shirt made of heavy cotton. It had the letters PDE emblazoned on the right side. "Try this on."

The small confines of the space made dressing difficult. He shrugged into the top. It was a little on the small side and the buttons looked like they might pop open. He had obviously worked hard to get back into shape after his injuries. She had to admire not only his physique, but also his work ethic.

He grabbed her waist and turned her, then tied her apron at the back. Once he was done, he wrapped his arms around her and pulled her closer so her back was against his front. He kissed her neck. "Tonight," he whispered.

That one word brought up an image of him behind her, pounding into her as she came. It was the promise of another night of lovemaking.

He released her and snatched a bucket with some window washing tools off the floor.

She grasped a long-handled duster.

He raised an eyebrow. "A maid with a duster? All you need is the little black outfit."

She gave him a hard look. "Remember, I'm armed."

One side of his mouth curved up in the beginnings of a smile. "You're not into it. Okay. Moving on."

He eased the door open and checked there was no one in the corridor. Once he was sure they were safe, they exited the closet and headed for the stairs.

"Human skin cells make up about seventy percent of dust. That means there's always something that needs dusting." He gave her a sideways glance.

"What a disgusting thought. And why the hell are we talking about dust? We should be focused on the task at hand."

"We look like soldiers going into battle. I was trying to loosen you up and lighten the mood. If we talk about boring things, we might blend in. For example, have you ever dusted your place?"

"Of course, I have," she lied.

He smiled, revealing his white teeth and dimple. "We have to go to the fifth floor."

By the time they'd reached the third level, she was grateful she was in good shape. "Go over the plan again?" They needed to be on the same page.

"There are two offices and a conference room. The last time I was here, the secure server could be accessed from two terminals, one in each office."

"Who do they belong to?"

He shrugged. "I don't know, now. It was Marshall and Lucy."

"What if someone's there?" she whispered as they reached the fifth floor.

He peered through a tiny window in the door. "Then PDE get their offices cleaned for free. We can always find somewhere to hide until they go home." He paused, grabbed the door handle, and then said, "All clear."

The fifth floor had a large reception area, which was decorated in brown and orange. She glanced at the overhead red LED display of the elevator to make sure the doors wouldn't ping open and surprise them. A large glass-walled conference room lay to the left of reception and two ornate wooden doors to the right. There were no signs on them to indicate which one belonged to Lucy. Michael put his ear to one door while she listened at the other.

Faint voices echoed from inside. She pointed to the room and made a movement with her hand to mimic talking. He nodded his understanding. She crept to his position.

He pointed at the handle, telling her he was

going to open it.

"Remember, if there's someone in there, let me talk. I can speak in Spanish and pretend I don't understand them," she whispered, reminding him of their plan.

He peeked his head inside. The room was empty. They entered and closed the door silently behind them.

The office was massive, bigger than her apartment. Evening sunlight streamed through a large picture window that overlooked the Granite City Square. A carved wood desk sat opposite the window.

"This was Marshall's office," Michael murmured. "Lucy hasn't changed a thing."

"Surprised?"

"Yes." He rifled through the desk until he found the terminal. "Damn, the battery's dead."

"Can you charge it?"

"Of course, but it'll take time." He tugged a long cord from the drawer and plugged it in. "I'd be surprised if anyone's used it since he died."

"I just hope it works after all this time." She stood behind him, looking over his shoulder.

They waited a few minutes in silence until the screen started blinking.

Then he typed a series of letters and symbols, which seemed like nonsense to her.

"I'll connect it to the internet that way I can explore the system from a distance." He inserted a flash drive into the computer.

She pointed to the keyboard and whispered, "How long will this take?"

"That depends on how much security the program has to work through," he answered in the same hushed tones.

An image appeared, which showed the program loading.

Voices sounded in the hallway. The people, whoever they were, had left the office next door. The volume and manner of their speech patterns suggested they had stopped moving and were waiting for the elevator.

Michael placed the terminal under the desk.

Sinclair held her duster near a picture frame, ready to play her role as janitorial staff.

After a few minutes, a ding sounded, followed by a hiss that told her the individuals were no longer on this floor. Sinclair sighed in relief at the mechanical sound of the carriage descending.

Neither of them moved. They were still listening, but there were no footsteps, no doors creaking, nothing.

Michael placed the terminal back on the tabletop.

She was starting to get antsy. This was taking a lot longer than they had anticipated. "Is that thing done?"

"It's done." He pulled the drive out and stuffed it in his pocket. "I should be able to access their secret network from my computer."

"Good." She opened the door a crack and peeked out. "Let's go."

****

Ethan stood behind Ludlow and Kemp as they descended in the elevator. He could kill the two of them without a second thought. He mentally gave his head a shake. He'd always prided himself on being a professional and not letting his emotions get in the way of the job. But he'd lost his detachment, which meant he'd either have to act or bow out. Fortunately, the holding pattern they'd been in since yesterday was over, which meant he wouldn't have to spend much more time with the two idiots.

"It's lucky the girl used the phone," Ludlow said.

"How are you going to shoot like that?" Ethan pointed to Ludlow's cast, which immobilized his hand so he could only wiggle his fingertips.

"I can use my other hand."

"Yeah, but can you shoot anything with it?" Ethan tried to make his tone jovial. Ludlow didn't strike him as the kind of guy who would train for hours to become ambidextrous.

Kemp chuckled. "No, his aim is shit."

"A lot you know. I've been practicing," Ludlow growled.

"You've got this?" Ethan needed to contact the Trainer so he could verify that Lucy's human trafficking had been endorsed by the Syndicate.

"The boss won't like it if you're not there,"

173

Ludlow said.

He didn't give a fuck if Lucy liked it or not. "I need to hit the head...had a bad burrito for lunch. It'll be ugly if I'm in the car. Go, I'll catch up with you."

If the Trainer wasn't available, he would snoop around. He was competent with computers. He couldn't hack, and code was a foreign language, but his position meant he had access to the secret network used by the Syndicate. All member's paid one percent of their profits into a fund for operational costs. If the slavery was sanctioned, then there should be something about it in the system.

He'd used the laptop in Marshall's old office on occasion. He headed for the stairs, not wanting to be picked up on the elevator camera. There was a good chance no one would check, but it paid to be cautious.

CHAPTER EIGHTEEN

Sinclair glanced around the room, making sure everything was in its place as Michael peeked out the door. Once he was confident there was no one in the lobby, he opened it wide.

They were halfway across the foyer when the stairwell door swung wide. A tall, slim man walked toward them. He had short brown hair and a red straight scar on his temple. It looked like he'd been burned with an iron bar. There was something about him that screamed enforcer. Maybe it was his posture or the way his gaze took in everything. It could also be that he'd just run up a flight of steps and wasn't out of breath. But she sensed this wasn't a man who spent his time behind a desk.

Thinking quickly, she stared at the ground and mumbled something in Spanish, hoping he would think they were just cleaning staff and ignore them.

"Don't I know you?" the man said as he continued to walk toward the office.

Her heartrate kicked up a notch as they shuffled past him, heading for the stairs. She gazed at the ground, watching his feet. In her experience, a person's feet moved before their upper body. She took a step closer, wondering if her duster would work as a fighting stick. No, that was stupid. She grabbed her baton but didn't extend it. Instead she said, "Today's my first day." She spoke in English with a Spanish accent.

"Not you. Him." He pointed to Michael, who stood with one hand on the door to the stairwell. Michael turned slowly.

"Papin!" His left hand went to the holster at his waist.

Shit. She flicked her baton open and wacked his arm, knowing that if the blow didn't break the bone, it would at least numb the limb.

"Fuck." He curled over, grabbing his injured elbow.

She shoved Michael to get him moving. "Go."

They ran down the first flight of stairs.

"Stop. I won't shoot," the man called after them. "I have information."

Michael halted and pushed her against the wall, so she was out of the line of fire. "What?"

"The girl used the phone. They know where you are."

"Why are you telling me this?" Michael

called.

"We don't have time for a discussion. Hurry back. You might still be able to save them. Go."

The color drained from Michael's face. He sprinted down the stairs, overtaking her as he jumped the last three steps of every flight.

Once outside, they raced for the truck. He stuck the car in gear and gunned the engine. They didn't bother with the secondary roads this time. They needed the fastest route.

"Who was that guy?" Her pulse had finally slowed enough that she could talk.

"Didn't you recognize him?" He tugged off his fake glasses and baseball hat and threw them onto the bench seat behind him, which had been all but useless in disguising his appearance.

"No, should I?"

"That's the guy who arrived at Tim's with a bloody knife. His name is Ethan Moore. Dana shot him in the head. I thought he was dead."

"That was how he got the scar." She yanked off her head scarf and twisted it around her hand.

His narrowed gaze slanted toward her. "If you hadn't seen him before, why did you attack him?"

"I thought he was going for a weapon, and I've learned to attack first and ask questions later." Because that was who she'd become. There were innocent reasons a man might reach for his belt, but her first response had been to assume it was a weapon.

"Your brother trained you well." Michael pressed the gas pedal, but the beat-up truck wouldn't go faster than sixty.

He'd been avoiding the most important part of their run-in with Ethan Moore. She had to ask, "Do you think he told the truth when he said Ava used the phone?"

"Yeah, I do. I should've known she'd get impatient and make a rash decision. I should've smashed it instead of just taking the battery and SIM card out, so—"

"Why would he warn you?" she said, shutting down his self-recrimination. There would be plenty of time for that once everyone was safe.

"I don't know."

"Do you think he's leading you into a trap?" She had to consider all the angles.

Michael stared straight ahead, his knuckles white as they gripped the steering wheel. "We'll know when we get there."

CHAPTER NINETEEN

Sinclair put a hand to her stomach to stop it heaving. Even at a distance, they could see a cloud of black smoke that spiraled up into the sky.

"No, no, no." Michael already had his foot to the floor, but the truck wouldn't go any faster.

Sinclair closed her eyes, praying his family would be okay.

Two fire trucks and three water trucks were parked in front of the house. Multiple figures in yellow fire-retardant gear swarmed about, managing hoses that were submerged into a large red square makeshift pool and being used to spray the flaming structure.

Michael jumped out of the vehicle before it had come to a complete stop and rushed toward the building.

Sinclair pulled the handbrake to stop the vehicle rolling, climbed into the driver's seat, and shifted it into park. Then she jumped out and followed Michael.

A policeman caught him and restrained him, preventing him from rushing into the burning cabin. Flames shot from the kitchen window. There was a loud hiss, and then an explosion to the side of the building. Everyone jumped, and the emergency personnel pulled back to a safer position.

"They pulled your Dad out. He's in the ambulance," a tribal police officer shouted at Michael, straining to be heard above the din.

Michael took off, heading to the ambulance that was parked on the other side of the firetrucks. Once again, she was close behind.

Milo lay on a gurney, blood dripping from a huge gash to his forehead. "They overpowered me. I couldn't stop them." His voice was thin.

Michael climbed inside and stood next to his stepdad. "What happened?"

They jumped me when I was working on the canoe. I tried to fight back, but they…" His hand went to his side.

The paramedic lifted his shirt to reveal Milo's misshapen ribs, which were already turning purple and black. "He has a head wound, a concussion, and we'll have to make sure there's no internal bleeding."

Michael put a hand on Milo's shoulder. "What about Mom and Ava?"

"They took them." He closed his eyes as his

voice faded.

Michael squeezed his eyes shut. He fisted his hands and then shook Milo awake. "Who did this? Did you see them?

"Big guy, beefy, and the other...other..." He faded again.

"What about the other?" Michael shouted.

"A broken hand." Milo, once again, closed his eyes.

Ice water dripped down Sinclair's spine. "They sound like the pair who attacked me."

"Are you escorting him to the hospital?" the paramedic asked as he hooked up an IV and plunged a needle into Milo's arm.

Michael's gaze jumped from Milo to her. He shook his head. "No."

His eyes were watery as he stepped out of the vehicle and stared at the cabin. Sinclair put a hand to his elbow in an attempt to show support, but he shook her off and walked away.

She resisted the temptation to indulge in self-pity and guilt. That wouldn't help find Nadie and Ava. They needed action.

She stopped the paramedic. All their phones were in the cabin. "I need to call a friend—"

"Here." He smiled and passed her his smartphone. "My plan only covers calls within Montana."

"Don't worry. It's a local number." She dialed Finn.

He picked up on the third ring. "Agent Callaghan."

"Finn, it's Sinclair. They found us."

"Was anyone hurt?"

"Michael and I were out, but Milo, Michael's stepdad, took a beating and they kidnapped his mom and sister. I have no idea what the play is. Taking them doesn't make any sense."

"It does if they want to exchange them for Michael. Kennedy and I are on our way. Don't go anywhere." He disconnected. He'd sounded rational and calm, which was both irritating and comforting at the same time.

She handed the smartphone back to the paramedic.

A brand-new Ford pickup parked behind the emergency vehicles, and a young man with short blond hair got out and was stopped by the same cop who'd intercepted Michael. "I'm looking for Ava O'Connell." He ran a jerky hand through his hair.

"Are you Caleb?" Michael stomped toward him.

"Yes." He took a step back. He was probably intimidated by Michael's obvious fury. "Ava called me and told me to meet her here."

"She gave you directions?" Sinclair clarified.

"Shit." Michael's gaze captured hers.

She could see his anger turning to frustration mixed with fear.

Ava had called her boyfriend and instructed him how to find the cabin. Which meant the

Syndicate had either been listening in or had tracked her phone using GPS. It didn't matter either way because the outcome had been the same. In the space of a few hours, Michael's family had been devastated, and there was no way to fix it.

CHAPTER TWENTY

Michael stared out at the Granite City Square from Finn's FBI office. Finn had deposited him and Sinclair in the federal building and had ordered them not to go anywhere. Then he and FBI Special Agent Morris had headed to the police station to talk to the detectives on the case.

The first thing Finn had done when he'd picked them up at the cabin, which was now a crime scene, was confiscate their weapons. Michael suspected Finn was trying to protect Michael from himself.

The only reason he'd obeyed Finn's commands was because he didn't have a place to start when it came to rescuing his mom and sister. The PDE building stood opposite, looming like a new age megalith, but there was no way they would be held in Lucy's headquarters. That was too obvious. If Michael was still a federal agent, Finn and the police might be inclined to share the details of the case. Who was he kidding? There was no way they would discuss the situation with anyone except the detectives working the investigation.

He closed his eyes, not wanting to think about what his mom and Ava were going through. Were they being tortured, beaten or—?

"Don't." Sinclair appeared by his side. "It won't help them."

"Do you have to be like this?" he snapped.

"Like what?" She put her hands on her hips.

"Cold, efficient. What does it take to upset you?" His world was falling apart, and she had the gall to tell him what to think.

"Tell me, how is being emotional working out for you? Is it doing any good?" If she could breathe fire and incinerate him, she probably would.

"That's easy for you to say. You don't show emotion. Nothing upsets you or gets to you. You're like a robot."

She flinched as if he'd slapped her.

He regretted the words as soon as they were out of his mouth, mostly because he knew they weren't true. If anything, she felt too much and had shielded herself in a cocoon, disguised as work, in order to bury her emotions. He opened his mouth to apologize, but she wouldn't let him speak.

"This is what I do. I deal with families whose children have been taken. Right now, I need you to shove your guilt aside." She turned away from him and then swung back, poking him in the chest. "Would it benefit us if I cried or tried to drink it away? Drown it with alcohol? Because I've done all that, and it didn't help one bit. My pain can't save them, and it won't bring them home, so I fight for them. Now, do you have the balls to join me or are you going to wallow?"

Her pale face, the pinched expression around her eyes, and the tremor in her hand told him she wasn't as unaffected as she seemed. She was right. He needed to be strong. This wasn't about him; it was about saving his family.

"I apologize. That was uncalled for. What do you want me to do?"

"Let's start by going over what we know." She grabbed a large notepad and sat at Agent Morris' desk, pen poised, ready to take notes. "Who has them?"

"The Syndicate."

She scribbled the answer down. "What do they want?"

"Me, presumably."

"Okay, so Finn and the police will put out an alert and investigate. We will follow your gut."

He already felt better by taking action, and working toward a goal was doing something constructive to get them back. "We can make a trade—me for them."

She shook her head. "There's nothing to say they will keep their word. When I've done exchanges, it's always been a straightforward purchase. The people I deal with value money above all else. Child Seekers buys the victims out of slavery. But this is different. They want you dead, and we know from their past with David and Tim they will kill anyone who threatens them." She doodled a figure eight next to her questions and answers. "Does knowing about their existence threaten them?"

"It seems that way."

"If that's the case, your death won't save anyone. They'll just kill all of you. And by making an exchange, you're playing right into their hands and giving them what they want. We need to be smarter. We need more information."

Finn strode into his office, followed by Agent Morris. "I've received permission to keep both of you with me until we know more. The police will need to talk to you."

Sinclair stood, vacating Agent Morris' desk. "What information do they have so far?"

"Nothing you don't already know. The state fire marshal and the police think this was an attack followed by arson. They also believe the fire was an attempt to kill your stepdad and dispose of his body. Unlucky for them and luckily for us, O'Connor has a hard head and regained consciousness in time to crawl out of the blaze."

"He'll need protection." Michael was sorry he hadn't escorted Milo to the hospital, but he couldn't do anything there.

"Already done." Finn slammed a file onto his desk.

"I need to call Lucy Portman." Michael blurted out the demand before he'd had time to think about it, but as soon as he said the words, he knew it was the right call.

Finn stared at him, open-mouthed for a second, and then said, "There are other avenues we can pursue."

Sinclair grabbed his elbow and swung him around to face her. "We just talked about this. If you hand yourself over, they will kill you."

Finn was shouting at him as he slammed his fist on the desk, and he thought he could hear Agent Morris talking in the background, but he didn't turn around to look at her. Instead, he held up his hands in a halt gesture, silencing everyone. "We need to play for time. We want them to think it's in their best interest to keep my mom and sister alive."

Finn took a deep breath and then nodded. "Okay, but we have to go over some instructions and, I'll need to set up a recording so I can use this as evidence."

He picked up his phone and dialed, presumably asking his headquarters in Salt Lake City to activate a recording on his office line.

While Finn was setting up, Michael fished his laptop out of his backpack. With a few clicks, he had Lucy's cell phone number.

Finn disconnected and said, "You can make

the call in a minute, but I need to give you some pointers first."

Michael crossed the room so he was standing at Finn's desk.

Finn kept his hand on the phone, guarding it. "This is a negotiation. You are playing for time. You can't just call, demand your mom and sister be released, and expect her to comply. It's not going to happen."

Michael nodded. "Understood."

"Most negotiators try and demonstrate empathy, but I—"

"It's not gonna happen." There was no way he could empathize with that vicious bitch.

Finn nodded his agreement, and then said, "This little trick might be useful. Let her correct you."

"What?"

"Get a fact or detail wrong so she can correct you. When kidnappers correct the negotiator, they often share useful information." Finn placed the phone on speaker and then pointed at him, signaling for him to dial. Michael locked his gaze with Sinclair. Their connection gave him strength. She answered with a slight nod. He dialed the number.

The ringtone buzzed until, "Hello."

"This is Michael Papin."

She drew in a long breath. "The famous Spider. Hacker extraordinaire, genius, and all-round bastard. I heard you lost your job when

189

you infiltrated my husband's organization. Marshall should have known better than to get involved with anything illegal." A denial of Portman's activities wasn't a good start.

Michael continued, "I will exchange my life for my mom and sister."

"I have no idea what you're talking about." She sounded confident and in control.

"I know you're part of the Syndicate. If you don't have them, then one of your colleagues does."

She laughed, the tone hard and hollow. "You're talking nonsense."

"I swear, if you harm them, I will hunt you down and kill every last one of you."

"I still don't know—"

"I'll call again," he said, cutting her off.

Michael slammed his fist down on Finn's desk.

"You did hear my instructions, didn't you?" Finn snapped and then let out a long sigh.

He stared at the phone. He couldn't answer.

"You didn't get her to incriminate herself, but you did a great job getting yourself implicated if she's ever murdered." Finn's voice was deadpan, giving nothing away. He'd already buried his frustration from a moment ago.

Michael put his hands on his hips and stared at the ceiling. Finally, he turned to Finn. "I know, but that shit doesn't matter. I want my family back, and now she knows the score."

CHAPTER TWENTY-ONE

Ethan Moore stood with his back to the wall in Lucy's office, using his KA-BAR knife to clean under his fingernails. It was an ineffective way to groom himself, and a stupid thing to do, but it sent a message to the two mercenaries, Ludlow and Kemp. He wanted them to know he was comfortable with his blade and was ready to use it.

The two of them were strutting around like they'd had a shootout with the Green Berets and won. When, in reality, they'd taken out a middle-aged man and abducted two unarmed women. They'd handed the women over to one of Lucy's operatives, a weaselly man with short dark hair in an expensive suit.

There was no way Papin could've gotten there in time. Ethan had sped past his rusted-out pickup on the highway and arrived in time to watch the cabin go up in flames. And once again, he'd been unable to contact the Trainer.

Ethan sheathed his blade and resisted the urge to scrub his hands across his face. Damn it all, he should've gone with them to the cabin instead of using Marshall's old computer on the fifth floor.

Since Marshall Portman's death, Lucy had taken measures to make PDE in Granite City her corporate headquarters for her numerous legitimate and illegitimate operations. One of those measures included taking out the internal camera system on the top two floors and the one by the entrance at the back of the building. She wanted the hired help, like him, to be able to come and go without being recorded. Little did she realize it had also enabled Papin to sneak in here, unnoticed, and do whatever in the hell computer geeks did.

Lucy finished her call and smiled. "That was Michael Papin. He's ready to make the exchange. I think I'll let him stew for a while. They say the waiting is worse than the pain."

She stared at Kemp, the older of the two thugs. "Where did you put the two women?"

"We gave them to the guy from the hotel. Like you said." Kemp almost bowed when he made that announcement.

"The hotel you mentioned before, on the east side?" Ethan asked. He was sticking his nose out, but he needed more info. If this was Syndicate business, Lucy might be forthcoming. He was, after all, the Syndicate's enforcer.

She shrugged and shook her head, her smooth blond hair cascading about her face. "If you'd have managed to get to the cabin on time, I might be inclined to tell you." She'd be a beautiful woman if she weren't such a bitch.

Ethan patted his stomach, "Bad burrito, it could happen to anyone."

She rolled her eyes and switched her gaze to Ludlow and Kemp, changing the subject. "I can't believe you've had this much trouble snagging such easy targets."

"'Cept the girlfriend wasn't easy. She broke my hand." Ludlow held up the offending appendage.

Lucy sighed. "And the other team were taken out by the family. These people—"

Ethan ground his teeth. He was out of patience. "You're in Montana. It's an open carry state. Everyone has a fucking gun and is trained to shoot."

Lucy huffed and plunked herself down in her leather office chair. "We got the job done...in the end." She sounded like a spoiled brat.

"Where are the mother and sister now?" He steered the conversation back to Papin's women.

"At the hotel," she said with a dismissive wave of her hand.

"What's the name of the hotel?" He was tempted to take his knife out of its sheath and slice her until she told him what he needed to know. He fisted his hands. He never allowed himself to lose his temper at work.

"I have a property on the east side of the city where I run an escort business," she hedged, giving him information he already knew.

"Escorts?" Ethan forced a smile, hoping it looked genuine. He didn't want Lucy to see his disgust. He wondered if the other members of the Syndicate were involved in Lucy's "escort" business. Then a thought pinged in his head.

"Did you say the hotel was on the east side?" He didn't wait for her to answer. "Is that why you had me stop those arsonists who were burning down their properties in that part of the city? Were they threatening your brothel?" His heartrate quickened. A month ago, he had robbed a bank so he could access a safety deposit box and hand the contents over to the police. He hadn't known why the papers were important. He'd just followed, blindly. The fact that his orders had come directly from the Trainer meant the brothel was a Syndicate-sanctioned business.

Lucy smiled. "I have to say, I was impressed with the cleverness of your plan. The way you used the tunnels to escape was shear genius."

He tried to look bored. "Are you still planning on using Papin's women?"

"They're good looking and they're Native American, which is a niche market. I can sell them at auction, but it might not come to that. There are other members of the Syndicate who might be interested."

He walked to the window and stared out over the city, considering everything she had told him. He spun back to face her. "I want them."

Both Ludlow and Kemp snickered. Ethan ignored them.

He stalked across the room until he was face-to-face with her. "I'm taking them, and I'm going to use them to kill Papin."

She stood and narrowed her eyes on him but didn't give in to his demand.

He stepped back and shrugged, feigning indifference. "Of course, if you don't need my services, I'll just let the Trainer know that I'm available for reassignment."

Her face twisted, changing her appearance from that of a beautiful woman into a vile caricature. "What's wrong? Have you gone too long without knifing someone? Do you need your fix?"

"Yes." He pinned her with a cold, dead gaze. He wasn't lying. He wanted to slice her and use his blade to rid himself of all his rage and anger.

Something about him, maybe his stance or the look on his face, made Lucy take a step back. "You can take control, but I want Papin dead. You aren't the only assassin on the payroll."

"What's the name of the place?" he demanded.

"They're at the Sun Down Hotel. I don't want them moved. They are a valuable commodity." She sat in her expensive chair with her back straight and her head held high, once again in control. "As soon as Papin's dead, I want them back. If you try to sell them out from under me, I will use the full force of the Syndicate to come after you."

"You don't have to worry. I won't sell them. You have my word." He inclined his head to one side in a gentlemanly gesture of agreement. He'd pushed her as far as she would go. He'd won, but knowing Lucy, she would probably eradicate him the next chance she got.

He strolled out of the room. It was obvious from his confrontation with Lucy that his time working for the Syndicate was coming to an end. But he couldn't just walk away. The Syndicate had assets all over the globe, and they had the resources to hunt him down. He had to be prepared to disappear completely.

CHAPTER
TWENTY-TWO

Finn Callaghan stared at the reports on his desk. The words blurred on the page. It was past midnight. He'd sent Kennedy to the hospital to interview Milo O'Connor.

He had the police report from the home invasion at Michael's parents place, the attack on Sinclair, and the interim report on the kidnapping and arson at the cabin.

Interestingly, Tate hadn't asked for details about the Syndicate, which in itself wasn't necessarily suspicious. The captain had probably been sidetracked by the amount of cases Sinclair and Michael were involved in. Finn hadn't connected the dots for Tate, but it didn't take a genius to realize the same two people were the victims of three different attacks in less than twenty-four hours. Four if he included the burglary at Sinclair's place of work. Between the two of them, they had escalated the crime rate in

Granite City-Elkhead County to new levels.

All the felonies showed a deliberate intent to get Michael, but why now? And why would they be so brazen?

Finn could only think of two answers: either Michael had done something to attract their attention, or they were planning something big and didn't want someone with Michael's skillset to undermine them.

His friend sat at Kennedy's desk, his laptop open as he tapped away at the keys. He could be investigating, but it struck Finn as classic blocking, which happened when someone, normally a suspect, would place objects between their person and the investigator in an effort to distance themselves from the discussion.

Sinclair sat on the couch at the far end of the office. Her elbow rested on the arm. Her head was supported by her hand and her eyes were closed. She seemed to be napping.

Under stress, the human body had three reactions: freeze, flight or fight. Her ability to save herself when faced with two assailants could only come with training and experience.

He fished his smartphone out of the pocket of his cargo pants and called David, Sinclair's brother.

"What's wrong?" David didn't waste any time with niceties.

Finn was momentarily taken aback. Sinclair had answered the phone with exactly the same attitude the last time he'd called her. In a low tone, so as not to wake her, he relayed everything that had happened, leaving out the details of the investigation. But he did explain his suspicion that the Syndicate had come after his sister and then taken Michael's family.

"Shit. How're they doing?" David didn't sound surprised.

"Michael's keeping busy, working on something, which he's going to share soon." Finn raised his voice, making sure his tone was forceful.

Michael glanced up, nodded, and then continued tapping away at the keyboard.

"That's a good coping strategy." David, who had been shot in the face on a rescue mission, knew all about trauma. "And Sinclair?"

"She seems fine, but you know her better than I do." Even though he was trained to read body language, Sinclair had always been a closed book. She was contained and controlled. He had never seen her disassemble, which was impressive in itself. Non-verbal responses were a product of the limbic system and couldn't be easily regulated.

"What can I do?" David asked.

"Call Tim and warn him. I want you both to be on the lookout in case these guys come after you."

"Don't worry, I have a contingency plan." David had probably been preparing for the day when the Syndicate would reappear since January when he had rescued Marie.

The minute he disconnected, Sinclair said, "How is my brother?" She hadn't moved and her eyes were still closed. There was absolutely no sign she was awake.

"He sounded good. Did you want to talk to him?" Finn shouldn't be shocked that she was conscious. How could anyone sleep with everything that had happened?

"Are you going to check out the break-in at Child Seekers?" Finally, she opened her eyes and stretched out her arms, working the knots out of her shoulders. "There's something not right about it, but I can't put my finger on it."

He searched through the files on his desk. "I have the report here. The robbery itself is troubling."

"It's not that. They stole my information. Why bother?" She continued to stretch, not looking at him.

He stared at her for a moment. The napping, the stretching, all her movements telegraphed blocking. Why hadn't he seen it before? He was way too close to this case. His emotional involvement meant his reasoning was compromised. When Kennedy arrived, she would be able to help him by providing some distance.

He forced his mind back to Sinclair's question. "So they could track you. Once they have your social security number, they know everything about you."

"Don't you think that's redundant? I mean, I've been trained to lay low, travel under the radar, and use only cash."

He rubbed his chin. He needed a shave. "Maybe they don't know about Child Seeker's standard operating procedure."

She shook her head and finally met his gaze. The bruises on her face were purple, but the swelling had subsided. "I would imagine any competent investigator would be able to find out what I do and draw conclusions."

"I agree." Michael didn't look up from the screen. "There's something hinky about it."

"What are you doing?" Finn asked. Michael obviously wasn't going to share.

"I'm checking to see if my virus worked or if it's been discovered and shut down."

"What virus?" Finn shouldn't be surprised by the announcement. Michael was a white hat hacker and a former investigator.

"When I was undercover at PDE, there were two computers set up to run on a separate network. I believe they are being used by the Syndicate. I installed a piece of code that will link it to the regular internet." Michael sat back in his chair and rubbed his eyes, another blocking mechanism. "We needed to know what they were doing so we could stay a step ahead."

Finn gritted his teeth to contain his reaction. If they weren't both going through hell, he would be cursing up a storm. "Let me get this straight. You used a virus to join an air-gapped system to the web. How did you upload this... code?"

Sinclair slumped on the couch. "We infiltrated the system in the PDE building."

"When?" Finn demanded.

"Earlier this evening while my mom and sister were being..." He fisted his hands then unflexed his fingers before he scrubbed his hands over his face.

Neither of them would meet Finn's gaze. *Shit.* "Why do you think they are after you now, after all this time?"

Michael shrugged. "I have a theory, but I needed to access their secure network to be sure."

"Do you think they attacked tonight because you were spotted?" Even as he spoke, he knew that didn't make sense. The kidnapping occurred before Sinclair and Michael had returned. Unless... "Did you go anywhere after you broke into PDE?"

Michael finally met his gaze. "That guy that tried to plant the knife at Tim's—"

"Ethan Moore, the killer." Even saying the name made the hairs on the back of Finn's neck stand on end.

"Yeah, him. We bumped into him. He warned us that they..." Michael swallowed and then continued, "He said Ava had used her phone, and if we hurried, we might be able to save them."

Finn gave a long, slow whistle. "You're saying that Ethan Moore caught you at PDE, and instead of killing you, he warned you. Why would he help?" As far as he could tell, Moore was an assassin for the Syndicate, so warning Michael, telling him about the attack, didn't make sense.

"I don't know." Sinclair stood and pulled her knees to her chest one at a time, stretching her leg muscles. "I got mixed signals from him."

"What do you mean?" Finn ignored that her torso was pointed away from him, something which normally meant the subject was uncomfortable with the conversation. Her distress could be caused by the fact that people under her protection had been taken.

Finally, she stopped and faced him. "Initially, he went for his weapon."

"A knife or a gun?" As far as he knew, Moore only used a knife.

Michael closed his eyes. "He was wearing a heavy-duty gun belt. His weapon—I think it's a Barretta—was tucked at the small of his back and his knife was at his side." He opened his eyes. "Does that help?"

Sinclair stared at Michael for a moment and then said, "Yeah, thanks. He didn't reach behind him. He was going for his side—"

"Which means he was going for his knife. Did he draw it?" Finn needed clarification.

She shook her head. "No, I tagged him with

my baton before he could, and then we ran."

That didn't make any sense, but everything in Sinclair's non-verbal communication told him she was being honest and forthright. "When did he warn you?"

Michael's tremoring hands hovered over the keyboard. "We were escaping. He called down the stairwell. He said we could still save them." He sat back, covering his face with his hands. "Obviously, we failed."

Finn ignored Michael's torment, not because he didn't feel sympathy for his friend, but because he couldn't follow Michael into his anguish-filled crater of guilt and misery. If he did, he wouldn't be any use to anyone. "Ethan warned you and didn't come after you?"

"But initially he went for his weapon," Sinclair added.

"That could've been a reflex," Finn said more to himself than his friends. "Maybe something's happened that's soured Moore's relationship with the Syndicate, or maybe he's playing a long game." Ethan had robbed a bank a month ago, put a number of customers in danger, set fire to the bank, nearly killed Detective Ramirez, and taken attorney Sophia Reed as hostage. Then, in a surprise twist, he had killed his fellow accomplices and given Ms. Reed proof that a group of businessmen were setting fire to buildings on the east side of the city. "There's no way to tell what Ethan's up to," he said finally. "We might as well deal with what we know."

"What do we know?" Sinclair sat on the couch, her gaze focused on Michael.

He stared at her for a long moment and then turned to Finn. "Lucy's financials don't add up. Years ago, she purchased several large properties abroad, worth millions, with money that couldn't be traced back to her legitimate businesses. When the recession hit, she sold them, and hey presto, she had clean money to prop up her companies. I didn't mention this before because I couldn't prove it."

"You suspect money laundering. What illegal activity is Lucy into that requires her to hide income?" Finn asked. As a former federal agent, Michael would've known the FBI didn't chase after half-baked suspicions.

"That's another reason we planted the virus. We needed to know what resources they had at their disposal, and we wanted to stay one step ahead of them," Sinclair stated.

Michael cleared his throat. "Whoever set up their system is brilliant. They're hiding their communications in signals from our own satellites. They've hacked military, government, research, and diplomatic organizations globally. If information is the new currency, these guys own the world."

Finn felt as if he'd slammed into a wall of ice. His hands and feet went numb, and it felt as though his heart had stopped beating. "Fuck. Can you tell what they're doing with it?"

"Not yet. I need to go into the dark web and, even then, it'll be hard to tell what they're up to. There's just so much data, it's overwhelming. I need to isolate a piece of info and then see what they're using it for. They could be selling it, and there's always blackmail, but that's just speculation on my part."

"What if it's not for sale. What if they're using it for their own purposes?" Sinclair asked.

"Umm…" Michael tilted his head. "The only way to really know is to hack their communications."

"I don't understand. I thought they were using our satellites, so you must be able to see their messages." Sinclair crossed the room and placed her hand on the back of his chair. It wasn't an overtly intimate gesture, but she was invading his personal space, something that didn't bother him in the least.

Michael turned to face her. "They're encrypted."

She narrowed her eyes. "Can you hack it?"

"If I can find the key to unlocking the code, then yes."

"How long do you think that'll take?" Finn wasn't really sure he understood what was going on.

"I don't even know if it's possible. When I dealt with this kind of encryption before, I would always plant a keylogger so I would have access to everyone's passwords before I started. Then it would just be a matter of..." Michael stared into space. He was completely motionless. It was as though someone had flicked an off switch and powered him down.

Sinclair waved a hand in front of his face.

Michael didn't flinch.

Finn emerged from behind his desk and stood next to Sinclair. "Has he ever done this before?"

She shook her head.

Suddenly, Michael gasped for breath, inhaling as if he'd stopped breathing for a while and then started again. "I remember."

"Remember what?" Finn had no idea what he was talking about.

Michael bounced out of his chair, grabbed Sinclair by the shoulders, and gave her a peck on the lips. Then he paced the room, his energy restored. "I remember what I did before Portman hit me with his car."

Sinclair laughed, her delight at Michael's statement apparent. "That's great."

Finn returned to his ergonomic seat behind his desk and waited for Michael to calm down.

His friend danced around, mumbling to himself for a few more minutes and then sat in his seat and faced Finn. "In their secure system I planted a piece of malware that can hack all their passwords and usernames. All I have to do is activate it and I'll have them."

Finn wasn't a slouch when it came to computers, but he needed clarification. "Let me get this straight. You designed two viruses to penetrate this secret network. The first one, which you planted back in January, stole their usernames and passwords. The one you downloaded this evening enables you to log in to their system via the internet?"

Michael's hands glided over the keyboard. "Yes, but I don't think I activated the first one. I put it in the system and planned to go back later when things had calmed down. It never occurred to me that I would get hit in the head and lose my memory."

"Is there any way to tell? Do you have some kind of storage for the information, a flash drive maybe?" Sinclair returned to her seat on the couch.

"Not a flash drive. I never store the information physically. Usually, I create a cloud account with a data storage company."

"A cloud account?" Sinclair asked.

"It works in the same way as most email accounts. You can open your Gmail from any computer or smartphone because Google stores it on the web. Cloud storage is also held on the web so all I have to do is bring up the data company and enter my account details. That way I can open it anywhere."

"You said you didn't trigger the first virus." Finn wanted to bring Michael back to the subject at hand. "If it wasn't you, who did?"

"One minute." Michael stared at the screen and then tapped a few more keys. "Huh. The IP address suggests that it was initiated from Lucy's terminal."

"Do you think she wanted the information, too?" Sinclair asked.

Michael frowned. "I don't see how, and as far as I can tell, no one has accessed my storage files. I think someone might have set it off by mistake."

Finn tapped his desk with the end of his pen. "And you didn't know about the first virus before today?" Michael had perfect recall. He never forgot anything.

"Concussion." He said the one word as if it explained everything, and maybe it did. Temporary memory loss from a head trauma was common.

"So you planted a virus in January to get their usernames and passwords but never activated it. Then someone gained entry to Lucy's office, set it off, and stole the passwords. When did they do this?"

Michael typed, searching for the data. Regaining his memory seemed to have revitalized him. "Two days ago."

Shit. That was just before Sinclair was attacked.

Michael continued working, seemingly unaware of the timeline he had just uncovered. He stopped and stared at the screen. "According to this, one percent of Lucy's profits are sent to the Global Democratic Coalition, which is also known as the GDC. They're a legitimate organization. Their website says they want to spread democracy around the world. I'll need to do some digging into them. It'll take time."

Finn stood and grabbed his jacket, which was hanging on his office door. "I'm going to talk to the detective in charge of the investigation into the break-in at Child Seeker's International. Then I'll talk to the fire marshal and the arson investigator."

"It's close to one in the morning. Will they be up?" Sinclair twirled a finger around a lock of hair, an action that told him she was stressed despite her seemingly calm manner.

"It takes hours to evaluate a crime scene and an arson where there are still hot spots to be extinguished. If they're not available, I'll head to my place and take a shower. We have bathroom facilities downstairs, so I'll bring back some toiletries and a T-shirt for each of you."

She smiled, but it didn't reach her eyes. "Thanks. Watch your back."

Michael didn't seem to notice Finn's departure. He was absorbed in his work.

Finn closed the door and headed for his SUV in the parking lot.

Michael had planted some malware while using an Army CID alias in an unsanctioned operation to obtain password information. And then, earlier this evening, they had broken into PDE and planted a second virus so they could access a secure, private network. They had done all this without a warrant. That meant there were legal implications to their actions. Not only could they be charged, but Finn couldn't act on any intelligence they'd provided. Any lawyer worth their retainer would claim it was fruit of the poisoned tree.

By the time he reached his car, he'd changed his mind about contacting Granite City-Elkhead County Police department and the fire marshal. They could wait until morning. He needed some space to figure out what to do next. He would have to tell Kennedy. It was bad enough he had a murder board behind his fridge, but if he kept Michael and Sinclair's actions from her, he ran the risk of making her an unwitting accomplice to their crimes.

He texted her, asking her to meet him at the Dumb Luck Café at six in the morning. Once he explained the situation to her, he would call Supervisory Special Agent in Charge Martin De-Luca and inform him of this development.

He started his vehicle and pulled out of the lot. What the hell was going on? The Global Democratic Coalition was an international political group. He hadn't seen that coming. He'd always believed the Syndicate's motive was greed. He'd grown up poor, so he understood wanting more, but this was something else—this was about power.

CHAPTER
TWENTY-THREE

Sinclair sifted through the printout Michael had given her. There were pages and pages of financial statements. With each business, she googled their location and their social media, trying to find anything that seemed out of place. Attempting to assess whether a company was legitimate was difficult for her. She wasn't an accountant or a hacker. Her work involved talking to people, asking questions, and a lot of legwork. This was way out of her comfort zone, and her lack of experience could, in the end, be a liability.

The pair of them were crowded together, sharing Agent Morris' desk. She took another sip of stale, acidic coffee, which made her stomach cramp in protest. It was two in the morning, and she had the beginnings of a fatigue headache forming behind her eyes. The facts and figures in front of her smudged together.

She stood. She wasn't going anywhere; she just couldn't stay seated and not fall asleep. This time yesterday she had been curled up in Michael's arms. The weekend they'd spent together at eighteen had always been important for her, although she had never realized why. Now she knew. It was because he made her feel like she belonged. She'd never felt at home anywhere except in his arms.

After years of meaningful looks and touches that lasted a moment too long, they'd finally gotten together. Unfortunately, it took more than love to make a relationship work. It was bad enough that Milo was seriously injured, but with Nadie and Ava taken...the guilt was just too much. At least it was for her. If she could go back in time and change her decision to join Michael on his mission to PDE, she would. She twisted at the waist, popping the ligaments in her lower back.

Michael hadn't moved, stretched, or done anything except work for hours. He also couldn't look her in the eye. He probably blamed her for what happened, which was understandable. Protecting people was her job. Finn had asked her to stay with the family because he knew how capable she was. Instead of doing her duty, she'd allowed herself to get distracted by their familiarity with the location and her own need to be loved. In doing so, she had let down her guard.

Finally, she sat and stared at the pages in front of her. The only thing she could do now was work to get them back. She straightened her spine and concentrated on the list of commercial properties held by PDE and Lucy Portman. The name of the Sun Down Hotel caught her eye. She remembered that establishment from when she had lived on the street. It was making an awful lot of money for a business that was situated in a derelict part of town known to locals as *East of Hell*. It was called that because it started at Hellebore Avenue and spread out from there. The area was notorious for its cheap boarding houses, druggies, and gang activity. They had avoided it when they'd lived on the street.

She elbowed Michael. "Take a look at this. Do you think this place is really making this kind of bank?"

He rubbed his face and then cleared his throat. "Sure, that seems legitimate."

He was dismissive of her, which pricked at her raw nerves. She was tempted to snap at him but buried the impulse. They were both tired and upset; losing her temper wouldn't help. "What are you working on?"

He sat back in his chair, still not looking at her. "I'm trying to identify the members of the Syndicate before they find my virus and shut it down. I'll hand the information over to Finn. That way, if the worst happens, he can stop them."

Pain shot through her chest, and she suppressed a gasp. What he hadn't said but meant was *if they kill me*, which was a real possibility. She couldn't let that happen. If she stuck by his side, then perhaps she could stop it, stop him from throwing his life away. Huh, she was creating her own emotional Gordian knot, an unsolvable problem. She felt guilty for going with him to PDE, leaving Nadie and the others unprotected. At the same time, she needed to protect Michael and couldn't stand the thought of anything happing to him, which was why she'd accompanied him in the first place.

"Instead of doing this..." She pointed to the list of businesses in front of her. "Perhaps I should look for properties where they would likely be held. I know from experience abductors whisk their victims away to a different geographic location. Within hours, they could be in another state and look totally different."

"Good point. They might still be planning to go through with an exchange, or at least use them as bait. If that's the case, then they'd be held locally. Make a list of everywhere you think is a possible location, include warehouses, empty office buildings, and hotels. Anywhere they could stash two women unnoticed." His screen had gone dark while they were talking. He tapped a key, and it sprang to life. Once again, he returned to his digital investigation.

She picked up the printout, grabbed the notepad that sat on Agent Morris' desk, and got to work. She would stay close to him for as long as was necessary to assure his safety.

****

Michael rubbed his eyes. His back hurt, as did his left hip, and pain was shooting into his head from the trapped nerves in his shoulder. Common sense told him his muscles were tense and had aggravated his injuries. Plus, sitting hunched over his computer didn't help. Although, compared to the pain he'd been in eight months ago, it was nothing except a distraction.

Finn slammed into the office and plunked a tote on his desk. "In here you'll find two T-shirts, shampoo, toothpaste, and new toothbrushes. The showers are on the ground floor." He headed for the door.

"Where are you going?" Michael asked.

Finn stopped with a hand on the doorknob and turned in his direction. His jaw seemed to be clenched tight and his lips were pressed into a thin line.

Michael had never been good at reading body language, but even he could tell Finn was pissed. "Forget I said anything."

Finn left without another word.

"He's easily riled." He stood and grabbed one of the coffees from Finn's desk.

Sinclair sat back and folded her arms across her chest. "Really, you think it's Finn?"

He shrugged. "Yeah, I mean it's okay. It's the

middle of the night. He's probably just tired."

Her eyes widened as though he'd said something shocking. "You don't think you were out of line asking him where he's going? He doesn't answer to you. We have taken over his office. You were a federal agent, weren't you?"

He nodded.

She didn't seem angry, but she wasn't going easy on him either. "Would you have talked about a case in front of two victims? No, you wouldn't. The only reason he hasn't kicked us out is because we're his friends. I'd be amazed if his partner has any such considerations. She will insist we move, and she'd be correct."

He rubbed the back of his neck. "You're right. I shouldn't have questioned him. I get so engrossed in what I'm doing, I don't consider others. I'll apologize when he gets back. We'll have to find another place to do our research." He closed his eyes for a moment too long and then forced them open. "I can't think of a place to go. Can you?"

"I can't think, period. We need rest—"

"No, we have to keep going." He shook his head. "God knows what's happening to them. I need—"

"No." She walked across the room to stand in front of him, her hands on her hips in a don't-mess-with-me stance. "I get it. You feel guilty. Well, you're not the only one. They were under my protection." She swallowed. It was as though she was gulping down her pain. "I should've been there, but Nadie insisted I go with you." She turned her back to him. "I wanted to be with you, so I didn't argue, but I should've known better."

He grabbed her shoulders and gently turned her, but she wouldn't look at him. He understood. He felt the same. He should never have gone off. Why did he always think his way was best? When it came to Sinclair, he was wrong more often than he was right. "We have survivor's guilt, don't we?"

She nodded. "I want to keep looking, but I can't think. My head's fuzzy, and it hurts. You know what that means, don't you?"

"Fatigue." Symptoms included a decrease in cognitive reasoning, impaired decision making, and irritability. They could have overlooked something vital because they were too tired to think. They both needed some shuteye. Just an hour would refresh them and help their brains function.

"Come on." She held his hand and led him to the couch. "You go first and get comfortable. I'll fit in around you."

He did as he was told, laying on his right side, supporting his head on the armrest at one end. Then he patted the seat, urging her to cuddle up. She fitted her body into his so they were spooning. He wrapped an arm around her waist, reassured by her presence. No matter what happened, he could rely on her to always point him in the right direction. "I don't know what I would do if I didn't have you." Then he closed his eyes and allowed himself to drift off.

CHAPTER TWENTY-FOUR

Ethan opened the door that accessed the sixth floor from the stairwell. He'd waited until five in the morning because he needed to scope the place out, and in his experience, this was the most likely time for lookouts to fall asleep. Unfortunately, the security surrounding this dump was top notch. He'd thought he'd be able to sneak in, but the guards had stopped him. It had taken a phone call to Lucy to allow him access. There was zero chance he'd be able to get anyone out.

But he had managed to override the CCTV camera in the room where they were being held. He had connections with several trusted individuals who worked on the wrong side of the law and were professionals, like himself. One of them was a hacker who had explained that the average smart phone had better security than web-connected security cameras.

Ethan had simply ran a program from his laptop that kept trying different passwords until it got the right one. Once he had access, all he had to do was loop the video feed to hide the conversation he was about to have with Papin's women.

A dim overhead lightbulb showed the dirt and grime that covered the walls. If the décor and smell of mold hadn't been an indication of how old and rundown the place was, using a key instead of a card to open the door was a dead giveaway.

He couldn't trust Lucy to keep her word even though she'd given him control of the women. He was just a fixer. People like her stomped on people like him. Sooner or later, her need to dominate the situation would become more important than her promise to let him use the women to lure Papin into a trap to kill him. Which meant he probably had twenty-four hours at the most before the women were sold, and even that was stretching it. He wouldn't be surprised if she'd already made contact with the interested parties.

He opened the door to the hotel room and reached for the light switch on the wall. The punch came out of nowhere. A blow to his cheek. It stung but didn't incapacitate him. He blocked the second jab aimed at his throat. Then he grabbed the woman's hands and held her still. He didn't care if he was hurting her. There was more at stake here than a few bruises. He kicked the door closed with his left foot and then concentrated on his attacker. He grasped both of her wrists with one hand and flicked on the light.

From the corner of his eye, he spotted a teen girl. She had the drawer from the nightstand above her head, ready to slam it into him. He pushed the older woman back. She bounced as she landed on the bed. Using his right foot, he kicked the young one in the knee. She went down hard.

He pulled his gun and aimed it at the daughter. "Stop, both of you."

The daughter stilled and the mother, who had regained her footing, froze.

"I'm not here to hurt you." He held his free hand up in a show of surrender, which meant nothing because he was still holding a gun on the kid.

"Then why are you here?" The mother fisted her hands, ready to fight.

"You were taken to use against your son, Papin, I'm protecting you. But the bitch who took you will never let you go. You're to be sold."

He could tell by the look on the older woman's face that she didn't understand. "This is a sex trafficking operation, and you are going to be auctioned off. I want to stop that from happening."

She narrowed her eyes. "Why would you help

us?"

That was a question he didn't want to answer. He had always enjoyed his job and had believed he was a man without a conscience, but when faced with the rape of multiple people, for profit, he realized he was human after all. It was a revelation he had yet to come to terms with, but one he accepted as true. "I kill people. I don't abuse them."

"You're here to kill us?" Her stance was rigid, and her nostrils flared as if preparing for a brawl.

This could escalate if he didn't find a way for the women to trust him. But he'd never been good at communicating. "No." He lowered his weapon, pointing it at the ground.

He'd murdered drug kingpins and CEOs without batting an eyelash, but he'd never been called upon to murder women and children. For most of his adult life, his goals had been simple: kill and get paid. Occasionally, he'd wondered about getting some hobbies and maybe starting a normal life, but he hadn't because he enjoyed his job and he wasn't interested in much else. Once his work with the Syndicate was over, he'd be adrift. He pushed the thought aside and focused on the woman in front of him.

She grabbed her daughter, shoving the young girl behind her. "Are you going to kill Michael?"

"Yes. I was supposed to kill him. Papin knows the score." Ethan suppressed a smile. There was a chance that like his friend, Morgan, Papin would've put up a fight. Ethan would've enjoyed that, but he had to let it go.

"Supposed to?" the girl asked. Her long hair was strung across her face as she collapsed onto the bed, rubbing her knee.

"I need to find him. Where would he go?"

The mother shrugged. "I don't know. We hadn't seen him for months. He turned up at the same time as the men—"

"Papin killed them?"

She nodded.

"How do I get in touch with him?"

The older woman lifted her chin in defiance. "Call the FBI."

"I want a real answer." He grabbed her by the front of her shirt and twisted it so it choked her. He might be trying to save her from a lifetime of rape, but he wasn't about to put up with any crap.

The daughter elbowed her way between them, in an attempt to shove him away. "That is a real answer. He has a friend in the FBI, Finn Callaghan. Call him."

He knew about the FBI friend and realized they were telling the truth. He let go of the mother and stepped back. "Do not leave this room. You're safe as long as you're here." He walked to the door, but stopped with his hand on the doorknob. He was leaving them defenseless. He turned his Barretta in his hand so he was holding the barrel. "Do either of you know how to use this?" Giving them his weapon was a risk. They might shoot him in the back, but his instinct told him that neither of them were that coldblooded.

The older woman nodded and took the handgun from him.

"I'll come back with food. I cannot emphasize this enough—don't leave this room and barricade the door with the dresser after I leave. There are guards everywhere. If they catch you trying to escape, they will hurt you."

"How will we know it's you when you return?" The older woman was checking the cartridge to make sure it was loaded, which was something he would've done.

"I'll knock like this." He tapped out a rhythm on the door. "You got that?" He tapped it out again.

They both nodded.

"If anyone else enters, shoot them. Do not hesitate." He locked the door after him and listened. He was gratified to hear the muffled sound of furniture being dragged across the floor. He headed to the fire exit at the rear of the hotel.

Going to Special Agent Callaghan was out of the question. He would be arrested for bank robbery and murder. If he ended up in the system, the Syndicate would suicide him for sure. They had plenty of people in the prison system who could kill him and make it look as if he'd done it to himself. It wasn't that they had an associate in every police station, but they knew the right people, and it would be easy to hire someone to do the dirty work.

He could go to Tim Morgan, but that was just as dangerous. As an ex-Ranger, Morgan considered himself a man of honor. He probably wouldn't attack unless it was necessary. But Morgan's skill with a blade matched Ethan's, and he still had the scars from their last encounter. Why take the risk?

He made his way out of the building. The security guard, a plainclothes man with an AK47, waved at him, letting him know he was under surveillance. Ethan waved back and strolled along the back alley toward his truck.

An image of the pretty defense attorney, Sophia Reed, appeared in his mind. She was tougher than she looked and had a brilliant legal mind. Although he'd taken her hostage, he had also saved her from being jumped by one of his accomplices in the robbery. She would listen. He'd get a few hours' sleep to sharpen his mind and would be waiting at Sophia's office when she arrived for work.

He hated to leave the Syndicate. Unfortunately, he couldn't get past the sex slavery and the horror of his own childhood. He wanted Lucy and the rest of her operation to suffer. The realization struck him like a kick to the kidneys. He didn't just want to take them down; he wanted to hurt them so bad they would pray to be allowed into hell.

CHAPTER
TWENTY-FIVE

Finn spotted Kennedy walking toward him as he was leaving the Dumb Luck Café. He thrust a coffee into her hand. "Let's talk in the car."

"What's going on?" She followed him across the Granite City square.

"Michael and Sinclair are camped out in the office, and I don't want to discuss any cases in front of them."

She frowned. "You left them alone in our office? That breaks all kinds of rules and jeopardizes the integrity of our files. You know that, don't you?"

He put a hand to his head, knowing he was eye-blocking, shutting out what she was saying. Finally, he dropped his arm and squared his shoulders. He was conflicted, and there was no way he could distance himself from whatever was going on. "I need you to take the lead, liaise with the Granite City-Elkhead County PD, and deal with the terrible twosome up there." He pointed to the federal building. "I will back you up a hundred percent."

They continued on in silence until they reached the lot where his government-issue Ford SUV was parked.

She took another sip of her coffee. "This is good, but next time I'll have sugar-free hazelnut in my latte."

"Noted." She never failed to keep him on his toes.

She climbed in, swiveled in her seat so she was facing him, and waited until he had closed his door. "Okay, what have you got?"

"One of the dead men from the home invasion has a Russian orthodox cross tattooed along his spine. Interpol are running him now to see if they can get an ID. The other two shooters have no distinguishing features and aren't in the system."

"I take it Interpol are checking them out, too?

"As per my instructions to Detective Ramirez, yes."

"And they all died by gunshot wounds?"

"Yes. Which matches what we saw and Michael's version of events. He shot two of them when they were trying to gain entry into the basement, and I got the last one."

"And ballistics supports that?"

"Verbally, yes, but I haven't received the written report yet."

She pulled a small notebook and a pen from her cargo pants.

He pointed to the pad. "Why didn't you get that out before?"

"I didn't think of it." She held her pen to the paper, ready to write. "And the break-in at Child Seekers?"

"Ramirez doesn't believe it was a robbery. Nothing was taken. All they did was look through the files and tear the place apart. Sinclair's documents were lying open on a nearby table."

"Like someone wanted them to be found?" She recorded everything in neat, compact letters.

"Exactly." He had no idea how she managed to write so fast and yet still have tidy penmanship.

"That sounds more like intimidation than robbery."

"Which is weird because you'd think jumping her in a back alley would be intimidating enough." He tapped his fingers against the steering wheel.

"Maybe they thought she would go home or use her credit card. Perhaps they don't understand what she does for a living."

He placed his elbow against the driver's side window and stared out at the lot. "It doesn't make sense."

Kennedy underlined her notes and turned the page. "Let's put a pin in that one and talk about the cabin. I went to the hospital like you asked. By the description Milo O'Connor gave us, I think it was the same two guys that attacked Sinclair in that back alley."

"Really?"

She nodded. "Yes. In her report, she said she hit the smaller one in the hand and she said the big one looked like an ex-fighter."

"There's a connection." If this was the Syndicate, then it would make sense the same men would be present at both crimes.

They sat in silence for a moment and then Kennedy said, "You think it's the Syndicate, don't you?"

Her ability to read his mind always amazed him. "You don't?"

They were both in attendance at the meeting at FBI headquarters in Salt Lake City with Special Agent in Charge Martin Deluca when they had discovered that evidence collected by Michael had gone missing.

She tapped her pen against the center console. "But why go after him now? We're missing something."

He tasted his coffee. It was nearly cold. "Do you know what I think?"

"No, but you're going to tell me."

"Michael's not as smart as he thinks. When he was undercover at PDE, he installed a virus that hacked all their passwords."

"Dear God." She stared blindly out the window. "Do you think they know it was him?"

"You're supposed to attend a seminar at Quantico in a couple of months. They will explain there are a lot of hackers, but very few of them can write code."

She gave him a look that suggested she didn't know what he was talking about. "I thought that was what made a hacker, the ability to write a series of squiggles and dashes, which can disrupt the world."

He shook his head. "Most of them just seek out and copy the squiggles and dashes."

"But Michael is one of the few who can actually make stuff up." She added that detail to her notes.

"From what I understand, it's like talking with an accent. Everyone who writes—"

"Has their own accent so they're identifiable, which means they know it was him."

"Exactly. He should've known as soon as he infected their computers he was putting a target on his back."

"So why didn't he take measures?" She flicked another page over as she continued writing down everything they discussed.

"Concussion. He lost his memory." Michael hadn't mentioned what he'd planned to do to cover his tracks, or maybe he hadn't planned that far. He'd seen an opportunity and seized it.

"Shit." Her use of a curse word confirmed his feeling of doom.

"It gets worse."

She gave him a pained look. "How?"

He told her about Michael and Sinclair's trip to PDE, how they had planted malware on the secure system to connect it to the internet, their encounter with Ethan Moore, and how Lucy was paying large sums of money to the Global Democratic Coalition.

She put a hand to her head. "This is almost too much. Could they be charged with breaking and entering? And why would Moore warn them? What's he playing at?"

"Plus, we can't use anything they uncover."

"Fruit of the poisonous tree." She nodded and then doodled a flower on her notepad. "We shouldn't push the panic button just yet. We haven't acted on anything they've discovered." She stopped writing. "How much should we tell our friends in local law enforcement?"

"My gut says tell them everything. I don't want anyone from the Granite City-Elkhead County Police Department to get hurt, and we still have to maintain a good working relationship with them once this is over."

"Despite what Deluca said, you think we should tell them about the mole?"

He nodded. "And how they've accessed my records. I don't want the Syndicate doing the same to them."

She drew in a breath. "Okay, we'll go and talk to Tate and Ramirez, but first things first. Let's deal with your friends who are living in our office."

He rolled his eyes. "I can't kick them out, but at the same time, they're driving me nuts."

She tried to hide her smile behind her coffee cup.

"Is that why you stayed out of the office last night?" He'd expected her back after she'd finished her interview, but she'd texted him to say she was heading home.

"No." She pursed her lips. A sure sign she was lying.

For the first time since Sinclair was mugged, he smiled. "You went home, showered, and slept in your own bed and left me to deal with them."

Her grin was positively gleeful. "I didn't neglect my duties, and you would've called if you needed me. They're your friends. I figured you could deal with them."

"I gotta tell you, I'm not doing a good job."

She frowned "Sure, you are. You had the sense to get me to take over so that puts you ahead of most." She sighed and then continued, "These people aren't just friends. They're your family. You can't cut them free when they have no safe place to go, and God knows we can't call the DOJ. Right now, they're in a building that has security at the front door and the FBI occupies the second floor. Let's put them in the conference room for now. That way we can keep an eye on them, and they'll still be safe. We'll come up with a long-term plan when things calm down."

"That'll work." Why the hell hadn't he thought of putting them there?

She opened the passenger door. Their chat was obviously at an end. "Do you want me to tell them?"

"No. It's like you said, they're family. I should do it." He opened his door and followed her into the building.

CHAPTER
TWENTY-SIX

Defense attorney Sophia Reed needed better security at her downtown office. He'd kept an eye on her since the bank robbery last month. Not because he intended to harm her, but because he never knew if he might need a good lawyer and she was the perfect go-between.

She was a creature of habit and arrived at work the same time every day. Her evening schedule did vary, however. He assumed she stayed later, depending on her workload.

It had been easy to jimmy the lock and, like most professionals, he had the electronic equipment needed to defeat the alarm. He left the cameras running. The cops could use the video to identify him. He smiled. Never in his life had he imagined he would be sharing information with the police and would want them to track him.

He locked the front door and reset the system. He didn't want her to call law enforcement before he'd had a chance to talk to her.

Her office wasn't as fancy as he'd expected, but it was tastefully decorated, and at the same time unassuming. She'd used the space well. Her desk was at one end of the room, and a sitting area with a couch, two armchairs, and a coffee table sat at the other. It conveyed success without being ostentatious.

He made his way to her private bathroom, which held a toilet and a sink. She had personalized it with scented hand soap and matching lotion. There was also a clean blouse hanging on the back of the door.

He listened as she entered. She paced around for a few minutes and then, finally, the door to her office clicked shut. When he heard her chair creak under her weight, he stepped out of the bathroom and walked toward her. "You might want to keep your hands where I can see them."

She jerked and let out a small squeal. "You—what—no!" She lunged for her purse, which was on top of her desk.

He dived, snatching the bag out of her grasp. "Sit down."

She obeyed his instruction. Her hands were shaking, and all color had drained from her face.

He tipped the contents of her bag onto her desk. Out tumbled her cell phone, a wallet, a pack of tissues, sunglasses, and a small can of pepper spray that would fit into the palm of her hand. He slipped the non-lethal weapon into his pocket. "Good choice."

"You looked different the last time I saw you." She sat with her back ramrod straight and her hands palm down on the tabletop. Every muscle in her body was rigid and tense.

"That's right, I was balding. It doesn't take much to change the description of a suspect, which messes with law enforcement and creates doubt."

Her eyes widened and then narrowed.

He could almost see her sizing up the situation and going through her options. "No one will be able to save you if I wanted to kill you."

"What do you want?" Her voice quivered.

He threw her purse on the desk and held up his arms, wiggling his fingers, showing her he had no intention of going for the knife at his waist, which probably wasn't as reassuring as it seemed considering he had the ability to kill with his bare hands. "I'm trying to protect two women and stop a human trafficking ring. I need you to get a message to Michael Papin."

"Who?" She shook her head. "And why should I believe you?"

He paused and then decided to be honest. "I can't think of a reason. If I'd been asked to kill the women, I would've done it quick so they didn't feel a thing, but they don't want them dead. They want them to suffer, and I don't do that."

"Who's they?" She seemed less frightened now that he had piqued her curiosity.

"Ask Michael Papin. He knows more than he should. That's why they want him."

She grabbed a pad of paper and a pen from the far side of her desk. "I don't understand. Who is Michael Papin? What has he got to do with these women? And why do you want to stop a trafficking ring?" She scribbled Papin's name on the paper.

He was only prepared to answer one of her questions. "The women are Papin's mother and sister."

She wrote down the words *mother* and *sister*. Then she pursed her lips and looked at him. "And you want to save them?"

He leaned in, wanting her to understand the seriousness of the situation. "Go see FBI Special Agent Finn Callaghan. Papin is with him."

"The FBI?" That got her attention.

"Yes. Papin plans to exchange himself for the women, but they will kill him and sell the women at auction."

Sophia gasped.

Ethan nodded, satisfied she recognized the gravity of the situation. "Yes, it's as bad as it sounds."

"Why are you helping them?"

"You should know why. I saved you from being molested, didn't I? I like killing but I don't rape, and I won't hurt a child. My reasons are my own."

"What's the message?" Her pen was poised in her hand.

"Tell him they are in room six-one-five on the sixth floor of the Sun Down Hotel.

She jotted down his instructions.

He pulled the pepper spray from his pocket and turned it over in his hand, inspecting it. "This is only effective if you can get to it in time to use it. Carry it in your pocket. That way it's handy if you need it." He placed it on her desk and walked out without looking back. She would probably call her cop boyfriend and then contact FBI Special Agent Finn Callaghan. Even if they didn't believe Ethan, they would have to investigate.

CHAPTER TWENTY-SEVEN

Michael stood and limped around the room. His left side had stiffened, making walking difficult.

Sinclair sat up and yawned. Her long hair fell about her face. He loved watching her as she woke up. If it wasn't for the dark circles shadowing her eyes and her paler than usual skin tone, he could almost imagine she'd just stirred from a beautiful dream.

But this wasn't a dream. It was a nightmare.

Finn had roused them when he and his partner, Special Agent Morris, returned. He had probably slept for less than an hour, but he was revitalized and ready to find his mom and Ava.

Special Agent Morris was brisk, efficient, and Michael got the impression she wasn't a pushover. There was no way in hell she would let them stay here. She hadn't said anything...yet. Although, everything about her, from her stern expression to the way she stood like a soldier on parade, suggested they were about to get their marching orders.

"I can't see them being held in a business that's open to the public. It would be harder to control the situation if there are customers coming and going. My guess would be they're in a warehouse somewhere," Michael announced. He wanted one last chance to brainstorm while they were all together.

Sinclair stood, walked to Agent Morris' desk, and began to tidy up the records she'd been reviewing. "Maybe...but I don't think we should rule out that hotel Lucy owns. I heard a rumor there was an upmarket brothel operating in the city. Maybe it's being run out of this hotel. That would explain the income."

Finn folded his arms as he sat on the edge of his desk. "Did you contact the police about this establishment?"

She stopped what she was doing and looked at him. Her head tilted to one side as though she was considering how much to tell him. Finally, she shrugged. "First, it's not my case. I just overheard my partner, Jake, talking about it and, second, no, I rarely call the cops to a brothel unless I'm investigating sex trafficking in a location where prostitution is legal and there's no chance of the women being charged."

"Why not?" Special Agent Morris placed her coffee on her desk, taking back her space.

Sinclair stacked the papers into a neat pile. "No disrespect to any of you, because I know you're the good guys, but there are police officers who would arrest the girls and not the pimps or johns. The threat of prison time is one of the tools traffickers use to keep the girls in line."

Her words rang true even though, as an ex-federal agent, Michael didn't want to believe them. "But the girls are the victims?"

She held the bundle of files in her arms and walked back to the couch. "It doesn't happen too often, but when it does, it's devastating for the women. I had one eighteen-year-old charged with prostitution after she'd been beaten and repeatedly raped. We managed to get the charges dropped, but it was another level of abuse she was forced to endure."

Finn sat in his chair and put his feet up on his desk, getting comfortable. "How do you free them if you don't use law enforcement?"

She sat, looking as deflated as he felt. "For cases that involve prostitution, we try and buy them out, or we steal them away. If it's a big ring run by a cartel, or if a case involves slave labor or someone stealing organs, I always call the authorities."

They'd gone off-track, discussing Sinclair's work, and he needed to bring them back to the subject at hand. "You said there was a hotel in town?" Michael crouched down in front of her.

Earlier, he'd dismissed her instincts and her experience. That had been a mistake born out of guilt. First, he'd allowed himself to become obsessed with Sinclair, and then he'd gone to PDE thinking if he knew what the Syndicate were up to, he could somehow save his family. But instead of saving them, he'd abandoned them when they needed him the most.

She thrust the financial records at him. "Yes. According to these statements, she's collecting money from the Sun Down Hotel. Do you remember how bad it was East of Hell? There's no way I can see a hotel in that area raking in this kind of cash." She seemed energized by the notion they might have a lead.

He placed the records on the ground, grabbed her face and gave her a quick peck on the lips. "I'm sorry I was so grumpy earlier."

She raised an eyebrow. "You weren't grumpy."

"I wasn't?"

"No." she smiled. "You were a jerk."

He shrugged. She wasn't wrong.

Special Agent Morris clapped her hands, getting their attention. "This is all very sweet, but you two need to move to the conference room. Now."

Michael slapped his laptop shut and unplugged it from the outlet. "Thank you for being so patient with us and letting us use your desk."

She graced him with a genteel smile.

"Oh, and for the record, we didn't look at any

files, not even the ones Finn left out on his desk." Michael knew it was mean, but he couldn't help teasing his friend.

Special Agent Morris gasped.

Finn threw his body over his desk as if that would help with his breach of protocol.

Michael headed for the door. "Don't worry, we won't tell anyone. Now, which way is the conference room?"

"What are your plans?" Special Agent Morris demanded.

He couldn't tell who she was addressing, but he assumed the question was meant for him. He stopped at the threshold and turned to face them, suddenly feeling tired, as if his nap had never happened. "Lucy hasn't contacted me to make an exchange."

"Did you think she would?" Finn stood and walked to the front of his desk.

Michael shrugged. "I hoped. This is about getting at me, isn't it?"

"It would be the logical move, get you out in the open and kill you. Without you to use as a bargaining chip, we have no way of getting your family back," Special Agent Morris said, pointing out the obvious.

He had nothing to add to her observation, so he decided to answer her earlier question. "I'm going to see if I can track down Lucy's haunts. Maybe she's keeping them close, and then I'm going to look into this Sun Down Hotel. If Sinclair thinks there something shady about it, then it's worth investigating."

"How are you going to track Lucy?" Finn asked.

"Nothing illegal. I have an algorithm that searches social media for photos of a chosen subject." He lied. They were FBI agents, and they needed deniability.

"Where's the conference room?" Sinclair inched past him, her arms still holding the printout he'd given her.

"Four doors down on the left." Special Agent Morris pointed the way.

He acknowledged her directions with a nod and closed the door behind him.

Once they were in the hallway, Sinclair whispered, "What are you really going to do?"

He should have known she'd see through his lie. "Figure out when Lucy Portman will be at her most vulnerable and kidnap her."

****

Sinclair stared at the PDE building that stood dark and foreboding in the early morning light. She rubbed her temples, trying to ignore the dull, fatigue-induced headache. Michael had been tapping away at his computer since they'd moved to the conference room an hour ago. She assumed he was focused on his goal of pursuing Lucy. A rich, powerful woman like her would probably have armed bodyguards, which meant there was a good chance his plan would get him killed.

She paced around the room and then stopped next to him. "You know your personal involvement puts you at a disadvantage."

He murmured something unintelligible but didn't look up from the screen.

"Your judgement is impaired," she shouted, trying to break his concentration and force him to listen.

She was tempted to haul him out of his seat and give him a good shake. But that wouldn't do any good. She couldn't convince him when he didn't want to listen. He was shutting her out. That was why a relationship between them would never work. He didn't share or communicate with others and she needed... She wasn't entirely sure what she needed, but she knew she couldn't trust him to include her in his world. He'd pushed her away sixteen years ago, and he was doing it again now. It didn't matter how much they cared for each other. Sometimes love wasn't enough.

She paced to the window and drummed the windowsill with her fingertips, hoping to come up with another approach. She suspected she'd discovered the source, or one of the sources, of Lucy Portman's illicit funds, but what would the original crime be? If Michael was right, and her legitimate holdings didn't account for all her money, then what kind of business could she be caught up in that led to a hotel in a rundown part of town? Her first choice was always human trafficking since it involved obscene amounts of money. That might be a bias on her part because she understood how it worked. Even small local operations made millions. The cabals that worked international sex slavery businesses made billions of dollars off their crimes.

The victims weren't just women, and it wasn't all about sexual exploitation. Hundreds of thousands of people were also trafficked for forced labor, domestic servitude, child begging, or the removal of their organs.

She faced him, her hands on her hips. "At least tell me what you're doing."

He rubbed his eyes and then continued to stare at his laptop. "I've accessed the Syndicate network. The members are listed by email and code names only. Lucy is sexgoddess, all one word."

"Yuck."

He nodded to show he agreed with her assessment. "I'm using her info like a key to a map to help figure out the names of the other Syndicate members. I have a hunch they are all connected through the Global Democratic Coalition."

"You've abandoned the idea of kidnapping Lucy?"

He pinched the bridge of his nose, took an exasperated breath, and said, "No, but I want to give Finn a list of the Syndicate's members. That way, if anything happens to me, he can still take them down."

The words "if anything happens to me" hung in the air like a thought bubble in a cartoon. She stared at him but couldn't form a coherent sentence. Every cell in her body turned to ice at the notion of him dying. She'd felt the same way when she'd watched Portman drive into him. She couldn't let him throw his life away. There was no hope of a future for them as a couple, but she wanted him to live.

He turned his attention back to his computer, dismissing her, not noticing her agitation.

Which was not a surprise given the fact that he was emotionally compromised and closed off. Normally, she would trust his judgement, at least in operational matters, but he felt responsible for Nadie and Ava and would do anything to make it right. She suspected that, in his mind, losing his life in an attempt to save them was preferable to living without them. Arguing with him would be counterproductive. First, he didn't want to hear what she had to say, and he had also been proven right too many times. It would be impossible for him to see that, in this instance, he was wrong.

She swung back to stare at the PDE building opposite. Lucy was making an awful lot of money from the Sun Down Hotel. Sinclair had a gut feeling that the establishment, in the rundown part of town, was a piece of the puzzle. Her experience had taught her that law enforcement agencies needed evidence, and her instinct wasn't enough. Besides, if she were wrong, she would be wasting everyone's time.

Because the case was local, Jake had been assigned to assess the situation and determine whether further investigation was warranted. She had no idea if he'd made a determination or if the Sun Down Hotel and the brothel in Jake's case was the same place.

She headed for the door. "I'm going to grab a shower. I'll be about half an hour." She could have told him the truth, but she didn't want him to worry.

Michael didn't look away from the screen. He just said something unintelligible and waved a hand, dismissing her.

Huh. She shouldn't have bothered lying. He wouldn't even notice she was gone. She left the conference room and headed along the hallway, checking each office door.

The first two were bolted. She crept past Finn's and tried the last room on the floor and was relieved to find it unlocked.

"Have a phone, have a phone…" She repeated the mantra under her breath as she searched the space.

There wasn't much. Just a locked filing cabinet and a cord that ran from the wall into a desk drawer. She opened it and was relieved to find a telephone. Lifting the receiver, she was ecstatic to hear a dial tone. She punched in Jake's number.

Her partner answered on the first ring. "Hello."

"I need some information." She knew she was being rude but didn't care.

"Sure, what do you need?" he growled. His raspy voice was a symptom of his smoking habit.

"There's a hotel on the east side, the Sun Down. Is that the place you were investigating as a brothel?"

There was a moment of silence and then the faint sound of a puff, telling her he'd just taken a drag of his cigarette. "How'd you know?"

"Just a hunch. I need all the information you have on it."

"Does this have anything to do with the break-in?"

"I really can't say." Why she was hedging, she didn't know, but telling him everything seemed wrong. Besides, she had no idea why someone had broken into their office, and given the circumstances, it wasn't high on her list of priorities.

"I'll meet you at the Dumb Luck Café in fifteen minutes." He hung up before she could tell him to come to the FBI offices. Fifteen minutes wasn't much time for him to drive to the coffee shop. Maybe he was already close by.

They'd been holed up at the federal building all night because Finn believed they were in danger, but did she really need special protection? Probably not. She'd been attacked in an attempt to get to Michael. Now that the bad guys had Nadie and Ava, they didn't need her. If she couldn't come up with another option, Michael would go after Lucy Portman. There was no way Finn would help, and knowing Michael, he wouldn't drag David and Tim into anything illegal. Which meant he was on his own. No matter what happened between them, she had to save him. She loved him. She always had, which meant she had no choice.

CHAPTER TWENTY-EIGHT

Detective Mateo Ramirez barged into Finn's office and collapsed into the vacant seat at his desk.

Finn said nothing at the unannounced intrusion, but he did raise a questioning eyebrow in Kennedy's direction.

She joined them, standing to the side of his desk so she could see both their faces.

Ramirez straightened his tie, which was a unique pattern that matched his suit perfectly. "I've been going over the break and enter at Child Seekers and want to talk to Sinclair Quinn about her schedule."

In the last year when they'd worked a few cases together, Finn had always found him to be honest and conscientious.

"Why? Do you think she has something to do with it?" Finn asked.

"Only as much as it was her information the

perp was after, and the timing is curious."

"How so?" Kennedy folded her arms and scowled at Finn.

"Her plane touched down at five. I'd give her and her partner"—he checked his notebook —"Jake Cox, thirty to forty-five minutes to collect their luggage and get through the airport. They split up in the parking lot. She drives to Granite City. Let's say she's done her grocery shopping by six-thirty."

"And she was jumped before seven. Where are you going with this?" Kennedy spoke before Finn could say anything.

"Child Seekers in Granite City is run out of a small office at the back of a church." Ramirez shifted in his seat, getting comfortable.

"I thought it was a big outfit." Kennedy pointed to Finn's notebook, silently telling him to take notes and at the same time reminding him she was in charge.

Ramirez shrugged. "They are and they aren't. They're a non-profit that devotes all their money towards operational costs. They have a lot of dedicated volunteers, a couple of paid administrators. Agents like Sinclair and her partner are paid employees. Although, I'm glad I don't have to live off her paycheck."

Finn smiled. "That bad, huh?" He knew Sinclair wasn't about the money.

"Oh, yeah."

"You were figuring out the timeline," Kennedy said, drawing him back to the subject at hand.

"Yes." He shook his head. It wasn't like him to get distracted. "I was thinking why break in and go through her files? Given her instruction and Child Seekers own guidelines, the only thing I can come up with is that the perps wanted to know what time her flight landed."

"That was in her records?" Finn scribbled down the information.

"Yep."

"How close are you to narrowing down the time of the robbery?" Kennedy dragged the chair from her desk over and sat in it.

Ramirez, once again, checked his notes. "The volunteer who does their office work, a very nice woman named Amy, left at five-thirty. The crime occurred sometime after that."

"That's cutting it a little close, don't you think?" Finn couldn't see someone breaking in just to see what time Sinclair arrived back in the country, and then within an hour, attacking her in an alley. It could have happened, but it didn't feel right.

Ramirez shrugged. "It's just a theory. Tell me about this Syndicate? We didn't get into it in Tate's office."

"What we know is sketchy, and what I'm going to tell you is just my opinion—"

"Our opinion," Kennedy corrected.

"They're a powerful group of businessmen

who are behind multiple crimes. Michael Papin secured proof they exist and handed the evidence over to the FBI."

Ramirez shifted in his seat. "The feds are investigating?"

Finn took a deep breath. Kennedy gave him a knowing look. How much did he want to tell?

Kennedy inhaled and then said, "The Department of Justice is compromised. The evidence Papin acquired was stolen, witnesses have been killed while in the custody of the U.S. Marshals, and they have Finn's personnel records." The words seemed to tumble out of her mouth.

As soon as she finished talking, Finn knew she'd made the right call.

"Fuck me." Ramirez uttered the curse under his breath.

Finn nodded. "Exactly."

"This powerful group of businessmen, are they international?"

"I think so, but that's just a theory, not fact. Why do you ask?"

"I was just wondering why they're showing up in a backwater like Granite City, Montana."

Finn stared at Ramirez and then switched his gaze to Kennedy. Why hadn't he thought of that?

There was a knock at the door, and Sophia Reed burst in without waiting for an answer.

"The desk sergeant told me you were here." She clutched Ramirez's hand.

"You're shaking. What's happened?" He

hugged her, holding her in a way that suggested the pair were an item. Their relationship had come to light after they'd been taken hostage during a bank robbery. Ramirez stepped back. "We should probably leave."

"No, Ethan wanted me to give them a message." The pretty dark-haired lawyer met Finn's gaze.

"Ethan?" Ramirez snapped.

"The same man from the bank robbery." Finn's heartbeat thundered in his ears as an icy chill inched down his spine.

"That freak came to see you?" Ramirez's skin flushed, and the veins of his forehead bulged.

She nodded.

"This guy needs to be stopped. He's targeting her." The detective thumped Finn's desk with his fist.

"Take a seat." Finn pointed to the chair Ramirez had vacated just minutes ago.

Ramirez ignored his suggestion. His rage was apparent in his wide stance, his fisted hands, and the way he clenched his teeth. But his hold seemed gentle as he urged Ms. Reed into his vacated chair.

Her face was pale and her movements jerky. She was obviously terrified. Everyone in law enforcement knew, respected, and feared her. She was the top criminal attorney in Granite City. Finn guessed her to be in her mid-thirties. She looked like the kind of woman who would be more at home driving her kids to little league, which generally worked in her favor because people tended to underestimate her. She was tenacious in her defense of her clients and had grudgingly earned Finn's respect.

It was unlikely Ramirez's temper would subside anytime soon so Finn might as well interview her now. He reached for a notepad and smiled at Ms. Reed. "Why don't you start from the beginning?"

Kennedy cleared her throat and locked her gaze on Finn, as if silently urging him to keep to their agreement and allow her to take the lead. He acknowledged her with a nod. "Special Agent Morris is running…" He almost said *interference* but stopped himself. "Acting as liaison in the cases we talked about yesterday." Damn those words were hard to say. He wanted to tell her to back down. Instead, he clamped his mouth shut.

Ramirez stared at him. Surprisingly, the announcement had shocked him enough that he was distracted from his anger. "Why?"

"I'm too emotionally involved. Michael Papin is a friend." Finn stepped out of the way, allowing Kennedy to take his chair.

It wheeled away from the desk. She dug her toes into the carpet to prevent it from rolling and then lowered the seat so her feet were flat on the floor. Then she gave him a dead-eyed glare that suggested he not smile or laugh at her predicament. He stared back, using his best poker face.

Kennedy picked up a pen and addressed Ms. Reed. "You saw Ethan Moore?"

Ramirez banged the arm of the chair. "I swear —"

Kennedy held up her hand in a halt motion "You're a detective. You know how this goes. You are emotionally involved, too. There's obviously a relationship between you two."

Ramirez paced to the window and then turned to watch, distancing himself from the conversation.

"This has to be informal. We're not on the case," Kennedy said to Ms. Reed. "Why'd you come to us?"

"Ethan told me to talk to Special Agent Callaghan." Ms. Reed's voice was low but audible.

Kennedy made a note, focusing on her job. She didn't look at Finn, but he knew she had to be wondering what the hell was going on. Once she was done, she said, "Let's get the info, and then I suggest Ms. Reed files a report with Captain Tate." She gave the detective a pointed look.

Ramirez nodded. "Okay." He seemed to be over his initial outburst.

"And detective..." Kennedy poked the air with her pen. Her back was straight and her muscles tense. Everything in her body language said don't-mess-with-me. "We need Ms. Reed to be able to tell us what happened. Normally, I'd ask you to wait outside, but as this is an informal setting, I will let you stay as long as you don't interrupt or interfere in any other way."

He gave a terse nod and crossed his arms, leaning against the window.

Kennedy smiled at the attorney. "Why don't you start at the beginning?"

The words rushed out of Sophia Reed's mouth. This wasn't the restrained, controlled lawyer Finn was used to seeing in the courtroom. Her hands moved as she talked, emphasizing every detail. The more a subject moved, the more likely it was they were being open and honest. Despite her fear at finding Ethan Moore in her office, she was able to recall the smallest detail. Which was impressive and explained, in part, why she was so successful in her chosen career.

Finn had questioned her when Ethan Moore had committed a bank heist a month ago. Afterward, Ethan had provided her with proof of a criminal conspiracy to commit arson. Moore's motive remained a mystery to this day.

Ethan had obviously latched onto Ms. Reed as some sort of proxy. Maybe it wasn't so surprising that he had a special interest in her. She was smart and posed no physical threat to him. She was the perfect person to use as a go-between.

"Let me get this straight. Moore is protecting Nadie and Ava O'Connor until we can rescue them, and they're being held at the Sun Down Hotel." Kennedy stared at Finn. "Isn't that the place Sinclair mentioned?"

Finn pictured a map of the town in his head. "Yes, she noticed it. I also have to wonder if the criminal conspiracy and arson Ethan uncovered in the bank heist was actually about protecting the area in order to keep the Sun Down Hotel from being discovered."

Sophia Reed cleared her throat. "He didn't mention that, but he made it clear the two women were to be sold. I don't know when, and he didn't say."

Finn silently cursed. This whole thing was a lot darker than he imagined. He'd thought they were waiting for the Syndicate to contact them to make an exchange. Which in itself was bad enough because he knew they would kill Michael and probably his mother and sister, too. He also found it hard to believe that Ethan was protecting Michael's family until the Sun Down Hotel could be raided. There was a good chance this was an elaborate trap.

"Did he say why he was sharing this information?" Kennedy must be thinking the same thing.

Sophia Reed gripped the hem of her jacket so tight her knuckles turned white. "Our conversation wasn't a cross-examination. He said what he had to say. And to be honest, I was too scared to ask any useful questions. But he did say he doesn't rape people and he doesn't hurt children. He just kills." She shrugged. "Maybe for him it crosses some sort of line. He did stop that robber from hurting me, but I always assumed he'd used me as a distraction because he killed both his partners. Even the young one who was never a threat."

There was no doubt in Finn's mind that she was telling the truth. When she explained the details, she talked with her hands. But when she talked about Ethan, she clamped onto her clothing with a vice-like grip, which was an understandable nervous response.

"Just to confirm," Kennedy said, going over the account, looking for any inconsistencies. It was standard practice to question a witness more than once, not because Kennedy didn't believe her, but it paid to be thorough. "Michael Papin's mother and sister are being held at the Sun Down Hotel, and they are to be sold—"

"Has anyone seen Sin— Did I hear you say sold?" Michael stood at the door, balancing an open laptop on one arm.

Finn cursed under his breath. "Haven't you heard of knocking? You do not have the right to burst in."

His friend's gaze flickered from Ramirez, to Sophia Reed, to Kennedy, and then settled on him.

Michael walked into the room. He wasn't inclined to back down or apologize. "Sinclair was right about the Sun Down Hotel. It's making way too much money for its size and location. And it also belongs to Lucy Portman."

Sophia stood. "You're Michael Papin, aren't you?"

Michael nodded and placed his computer on Finn's desk.

Finn said nothing. He could've shut this down and told Michael to wait outside, but he didn't. Remarkably, Kennedy hadn't said anything either. They seemed to be working way outside the rules on this one.

Ms. Reed took two steps toward Michael and said, "Ethan said your mom and sister are at the Sun Down Hotel. He said you plan to exchange yourself for them, but it's a trap. They aren't going to release your family. They're to be auctioned."

Michael paled and blinked rapidly. Then his nostrils flared, and his expression grew hard, unflinching. "I will kill every last fucking one of them."

Ramirez leapt across the room and caught his arm. "She's just the messenger, back off. We'll help you, but you cannot make hasty or stupid decisions."

Michael stared at Ramirez's hand and then his face. "Who are you?"

Finn could tell Michael had hesitated and stopped himself from letting lose a string of curse words.

"I'm Detective Ramirez, and this is my fiancée, Sophia Reed."

Michael ignored Ramirez and addressed Finn. "What's going on?"

Kennedy stood. "According to Ms. Reed, Ethan Moore is keeping your family safe until you can rescue them."

Ms. Reed nodded. "They're on the sixth floor, room six-one-five."

CHAPTER TWENTY-NINE

The L-shaped coffee shop was more up-market than Sinclair remembered. As a teen, she'd slept in the doorway on cold winter nights. Any place out of the wind was good, and The Dumb Luck had a deep entrance that allowed the four of them to fit comfortably.

Of course, it wasn't called the Dumb Luck Café back then but the Alley Cat Bistro. The owner, who was also a chef, had been a jerk who had threatened them with a meat cleaver whenever he caught them trying to stay warm.

She didn't order coffee, preferring to wait for Jake. She eyed the blueberry and white chocolate scones. Her plan to spend her days off from work baking with her neighbors and giving surplus to the homeless seemed like another life; so much had happened in three days.

Jake limped into the coffee shop. He was an older man who always looked a little raggedy. Everything about him seemed tired, even his gray moustache. His regular uniform was a shabby suit and trench coat, which appeared to have been purchased when she was still in diapers. He insisted on wearing a shirt and tie, even though Child Seekers had a relaxed dress code. Maybe his clothing choices were a throwback to his time as a cop. Not that it mattered. As long as he was one of the good guys, she didn't care how he looked.

She stood to join him, but he waved her back. "You stay there. It's packed in here. I don't want to lose the table."

She peered out the window. Rain was moving in. That was bound to aggravate his bad knee. She stayed where she was, watching him order their drinks and then hobble to a side counter to add cream to his coffee, which was odd because he normally took it black. Maybe he was getting soft in his old age.

Finally, he sat at the table and placed a rich smooth mocha in front of her. As much as she loved chocolate, she wasn't a fan of Mocha coffee, but she took a sip, not wanting to be difficult. As a twenty-year veteran of the LA police department, he probably didn't care to know the difference between a plain latte and an ultra-sweet drink.

"Is your knee bothering you?" she asked just to be polite.

"Yeah, I need a replacement, but my medical

won't cover it."

Sinclair took another sip and tried not to grimace. "Do you have any information for me?"

"No."

"Are you saying the Sun Down Hotel is clean?"

His expression was blank. "No, I'm saying this is none of your business."

She glanced at his coffee. It was black. What had he been doing at the creamer station?

"There are two missing women. Finding them is what we do."

"It's what you do."

"Who are you?" She could tell by his sneer and his hate-filled gaze that she was seeing a knew side to him.

"Working with you this last year has been the most exhausting of my life. You are such a tireless bitch. Why can't you just stop? For God's sake, do a half-assed job just once in your sad little life. What has saving the world got you? You live in a crummy studio apartment. You wear clothes until they get holes. You never take a vacation. When was the last time you got laid, for fuck's sake?"

He carried on talking, but she blocked him out. Her heart raced so hard her chest hurt. She stuck her hand in her pocket, looking for her phone, but it wasn't there. She hadn't carried one since this all began. She tried to stand, but her muscles were too weak to hold her, and she collapsed back into the chair.

"You…you…" Her mouth refused to work.

"I've been setting up this deal for a while. My buyer will pay millions to watch a gladiator like you. Sometimes they fight to the death. It's time for me to retire." He grabbed her arms and pulled her out of her seat. She tried to punch him, but her body wouldn't respond to her commands.

Jake was the leak, the one the Ukrainian prostitute had warned her about. She tried to think about all the implications, but her brain felt as though it was stuffed with cotton wool.

He put an arm around her waist and half-carried half-dragged her out of the coffee shop. "It's okay. She's just feeling unwell. I'm taking her to the hospital," he announced to the concerned patrons.

She was being stolen in broad daylight, and no one was going to stop him. She opened her mouth to scream, but no sound came out.

Everything became a kaleidoscope of disjointed images. The backseat of Jake's car, a parking lot, a hotel room, crashing into a bathroom, and then nothing.

CHAPTER THIRTY

Michael paced to the window and watched as Sophia Reed headed toward the police station, accompanied by Detective Ramirez. He felt as though a vice had tightened around his chest. All he had left was the faint hope that Moore was telling the truth and was protecting his mother and sister. But how likely was that? He recalled Ethan Moore arriving at Tim's house with a blood-covered knife. What was it people said about first impressions? He didn't know, and he didn't fucking care. If Moore really had them tucked away safe somewhere, why hadn't he just released them?

There was a knock at the door.

"Come," Kennedy called and then smiled at Finn.

There was an undercurrent between them that he couldn't define. He wasn't sure if they were close because they were colleagues, friends, or if it was something more.

The door opened, and Milo hobbled in.

Michael rushed to his side. "I thought you were supposed to stay in hospital for a few days."

"I couldn't." The pain in his gaze was a reflection of Michael's torment.

He helped his stepfather to the couch. The older man looked better than he had yesterday but that wasn't saying much. The three-inch gash that ran along Milo's forehead had been stitched together. Somehow that made the wound look worse, or maybe it was the swelling around the laceration.

He gave a raspy, wet cough and then winced and clutched his side. His lungs had probably been damaged by the smoke, which was another reminder he had endured and survived a house fire. "Get me up to speed."

"We know where they're being held. I had planned to exchange myself for them." The two FBI agents in the room might have preferred he not share the information, but he was way past asking permission.

"But?" Milo's gaze connected with his.

"What do you mean *but*?"

"Son, there's always a freaking *but*. Tell me everything." He gave another chesty cough.

"We've been told they don't plan to keep to their part of the bargain. They will kill me and auction Mom and Ava off as slaves."

Milo flinched and growled, "Where are they?"

"The Sun Down Hotel. It's on the east side of the city."

Finn cleared his throat. "I've contacted the Granite City-Elkhead County Police department. I've asked them to get their SWAT team ready, and I'm calling in the FBI HRT team from Salt Lake City.

Michael scrubbed his hands over his eyes and then said, "Sinclair's input would be invaluable right now. Saving people from human trafficking is what she does. Has anyone seen her? She said she was taking a shower." He wished he'd paid more attention to the time. She seemed to have been gone a while, but he couldn't remember when she'd left.

Both agents shook their heads.

"Didn't she come in here to grab a T-shirt and some toiletries?" He frowned. She couldn't have gone far. There was no way she would leave, not with everything that had happened.

Agent Morris narrowed her eyes. "How long ago was this?"

He shrugged. He didn't know. He'd been so engrossed in what he was doing he hadn't noticed. *Shit*. What was wrong with him that he'd tuned out the woman he loved?

He walked to the door. "I'll check the showers."

"No, I'll go." Special Agent Kennedy blocked him from leaving.

He frowned at her.

"They're women's showers, and you need to stay here in case they call." Special Agent Morris walked to the door.

"They're not going to call, and even if they do, it's a set up," he reasoned.

She stopped with her hand on the handle. "Yes, but they don't know that we know that."

Finn stared at her with an incredulous look on his face. "Did you really just use the they-don't-know-that-we-know sentence?"

Kennedy waved a hand, dismissing Finn's comment. "We need to play for time. When—"

"You mean *if*. Maybe Moore is setting us up, and this is their way of drawing me out into the open." Even as he said the words, Michael knew it didn't matter if it was a trap. If there was even a remote chance he could get his mom and sister back, he would take it.

"At this stage, we can't be certain of anything. They may call. Ethan might be planning a trap. The Sun Down Hotel is our best lead, and even that could be a lie. We don't know, and therefore we need to be prepared for everything," Finn explained.

They were right. They couldn't be certain of anything. All Michael had to go on was his gut, and it was telling him that Sinclair had zeroed in on the Sun Down Hotel because something about it seemed suspicious, and he trusted her instincts even if he questioned his own. "What will you do?"

Agent Morris opened the door. "We're trying to confirm their location, and we're going to let the Granite City-Elkhead County Police Department be at any exchange they set up. Just in case. That's all I can share with you. I'll see what's keeping Sinclair."

The minute the door closed behind her, Finn punched some numbers on his office phone.

Milo waved a hand, beckoning Michael to the sofa. "Tell me you have a plan B."

Michael rubbed his neck. All the what-ifs and variables were jumbled in his head. He grabbed his computer and brought it back to the couch. He loaded his TOR software and, with a few clicks, he was on the dark web.

In his experience, sellers on the black-market displayed their inventory beforehand. If Ethan was telling the truth, and his mom and Ava were to be auctioned, there would be a record of it somewhere. With a few more taps, their photos loaded. Underneath the image, in bold letters, it read: *Bidding starts in two hours.*

"Shit." He placed the computer on the cushion between them so Milo could see it.

His stepdad gasped as his body jerked and his hand flew to his mouth.

Michael glanced at Finn who was still on the phone. He adjusted his position, so his back was to his friend. "Milo, tell me the truth. Are you well enough to fly?"

"If I have to control the damn helicopter with

my teeth, I'll get it off the ground. What do you have in mind?"

He grabbed a piece of paper from the desk and scribbled David Quinn's number on it. "He's ex-Special Forces. He'll help us get what we need."

Milo took the paper and stuffed it in his pocket.

At the same time, Kennedy barreled through the door. "Sinclair left the building."

Michael stood. "She what?"

"When I didn't find her in the showers, I spoke to security. She left. They said she was on foot, heading west but…" She shrugged. "They don't know where she went once she was out of sight."

Michael put a hand to his head, wanting to block out the news. Perhaps he was worrying for nothing. Perhaps she was just following her own lines of enquiry or she'd skipped out on him. No, she would never do that.

"Can you think of anywhere she would go?" Finn moved to the front of his desk.

Michael shook his head, trying to remember everything she had said. "Even before Sophia Reed delivered Ethan's message, Sinclair was convinced that something was up with the Sun Down Hotel. I guess, in her line of work, they're trained to look for that sort of thing. I figured…" At that moment, the screen on his laptop, which was still sitting on the couch, refreshed.

A headline with the words *New Inventory: Gladiator* appeared, followed by a video of a tall, unconscious woman being dragged into a hotel room. It was black and white, but he could clearly see the bruises on her face and the jeans and shirt she'd been wearing.

The muscles in his legs turned to jelly. "No, no, God no. They have Sinclair."

CHAPTER THIRTY-ONE

Michael doubted either of the FBI agents would notice if he walked out. Both Special Agent Morris and Finn were on the phone. The time was counting down on his screen, and he had no idea if they could get there in time to save them.

What would the Syndicate do to Sinclair, a woman who had fought against human trafficking for most of her adult life? He couldn't rely on Ethan protecting any of them once they were auctioned. He almost laughed at that idiotic thought. He couldn't trust Ethan at all. This could be a trap, but given that the clock was, literally, ticking, he had no choice but to act on the intelligence the assassin had provided.

Had Sinclair had a lead and told him where she was going, and he'd ignored her? That was a distinct possibility. He'd been so focused on himself and his own feelings he'd shut her out.

Growing up, she'd endured one hardship after another, which had forced her to become strong and independent.

He'd asked her to let him in, which was a giant leap for her. Relationships required a certain amount of vulnerability. At eighteen, he'd betrayed her when they were supposed to be friends...more than friends. No wonder she didn't want to get involved with him when he had, once again, proved himself untrustworthy. And now he had thrown away any chance they had to be together and put her in danger.

He inhaled, pushing back against his overwhelming guilt. Sinclair would never allow him to wallow. She would fight to her last breath, and so would he.

The phone on Special Agent Kennedy's desk rang. She grabbed the receiver. "Hello." After listening for a moment, she waved at him. "It's them."

Finn ended his call with the push of a button and punched in another number, probably calling his headquarters in Salt Lake City so they could record and trace the call.

Michael clutched the handset, took a deep breath, and said, "Hello."

"Be at the fountain in Granite City Square in one hour," a computer-generated voice demanded.

"I'm not going anywhere until you prove my mom, Ava, and Sinclair are alive." No matter what action he chose to take, he needed proof of life.

"I've sent videos to Special Agent Callaghan's work phone."

Michael nodded to Finn, who was tapping the screen. His friend's eyes widened before he stood and strode across the room, holding his smartphone up.

A film played of his mom and Ava sitting on a bed in a dingy hotel room.

Finn swiped. Another recording came into view. This was the same one he'd seen on the dark web of Sinclair being dragged into the hotel. Which he knew didn't depict her current status. He was about to tell the caller that but stopped. If he revealed he'd already seen the playback on the dark web, the Syndicate would realize he also knew about the auction. Instead of challenging, he said, "What guarantee do I have that you'll let them go?"

"Why would we want them?" Even though the voice was genderless and mechanical, he sensed the glee in their tone.

"Did you say one hour?" He was playing for time now, hoping the FBI techs could track the call.

The voice laughed and then said, "Stalling won't work. They can't trace me. It's the same with the email address. You can use your last hour talking to me if you want."

He slammed the phone down.

Fuck. Now he had a choice to make. Did he take a chance and trust the voice, or should he believe Ethan, the psycho with the knife?

It all came back to the Sun Down Hotel. Michael took a deep breath in an effort to center himself. He believed Moore was telling the truth, but only because Sinclair had been convinced there was something suspicious about the Sun Down Hotel, and he had faith in her.

He needed to act if he was to save them. Once he didn't show at the meeting point, the Syndicate would know he was up to something.

Finn and Special Agent Morris were busy on the other side of the office, whispering to each other, probably figuring out a plan.

He grabbed Milo and hoisted him to his feet. "You need to leave now. There's a phone at security you can use to make your call. Meet me at Granite City Helicopters. I'll only be a few minutes behind you."

His stepdad looked pale and tense, which was probably a combination of worry and pain, but he nodded and hobbled out.

Finn got a call. He glanced at the door closing behind Milo and then turned his back and started talking.

Michael grabbed his computer and hit a few buttons, pulling up an image of the Sun Down Hotel. It was a large brick building. He clicked on an arrow so the picture rotated, giving him a three-hundred-and-sixty-degree view. There were a few powerlines but none of them looked to be too close. Then he changed to an aerial view. Now he could recognize the location, even from above.

He stomped to the door.

"Where are you going?" Finn, who'd just hung up, stopped him as Michael reached for the door handle.

"The little boys room." He rubbed his stomach. "I feel sick." He hated lying, but Finn needed to play by the book, and as far as Michael was concerned, they needed to throw the book away. He would do what had to be done to get his family back.

****

Kennedy stood in front of Finn, her hands on her hips. Finn didn't need to look at her face to know she was pissed, but he met her gaze anyway.

"You shouldn't have let him go." Her facial muscles were pinched and tense. She was mad.

He raised an eyebrow, hoping he managed to look surprised. "To the washroom?"

She curled her lip. "You don't believe that, and neither do I. He's going to do something stupid."

Finn met her in the middle of the room. "Maybe. But you're the lead agent. Why didn't you stop him?"

She slapped her forehead with her palm. "I'm not used to being the boss, and he's your friend.

What if he gets in the way of the police and gets shot? Or worse, prevents us from doing our job?"

"He won't be a problem. First, he's an ex-federal agent."

"And second?"

"The HRT team is two hours out. They'll never make it here in time to stop him being assassinated in the square, and we both know that's the plan."

"Of course it is, but he can't go off—" Her head tilted to one side. "Did he share his strategy?"

He almost laughed. "No. Michael got fired for going undercover without permission. He doesn't share what he's thinking unless he needs you to know. But I think in this case, he might be protecting us."

"Might be?"

Finn shrugged. "It's hard to tell when he's under so much emotional stress, but it's obvious what he's going to do."

"It is?" She was staring at him as if he'd gone insane.

"Milo, his stepdad, left suddenly. Why would he leave? We're trying to save his wife and daughter, and he has something better to do?"

"You don't think he's involved somehow?" Her hand covered her mouth.

"No, not at all. Milo was an Air Force helicopter pilot. His mom and sister are being held on the top floor. I would bet good money they're going to land on the roof and go in."

She stepped back, her eyes wide. "*Shit.*" Then she put her hands on his chest and shoved hard. "You should've stopped them."

He allowed her to move him back an inch. "Apart from the legality of a helicopter flying low within the city limits, it's not a bad plan. We could go in through the main entrance and create a distraction. That'll be less men with guns they have to deal with. It'll give them a better chance of success."

"But it's not coordinated. How will we know they're ready? And we don't have a warrant."

"We don't need a warrant. These are exigent circumstances." A clause in the fourth amendment allowed them to enter a building without a warrant if someone was in danger. And as far as Finn was concerned, kidnapping three women and selling them meant they were in danger and this was an emergency.

She slapped her head again. "Of course."

"But you're right about the coordination. We'll have to be in position. As soon as we see them, we'll go in."

She tapped a finger against her lip as she thought about the problem. "I wish there was some way we could talk to them."

"You know if we sanction this, there's a good chance we can kiss our careers goodbye."

"I wouldn't be surprised if they're over anyway, and I suspect Deluca's is, too. We know about the Syndicate. They're not going to let us keep investigating." She made a dismissive gesture with her hand, waving away her observation. "We'll talk about this later. Let's save these women first."

Finn glanced at the couch. Michael had left his laptop open. Finn snatched up the device. "It isn't locked. And yes. He's going to land on the roof."

"What?" She stood beside him.

"He probably has it set to lock after a few minutes of inactivity but forgot to shut it down." Finn moved the cursor to prevent the computer from timing out. He stared at an aerial view of the Sun Down Hotel. Then he placed the device back on the couch.

"Do you think Michael left his computer open because he wanted you to know what he was doing, or is he just upset and distracted?" she asked.

"It doesn't matter. We need to keep our focus on getting Sinclair and the others back." He tried to swallow the sour taste in his mouth. He had no idea if a rescue was possible or if Michael's unspoken plan would work.

"What resources does Michael have?"

Kennedy's question forced him to consider Michael's options. "If I wanted a helicopter and firepower, I'd call David Quinn and Tim Morgan."

"I thought Quinn didn't carry weapons."

"His wife's rich, so he'll be able to get the helicopter, and Tim has the guns."

He fished his smartphone from his pocket and dialed David's number. When he answered, Finn didn't mess around with small talk. "I need you to give Michael a message."

"I don't know—"

"Tell him to call me before he lands on the roof. We will go in the main entrance and create a distraction."

David hesitated.

"You got that?" Finn pressed.

"I got it. I'll pass on the message."

Finn disconnected, not giving David a chance to explain. "There, it's done."

A minute later, his phone rang. He recognized the number and glanced at Kennedy. "It's Ramirez." He pressed a button to put the call on speaker. "Detective, do you have any information for me?"

"I checked out the Sun Down. The place is crawling with guards, and not regular uniformed security either. I talked to Vice. They suspect the place is a brothel. Word is their customers are driven there in fancy cars. Even the neighborhood gangs don't mess with them. I didn't enter. I wasn't sure what the play was. Captain Tate has SWAT on standby."

Because of the small size of Granite City-Elkhead County Police department, members of the tactical unit worked as regular officers and volunteered for the specialized unit.

Finn smiled. "Tate's good people."

"Don't tell him that. He thinks he's a hard ass."

Kennedy grabbed her raid jacket. Their bulletproof vests were in the SUV.

Finn had a feeling that before the day was over, they would need both.

CHAPTER
THIRTY-TWO

Michael climbed out of the taxi at Granite City Helicopters, which was nothing more than a hanger and an airstrip west of town. Milo, David, and Tim were waiting for him on the tarmac.

"Did you have any trouble renting a helicopter?" He shook David's hand.

"There she is." David pointed to a small aircraft. "It was the biggest one they had, but you'll still be full coming back."

"You might lose money on this rental." Milo started his inspection.

What he was checking, Michael couldn't say and didn't care. As long as it got them to the roof and back, it didn't matter.

"Don't worry about it." David ran a jerky hand through his hair, his concern palpable. "Do you know how Sinclair was taken?"

Michael shook his head.

He frowned. "Do you know if she's at this hotel?"

Michael, once again, shook his head. All he knew was that she'd been dragged into a hotel room. He couldn't be sure it was the Sun Down. "Ethan Moore said—"

"The freak with the knife." Tim stared at him, his eyes wide. "We're trusting that psycho?"

"No, before he gave us this info, Sinclair zeroed in on the Sun Down. She said there was something hinky about it, and I trust her."

David and Tim shared a look.

Michael didn't know what that was about, and he didn't care. He needed to act soon. "I'm going whether you think it's a good idea or not."

"You know, if it wasn't for the lack of room in the helo, we'd be coming with you," David said.

"I need to go." He was done chatting.

Tim thrust a large gray tote into his hand. "There's a rifle and two handguns. They're all loaded and ready."

He took the bag but didn't open it. "Thanks."

"Call Finn." David pressed his cell phone into his free hand.

Michael grimaced. "I don't think—"

"He's planning to go in the main entrance and draw the guards away from you."

He nodded but didn't reply. His throat felt thick. His friends had come through. Even Finn, who obviously wasn't as by-the-book as he seemed.

"Call Tim's cell if you need backup," David added. "We'll come running."

Michael nodded, a gesture that covered both goodbye and thank you, and then climbed into the helicopter.

Milo pushed some controls, and the blades rotated, slicing through the air. He signaled for Michael to put on his headphones, and then they took off.

He unzipped the bag and checked the weapons, a habit born out of years of practice, first in the US Army and then as a federal agent.

He was prepared and ready. He just hoped their intelligence was correct.

CHAPTER THIRTY-THREE

Sinclair woke to find herself lying on a hard linoleum floor. An iridescent lamp over the sink caused a knifing pain to slice into her brain. She groaned and squeezed her eyes shut in an attempt to block out the light.

Her tongue smacked against the roof of her mouth. It tasted as though she'd eaten a cardboard box. Her stomach rolled, making her wonder if she'd washed the box down with acid.

What the hell had happened? She remembered being in the coffee shop with Jake and then...then... Her eyes flew open. The bastard had spiked her coffee. She winced, fighting the pain as she forced herself to her feet. Her knees were still weak, but they held.

She scanned her room. Like most hotel bathrooms, there were no windows, assuming this was a hotel. Only a brown and orange tile floor with a beige bathtub, sink, and toilet. The towel rack had been torn out of the wall. As had the fixtures for the tub and sink.

Killing would be too kind for the likes of Jake. A wave of dizziness overtook her, and she grabbed the scuffed countertop for support.

The sound of cheering and the roar of a crowd rang through the air. Whoever was in the next room was watching sports. Which was good because, in her experience, that meant the volume would remain at an ear-splitting level. If her captors didn't know she was awake, she would have time to plan her escape.

She needed to shake off the effects of the drug and get her act together because they, whoever they were, weren't going to stay on the other side of the door forever. If she had to speculate, she would guess her location to be the Sun Down Hotel.

She checked her clothing. All the buttons and zips were exactly as they should be, and she wasn't sticky anywhere, so she didn't believe she'd been molested. Why had Jake turned on her? When she shook her head, she instantly regretted it as another wave of dizziness and nausea overwhelmed her. She would deal with him after she got away.

They, the sports watchers in the other room, had left the light on, which helped because it would've been much harder to familiarize herself with her surroundings in the dark.

Her brother had always told her that, in a

fight, she should use whatever was at hand—anything could become a weapon.

The dingy countertop had been cleared. There wasn't even a glass to crack over someone's head. They'd also taken the mirror off the wall, which wasn't surprising. A mirror was just a huge piece of glass, and she would've been able to do a lot of damage with that. They had left the top of the toilet tank but that was too heavy. It would be hard to wield, and judging by the voices in the next room, there were at least two men.

When fighting in hand-to-hand combat, she often punched or used a baton. She rarely gouged because the idea of gouging someone's eyes out made her gag. It was the same with stabbing. A piercing wound usually meant a lot of blood, and she didn't want to go there. Avoiding either of those two options hadn't been a problem in the past because she had never planned an attack. Before, she'd only reacted to assaults. Her mission had always been to get herself and her charges to safety. Which was pretty much what she was doing here, except she was the one who needed saving and she had time to prepare.

She opened the cupboard under the sink. It was empty. The handle was nothing more than a cheap plastic knob, no help there. But the hinges that held the doors to the vanity were flat and about three inches wide. David had told her that a roll of quarters would improve the impact of her punch. She didn't have a roll of quarters, but she could use the hardware to make her hits more effective. With the edge of her thumbnail she set to work unscrewing them, hoping she could get them loose before the men in the other room came for her.

She should never have gone to the coffee shop, especially without telling someone where she was going. She could only imagine what Michael was going through right now. He might be mad at her, but he would also be concerned. He was already suffering the effects of guilt over Nadie and Ava, and now she had added to it. Not just because she'd been captured herself, but she wasn't there to help him save his family.

She managed to get one off. If she held it in her fist, with the flat edge pointing toward her assailant, it would work as an enhanced knuckle-duster.

Worse than all the recriminations was the idea that she might never see him again. When she'd decided to meet Jake, it had been in the hopes of saving Michael.

By the time she'd worked the first one free, the fingernails on her right hand were chipped and broken, which meant she couldn't get them in the grooves of the screw to work off the second piece. She twisted, trying to get her left hand into the corner.

The TV went silent.

She stood. One hinge would have to do, but

would it be enough for her to overcome two men? She needed a distraction, something to keep them off-guard. She undid some shirt buttons, revealing her bra. It was a plain white practical piece of underwear, nothing sexy, but it was all she had to work with.

The door handle rattled. She hid her right hand behind her back with her makeshift weapon pressed firmly in her fist.

The first man through the door was cheap suit guy from the alley.

Oh, shit.

He wasn't wearing a jacket and she could plainly see he had a handgun secured in his shoulder holster. It was a Glock, which meant there was no safety. "Sleeping Beauty is finally awake."

She gave them a sheepish grin. Using her free hand, she flicked her hair over her shoulder and did her best impression of a flirty teenage girl. "I've been waiting for you."

The big guy with the bent nose followed in behind him. He wore a weapon, too. Luckily, in the small confines of the bathroom, they couldn't surround her. They were forced to stand in line, which meant she could deal with them one at a time.

Cheap Suit eyed her suspiciously and then glanced at her breasts. "I'm not into anything kinky, but Kemp here"—using his thumb, he pointed to the big man behind him—"likes it rough."

She raised an eyebrow. "I think I might be able to accommodate him."

"We didn't think you'd be willing," Kemp said as he unbuttoned his shirt.

She suppressed her revulsion and fingered her open top, knowing the movement would draw their gaze to her breasts. "I know a joke. Do you want to hear it?"

Cheap Suit smiled. "Sure." The more sidetracked he was, the better. She'd deal with him first and then tackle Kemp.

She chuckled, playing her part. Not that she had any experience at seduction or being coy. The drug had worn off somewhat, but she definitely wasn't playing her A-game. "What did the wind say to the warrior?"

Cheat Suit grinned, still staring at her chest. "I don't know, what did the wind say to the warrior?"

"You cannot withstand the storm. And do you know what the warrior said?" She ran a finger down the side of his face.

Cheap Suit shook his head, smiling. "No."

"I am the storm." She grabbed his ear so he couldn't move and thrust the latch into his throat. He made a gurgling sound and stumbled forward so his head rested on her shoulder. She grabbed his weapon from his holster and fired two shots, aiming for Kemp, hitting him in the chest. He went down hard.

She stepped back, allowing Cheap Suit to slump to the ground.

She checked both men to see if they were breathing. If they weren't dead, she'd have to tie them because she couldn't afford to have them sneak up behind her. Neither of them had a pulse. She blocked the sight and smell of blood and buried her distaste for her own actions. She had to move. They probably had friends who would have heard the shots and would come to their aid. She grabbed Kemp's weapon and checked the magazine. Full.

With a pistol in each hand, she moved to the door of the bathroom. The main room held nothing but a bed and a TV. Once she was convinced there was no one else there, she made her way to the window, hoping she was on the ground floor. No such luck, she was on the top floor. A large street sign declared it to be the Sun Down Hotel. Having her hunch proven right didn't give her any satisfaction at all.

She tucked one of the weapons into her gun belt. Holding both wasn't practical. She needed a hand free to open the doors. Plus, she couldn't see in two directions at once.

The fact that guards hadn't rushed in after she'd shot her assailants suggested they were either on another floor, were making their way to this location, or gunshots were heard regularly so the sound was nothing new.

She turned the handle and stepped out into

the hallway with the Glock ready.

The lighting was dim, but she could make out the peeling paint and the torn carpet. Like all hotels, rooms lined both sides of the corridor. At the end of the hall on her right was the elevator. The stairwell lay in the opposite direction.

She turned left.

A door swung open. There was nowhere for her to hide. She raised her sidearm. A man stepped out, the same man who'd warned them when they were at the PDE building.

"You." She had no idea what his role was or whether he was one of the good guys or not.

He held up his hands in a show of surrender. "I'm not here to hurt you. You have to hurry. I heard the shots. They will, too." Then he spoke to someone inside the room. "It's okay. You're safe."

Safe? There was no way she would consider this situation safe.

Nadie and Ava rushed past him. Both greeted her with a hug.

She reciprocated with her free arm but kept her gaze, and weapon, fixed on the man known as Ethan.

"We knew you'd come," Nadie said, still hugging her.

Using all her strength, Sinclair pushed the women away. "No, I'm not here to save you. I mean, I will if I can but…"

"I don't understand," Ava sobbed.

"I was captured, too."

Ethan rolled his eyes in a save-me-from-these-idiots motion.

"I was drugged by my partner," she snapped, her temper flaring. "Now, be useful and tell me the best way out of here."

"There is no way." He shook his head. "If there was, I would've let them go. The ground floor is crawling with guards. You'll never get past them."

"Do you think they're on their way?"

Ethan turned on his heel and headed for the stairs. "Of course, they are." He pushed open the door with one hand, stopped, and pointed up. "Go to the roof and attract someone's attention. That's the only chance you have."

Then he headed down the steps, allowing the door to slam shut after him.

The elevator pinged, telling her someone was coming.

"Go!" Sinclair followed Ethan's suggestion and shoved Nadie and Ava toward the exit.

A shot rang out, and drywall splintered above her head.

She reached the door to the stairwell, turned and fired, hoping to slow the guards' progress. Then she followed the women to the rooftop.

It was empty except for a rectangular, metal, heavy-duty air conditioning unit. There were no heavy blocks or sticks or anything she could use to jam the door.

Ava and Nadie stood at the edge, screaming and waving for help.

She dived behind the unit. It wasn't sturdy and wouldn't make a great shield, but it was all she had. She aimed her weapon at the door. The minute someone tried to open it, she would fire.

CHAPTER THIRTY-FOUR

Finn strolled to the front desk of the Sun Down Hotel with Kennedy by his side. Both of them were wearing their bullet proof vests and their raid jackets. SWAT were assembled outside along with Detective Ramirez and Captain Tate, all ready to help if needed.

The lobby wasn't big, but it was stylishly decorated. The reception desk was made of dark, varnished wood topped with a pale granite counter, and the floors were polished stone. It screamed wealth and opulence, which was at odds with the dilapidated exterior.

The space opened into two hallways, the one on the right leading to the elevator. The left corridor seemed to lead to more rooms. The manager's office was behind reception on Finn's right. It had a frosted glass door, and he could see a figure moving around inside.

This wasn't the smartest idea he'd ever had,

but he couldn't think of any other way to get the guards' attention away from Michael. Finn had received a call from him a minute ago. It had been hard to make out what he was saying above the sound of the rotors, but they managed.

Before he could even open his mouth, the woman behind the desk said, "You need a warrant." He guessed she was in her forties but looked closer to sixty. Probably because her make-up was so thick it appeared as though she'd applied it with a trowel.

Finn tilted his head to one side, a response most people found non-threatening. "I need a warrant to enter the lobby of a hotel?"

"Yes." Her hands stayed in sight, but they didn't move when she talked. She also leaned back, putting some distance between them. Both were signs she didn't like their presence.

Kennedy walked to the corridor on the right and then the left, checking the place out.

"Are you telling me that only private customers come to this hotel?"

"Yes." She smiled, the corners of her mouth turning up, but there was no emotion in her eyes.

The manager's office door opened. A well-dressed man in a black suit stood at the door. He was handsome with short dark hair and had a debonair quality about him. Finn guessed him to be about forty. He wore a jacket, and a bulge under his armpit told Finn he was armed.

The manager made eye contact with the receptionist but said nothing.

Finn needed to establish if this was a legitimate business. He didn't want an innocent family to get caught in the middle if things went south. "I have family coming into town, and I thought I might be able to afford to put them up here. Do you have room rates?"

The boom of repeated gunfire rang out.

Kennedy looked up. "It sounds like it's coming from above us."

Finn drew his Glock 27 and pointed it at the guy from the office.

Slamming doors echoed from the hall to the left, followed by the rumble of people running.

From the corner of his eye, he saw Kennedy draw her weapon and cover his back.

The receptionist escaped into the office.

The manager reached for his handgun.

His intuition kicked in. Finn shot him twice in his chest. The people running toward them had to be private security. They were about to be outnumbered.

"Take cover," Finn yelled at Kennedy.

He dived over the reception desk and was gratified when Kennedy landed on the hard-stone tiles next to him.

He readied his weapon, but the barrage of bullets forced him to stay down. They were showered with hunks of drywall, wood, and granite. He threw himself over Kennedy.

"Huh." Pieces of debris pounded him, nicking his body. He covered his head. Then a sharp pain stabbed at his arm. A ten-inch piece of wood had impaled his left bicep.

Kennedy shoved him to the side, her Glock 22 drawn. He could tell she was shooting by the recoil of her weapon, but couldn't hear anything above the noise.

He grabbed his police radio. "This is FBI Special Agent Callaghan. We're under fire. Repeat, we're under fire."

CHAPTER THIRTY-FIVE

Michael's estimation of his stepdad had just shot up a thousand-fold. It was obvious Milo was in pain by his pallor and the sheen of sweat that covered his face. He gritted his teeth against the effort it took to control the helicopter. And yet he still managed to swoop between the buildings of Granite City with a precision that spoke of his years of service in the US Airforce.

Michael pulled the rifle from the bag and wedged it between the seats. "I'll leave this in case you need it. "We're looking for a rectangle, about a mile east of the square." He pointed the way, drawing on the aerial view he'd researched on his computer.

His breath lodged in his throat as the building came into sight. Ava and his mom were waving at them. Sinclair stood behind what looked like a square piece of sheet metal, firing at some unknown assailant who was behind a closed door.

They seemed to be trying to get onto the roof, and she was the only thing stopping them.

He said a silent prayer of thanks that she was with his mom and sister. Up until this point, he hadn't been sure they were being held together. It felt as if he'd been kicked in the chest as a chaotic mix of emotions flooded him. He was relieved that everyone was alive. At the same time, he was overwhelmed with fear for them. They were obviously under attack, and this could still go sideways. He was also so damn proud of Sinclair. She was a badass who would go down fighting to protect those in her care, and in this instance, that meant his family.

"You see that?" Milo's voice quivered, telling him his stepfather was not unaffected by the scene unfolding below them. He landed the helicopter on the roof of the building with a bounce, a reminder that he was still recovering and he wasn't as clearheaded as he should be.

Michael took off his earmuffs and jumped out.

Ava threw her arms around him, followed by his mom. "I knew you would come."

He untangled them, not wanting to waste time on a reunion. He loved them, but he had to get to Sinclair. "Go."

Gunfire reverberated across the rooftop, reminding him she was still holding back the assailants.

His mom gripped his hand. The pain in her gaze made her concern tangible.

"We'll be right behind," he promised. There was no way he would leave without the woman he loved. He shoved his mom and sister, propelling them toward the helo. Then he raced to Sinclair's position.

Another volley rang out from behind the door, forcing him to leap to the rear of the air conditioning unit. He landed so close to her he almost knocked her down.

"It's time to go," he shouted, pushing himself into a sitting position so his back was against the metal. They weren't the words of love he wanted to say, but this wasn't the time.

"Agreed." She twisted to the far edge of their shelter and fired at the door. Then she sat and drew another weapon from her belt. "I only have ten bullets left."

He held up both handguns Tim had provided. "Your ride awaits."

She gave him a sideways glance and smiled. "One, two, three…"

They both stood together and shot at the door, laying down a barrage of gunfire. He stepped toward the helicopter and was pleased when she followed.

They continued moving, all the while firing, preventing the guards from coming through the door.

Finally, her pistol clicked but no sound came out. "Empty."

He grabbed her hand and ran, forcing her into

the rear of the helo first. In his peripheral vision, his mom, who was in the front passenger seat, raised the rifle. He'd left it for Milo and had no idea if she knew how to use it.

She shot repeatedly, providing them with cover. He buried his surprise and shock at her ability. There would be time to ask later.

Milo took off and immediately leaned the aircraft to the right, presumably to get them out of range.

Michael rolled, taking Sinclair with him. He held her in his arms. She was safe. The terror that had been curled in his gut began to dissolve.

His mom slammed her door closed. Ava, who was buckled in, did the same with the rear door. The whup-whup of the rotors quietened somewhat.

Sinclair pushed herself up onto her elbow and smiled down at him. "A helicopter. That's a new one. What made you think of it?"

"Some gang in Montreal used a helo in a prison break. And it just so happens we have a pilot in the family." He brushed a thumb over a fresh scratch on her cheek. The bruises on her face were now green with a yellow tinge and were still swollen. "I owe you an apology. I'm an idiot. I get too caught up in my work. I promise you I will never ignore you again."

She grabbed his shirt, tugging him closer. "Yes, you will. It's who you are. But at least you had my back."

"Always." He covered her mouth with his. A familiar feeling of warmth came over him. It wasn't just about sex. Okay, some of it was about sex because he was still a man. But it was so much more than that. He hoped one day soon she would see they belonged together. They always had.

CHAPTER
THIRTY-SIX

Ethan smiled as he entered Lucy's office without knocking. He'd managed to make it out of the Sun Down just before the police surrounded the building. He planned on leaving Granite City tonight, but not before he dealt with a few loose ends.

Lucy lay on her desk with her skirt shoved up to her waist and her blouse open, revealing her breasts. Her stocking-clad legs were wrapped around the computer geek's backside. Tyler still wore all his clothes except his pants, which were pooled around his ankles. Sweat dripped from his brow as he pumped away, servicing his queen. Both of them seemed to be engrossed in their sex act.

Ethan's stomach heaved at the sight of her. He didn't find her repulsive because she liked sex and indulged at every opportunity. In his opinion, all consenting adults were welcome to do whatever they wanted, as long as it didn't harm anyone else. But Lucy used people for her own pleasure. It was as though she saw other humans as toys for her amusement.

He positioned himself behind Tyler, who glanced his way and then refocused on gratifying Lucy. *No small feat.*

"Do you mind, bro?" the kid mumbled.

In other circumstances, Ethan might have backed off and let him have his grand finale, but there was something that had been bothering him, and he needed to satisfy his curiosity.

He unsheathed his blade and held it to the geek's throat.

"What the fuck?" Tyler stopped what he was doing.

"Tell me about Papin's virus." Ethan could almost smell the blood pounding through the runt's veins. His own heartbeat kicked up a notch in anticipation.

The kid's Adam's apple bobbed. "I think he planted it when he was pretending to be Spider, and then he—"

Ethan dug the sharp tip of his knife into Tyler's skin. "The truth."

"I am telling the truth."

Lucy had disengaged from Tyler and was now sitting on her desk, facing them. Her eyes narrowed into two slits. She was interested in the answer, which worked in his favor.

He jabbed the knife a little deeper and then

ran his finger across the wound, allowing blood to collect on his hand. He almost groaned as the metallic smell made his nerve endings come alive. He held up his bloody fingers for Tyler to see. "Did Papin really activate it?"

Tyler tried to shake his head but couldn't manage the movement without nudging the blade deeper. "N-n-no. I did."

Lucy bared her teeth as her hands fisted. "Why did you do that?"

"Papin was the agent who sent me to prison for hacking into the Pentagon. Do you know what it was like for me in there? I couldn't get to him. I didn't have the resources, but you do. Besides, I was doing you a favor. He was going to come back and get you eventually. It was only a matter of time." Tyler clasped his hands together, pleading with Lucy. "Please, don't let him kill me. I did it for you."

Ethan smiled. Tyler was such a pathetic figure. His butt was naked, his dick was limp, and he thought she was in charge. It hadn't occurred to him that Ethan was the one who was actually in control.

"That's all I needed to know." He grabbed Tyler's chin and drew his blade across, slicing his carotid artery.

Ethan licked his lips and shivered as a wave of pleasure shot through his body. He would've liked to toy with Tyler, but this wasn't the time to play. He fixed his gaze on Lucy.

She jumped off her desk, shifting out of the way, as Tyler's body slumped forward. She stood facing Ethan. Her hands trembled as she struggled with the buttons of the blouse, as if doing them up could protect her. "Did you have to kill him here? This mess will be hell for the cleaners."

He closed the space between them and, using one hand, grabbed her by the neck. He forced her back until her spine hit the wall. Then he placed the point of the KA-BAR against her ribs.

"Please, Ethan. I have money. I can pay." Her unblinking eyes bulged, and her lips quivered. Her hands gripped his arm as she tried to loosen his hold.

"I don't remember my last name, but I know my first name is Ethan. I don't know where I was born or where I lived before I was taken." He was surprised at how calm and restrained he sounded.

She stilled. Maybe she wanted to listen to him, or perhaps she realized the futility of her situation.

"I think I was around three or four when I was bundled into the back seat of the car. The man, who called himself Father, dyed my hair and made me change my clothes. I cried when Father told me my parents didn't want me anymore and had given me to him."

He tightened his grip, blocking her airway, enjoying the knowledge that he could kill her with his bare hands. "That first night is burned into my brain like a tattoo, a memory that won't wear off."

When she made a choking sound, he relaxed his fingers. He wasn't ready for her to die yet.

She gasped for breath, inhaling large lungfuls of air. Once she was sufficiently recovered, she said, "I can help you find your family. I have money, resources—"

"It's too late." With a flick of his hand, he made a small incision in her ribcage. Not so deep that he hit bone but enough she could feel it.

She squealed and gave a slight shake of her head, which was all she could manage with him pinning her to the wall. From the vacant look in her eyes, it was obvious she didn't understand.

"As an adult, I knew Father had lied about my parents, but children believe what grown-ups tell them. Now, there's no going back. The years of rape and abuse destroyed the good man I might have been and turned me into the monster you see before you. That's why Father was my first victim." He nicked her again.

"I was fifteen when he told me I would be handed over to another man who preferred older boys. It's funny... I always thought the term 'seeing red' was just a saying, but I actually remember a red mist as rage washed over me. It was all I could see. I grabbed a steak knife from the kitchen counter and lashed out. I stabbed him again and again. "He slashed her stomach.

"Even now, after all these years, I derive immense satisfaction from the memory."

"I-I-I'm sorry." Tears streamed down her face. He knew she wasn't really sorry, not for him, anyway.

He moved his knife up to her cheek, making another small nick. "You're a bad girl, Lucy. You've been living off the suffering of others, and I can't let it continue. It has to end. Tell me who the Trainer is."

"I don't know."

He scored an X across her chin and inhaled deeply. The scent flooded him with warmth.

"Please." She wept, tears streaming down her face, streaking her makeup.

"Does the Trainer know about your human trafficking business?"

She hiccupped. "Yes. All the customers are Syndicate members.

"All this time, I've been working for a bunch of rapists?"

Her eyes held a distant look of shock, and she didn't seem able to respond.

Using the hand that was wrapped around her throat, he gave her a shake. "I'm going to burn it all down. I will destroy everything the Syndicate have built, and I will kill every one of them. Starting with you."

"Please, you don't have to—"

"No, I don't have to, but I will." He slid his blade between her ribs so it pierced her heart. He stepped back, allowing her body to slump to the ground as he was rocked with another surge of euphoria. Once it was over, he breathed deeply as he observed Lucy's body, lying in a crumpled heap on the floor.

It was a quicker death than she deserved. He would've liked more time to play, but he would have to move quickly if he didn't want to get caught standing over the body with a bloody knife in his hand. He wasn't sure if the Syndicate would suspect him in Lucy's death. Which could be a problem, but he had a backup ID ready should he need it. The Trainer would demand answers and, unlike Lucy, he wouldn't be put off with stories about a bad burrito.

He probably had less than twelve hours before the shit hit the proverbial fan. He needed to be ready and organized in case he had to make an exit. But before he left, he had one last job to do.

CHAPTER THIRTY-SEVEN

Sinclair marched into the Dumb Luck Café with Michael by her side. She had been questioned repeatedly by Detective Ramirez of the Granite City-Elkhead County Police. They had wanted every detail and had asked her to account for every second of her confinement. She'd done her best to comply.

By the time they were finished with her, she was tired and achy. Above all, she'd wanted to see Michael, to hold him and once again enjoy the sensation that she belonged.

She also needed to thank Finn, who had been injured when he'd created a distraction in the lobby.

But before she could leave, Ramirez had asked her to confirm Jake's identity before they made an arrest. She was happy to comply. Shockingly, he hadn't taken off after he'd drugged her and the Sun Down had been raided. Was he so greedy that he wanted to continue to use Child Seekers to grow his bank account? Or maybe he hadn't heard the news and thought he was safe.

The coffee house was basically a rectangle with one corner carved out as a serving space, which meant the seating area was an L shape.

Michael grabbed her hand and tugged her toward a table in the corner away from Ramirez and his fellow officers who sat on the opposite side. "If we sit here, he won't be able to see you from the door."

"That's a good idea." She was still shaken by what happened. She'd known Michael would come for Nadie and Ava, but he had refused to leave without her. Which shouldn't be a surprise because he was a good man. For him, that was a normal reaction, but it meant so much to her. She hadn't realized how isolated she'd become in the last year. Reconnecting with Michael had opened her eyes. She didn't want to walk through life alone. At the same time, she couldn't give up her work at Child Seekers. How could she turn her back on all that suffering?

Ramirez waved at her from across the room, telling her he was aware they were in position. He had arranged for Amy to call Jake, telling him someone wanted to share a lead. Apparently, Jake had refused to meet with the informant unless they were in a public place, which was standard operating procedure but still a pain.

Every single muscle in Sinclair's body tensed

as she waited. Why had Jake betrayed them? All Child Seekers workers, whether they were volunteers or paid employees, went through extensive background checks. Had he always been corrupt? Had she driven him to it? Although she couldn't recall his exact words when he'd drugged her, she did remember the hate that had oozed out of him, like a dark, evil entity from a horror movie.

Michael brushed a strand of hair out of her face. "Don't think about it." He cupped her neck, forcing her to look at him. She twisted, trying to turn.

He placed his forehead against hers. "Hush. Don't struggle. There's a guy with a gray moustache looking around."

"Tell me when I can turn." Even if she couldn't talk to him, she wanted to look him in the eye and watch his arrest.

Michael nodded and leaned back. "He's approaching the counter. Turn now."

She stood and spun around.

On the other side of the room, Ramirez jumped to his feet.

Jake stared at her for a minute. He seemed too stunned to move.

"That's him," Sinclair shouted.

Detective Ramirez sprang, ramming his gun into Jake's ribs so hard he almost lifted him off the ground.

"Jake Cox, I'm charging you with second degree assault and kidnapping in the first degree." Ramirez held Jake up against the counter while another officer with blond hair and a pock-marked face cuffed him. "You are also charged with filing a fake report in the break and enter at Child Seeker's International. You have the right..."

She grinned. As an ex-cop, he would suffer in prison, and he deserved every second of it. Part of her wanted to punch him in the face and smash him until he was nothing, but it was probably better if she let the cops do their thing.

Michael held her hand. "Are you ready?"

She would let the authorities deal with the fallout. She needed some well-earned rest. "Let's go and see Finn."

They walked out hand in hand.

CHAPTER THIRTY-EIGHT

Finn sat in a curtained cubicle of the emergency room, waiting for the doctor to tell him he could go home.

A tiny dark-haired woman wearing a white lab coat entered. "It took a lot of work to get the wound cleaned. That stick fragmented into tiny splinters. We think we got it all. You'll be on antibiotics for a while. And you'll need to check in with your doctor."

"But it was just my arm." He held up his injured limb and immediately regretted it as a throb of pain forced him to lower it.

She stared at him as though he was an idiot. "You damaged your muscle. That's going to take a while to heal."

"How long's a while? Weeks?"

"Months?" She held out several pieces of paper. "Here's your prescription and something for the pain. I also jotted down some instructions about caring for your injury so you don't forget."

"I won't need the pain meds. Over the counter stuff will work fine."

She made a humph sound, tugged the curtain aside, and left.

Kennedy waved at him. She must've been waiting on the other side of the screen.

He beckoned her closer as he tried to get his bandaged arm into his bloody and ragged shirt.

She clutched the fabric of the sleeve and tore it. "What the…?" He stopped complaining. There was no point. His shirt was ruined. He was going to have to throw it away anyway, so it didn't matter.

She took over the task of doing up the buttons. There were dark circles under her eyes. Her thick, lush hair was down, and there was a bruise on her chin.

He pointed to her face. "You're hurt, too."

She shook her head and took a step back, having finished her chore. "It's nothing."

He felt like a fool. Here he was receiving all this fuss over a stick, and she was just as beaten up. His concern wasn't just about her physical state. He was also worried about the effects of trauma. They'd walked into that hotel, knowing they would come under fire. As her superior, and her partner, he was responsible for her safety. "Deluca will have my badge for this."

She shook her head and gave a humorless

chuckle. "For the Sun Down? Not a chance. The FBI is sending the Child Exploitation and Human Trafficking Task force to go through their records and talk to the victims. They found a wealth of files that suggest it's part of a global operation."

"Sinclair and the others?" God, he was tired. He couldn't remember the last time he'd slept in his own bed.

"They're safe, as are the twenty women who were rescued. We did good." Her gaze didn't meet his.

"What aren't you telling me?"

Her eyes widened and then narrowed, which told him she was surprised by his question but still didn't want to answer.

"I'll find out eventually," he pressed.

"We're both on administrative leave, and your story is all over the news."

"We knew that would happen." The knowledge that his personal life was being sensationalized in the public arena was a kick in the pants, but he'd been mentally preparing for it. The only shock was that the Syndicate had sat on the information for as long as they had.

He eased off the bed. "They might want us to take a break after being involved in a shootout." That was probably the official explanation, but with everything going on, it was more likely they were sidelining him to evaluate his actions. He wasn't sure how he'd come out of the investigation that was bound to follow. He just hoped Kennedy was spared.

She met his stride as he made his way to the exit. "The others are waiting outside."

"Others?" He gave her a sideways glance. If by "others" she meant his superiors at the FBI, then he was leaving by the back door. He didn't want to talk to them until he'd had some sleep and his mind was clear.

She smiled. "Michael, Sinclair, David, and Tim."

"Oh." Them he could handle.

The minute he left the ward, Tim said, "Finn, you were hospitalized for a splinter. I guess FBI agents aren't as tough as they used to be."

Everyone laughed, him included.

Sinclair hugged him. "Thanks for everything."

He was surprised by her show of affection, but hugged her back. "You're welcome. Are you okay?"

Before she could answer, Michael thrust a folded piece of paper into his pocket and leaned in close, whispering in Finn's ear, "This is a list of all the members of the Syndicate. There are no other copies except for the one in my head."

He was amazed the Syndicate had taken so long to see Michael as a threat and move against him. Which had worked in his friend's favor. That time had given him an opportunity to recover, and judging by the way he held Sinclair's hand, he'd obviously managed to persuade her to take a chance on him.

The group made their way through the exit and out into the parking lot. It felt good to breathe in the cool night air and rid himself of the antiseptic smell that permeated the emergency room. "You should all lay low for a while."

"I have a bolt hole," David announced. "After everything that happened with Marie, we thought it would be a good idea."

Tim frowned. "I'm not that organized. I might be able to persuade Dana and Logan to camp in the mountains, but it'll be tough. She's the police chief and Logan has school. How long do you think it will take for things to calm down?"

Michael cleared his throat. "It could be a while."

Or forever. That thought appeared in Finn's mind out of nowhere.

CHAPTER THIRTY-NINE

Finn sighed as he unlocked the door to his apartment. All he wanted to do was take a shower, go to bed, and sleep for at least twelve hours, maybe longer.

His place wasn't upmarket or stylish. The décor was dated with way too much beige for his taste, but it was clean.

The vacuum had been moved and there were tracks in the rug. He was instantly alert, his senses going into overdrive. Someone was in his home. He always vacuumed the carpet before he left the house, brushing the pile in the same direction, so if anyone walked through, he would be able to see their footprints. Then he placed the appliance against the door so anyone entering would have to push it out of the way.

He drew his weapon and silently cursed because his arm hurt like a bitch. Ignoring the pain, he entered. First, he cleared the galley kitchen to the right and then the bathroom on the left. He inched along the short hallway, listening. The hall emptied into a living room, which was square in shape. From this angle, he could tell there was no one on the far side of the room, but there was a blind spot, one corner he couldn't see.

"I'm not here to kill you." Ethan Moore strolled into the middle of the room, his arms raised. "I'm here to say goodbye and to tell you I will be in touch."

"I don't understand." The morning light was behind Moore, so his face was shadowed, which made it impossible for Finn to read his responses.

"I've left the Syndicate."

Still holding his Glock on the assassin, Finn crept around him, forcing the suspect to turn. "Leaving them doesn't absolve you of murder."

Ethan smiled, his mouth turning up as his eyes lit. It was a genuine reaction. "No, it doesn't. I'll admit I enjoy killing, but I never would have worked for them if I'd known about the slavery."

He didn't seem like a demonstrative man who would communicate with big gestures, but he made small movements with his hands as he talked. His body faced Finn. Similarly, his feet weren't turned toward the door. If someone wanted to leave, their feet normally pointed the way. That wasn't the case here. Ethan was exactly where he wanted to be, which made sense considering he'd broken into Finn's apartment.

"They crossed a line, your line. That's why you helped Michael get his family back."

He nodded. "Yes."

Finn hadn't lowered his handgun, but he also hadn't put the cuffs on him. "Who's in charge?"

"I'm not sure. My contact was known as the Trainer." Once again, Ethan's hands moved when he talked.

"The Trainer?" That was a strange name for a boss unless... "As in a sports team?"

He shrugged. "Years ago, I worked for a group of businessmen who formed a syndicate to buy a racehorse."

"This is a different group from the Syndicate?" He used air quotes when he said "the Syndicate."

"Yes, but they work in the same way."

"Are you saying the Syndicate are a group of businessmen who have an individual who's their racehorse, and they are preparing them for... what? Politics? A political race?" That would make sense with their connection to the Global Democratic Coalition.

Ethan shrugged. "I've always believed any politician could be bought or blackmailed, which is why I've never had to kill one."

As cynical as that viewpoint was, it did make sense. "Then it would have to be someone high up in the justice department or maybe a judge."

Ethan shrugged. "Or some other government official with power."

The DOJ would make the most sense because money already manipulated politics, but the system of law and order was independent.

"I'm not here to discuss all the crazy possibilities with you." He pointed a finger at his temple and drew circles in the air as he took two steps back.

"Why then?" Finn glanced down. At some time during their conversation, he had lowered his weapon. He didn't raise it.

"Taking out the Sun Down hurt them. They'll come after you now."

"They already did. I'm all over the news, and I'm on leave. My career is over."

"I wouldn't be surprised if they go after your friends. I was expecting to get the order to take out Papin months ago when he ruined my plans at Molly's Mountain."

"But the order never came?"

"No, Ackerman was the one who wanted him dead, and he was out of the picture." He took another step back.

Finn closed the distance between them. He couldn't let Ethan leave without answers. "So why come after him now?"

"One of Lucy's computer geek's, a guy named Tyler, found the virus dormant in the system and activated it. Papin had put him in prison, and he knew it would force the Syndicate to hunt Papin down."

"Tyler," Finn repeated the name and then said, "What's his last name? We need to bring him in for questioning."

"He's dead." Ethan smiled.

Once again, it was a genuine response, which made ice trickle down Finn's back. This guy really enjoyed slaughtering people. "Did Lucy Portman have him killed?"

The creepy grin widened. "No. She's dead, too."

"Be a witness for us. We can protect you." As soon as he said the words, he realized he was lying. Not necessarily to Moore, but to himself. All the agencies under the Department of Justice were compromised. He'd served on the side of law and order for all his adult life. First as military police with the US Army and later with the FBI. The Syndicate were shitting on his life.

Ethan laughed and then said, "Liar. How many witnesses have you lost? You can't even protect yourself. Sooner or later, they will come for you and your friends."

"Special Agent Morris?"

"Everyone." He turned and headed for the front door.

"Shit." Finn didn't try to stop him. He holstered his sidearm and retrieved his phone from his pocket. He had to call Kennedy to warn her.

There was no way he'd get any sleep tonight.

CHAPTER FORTY

Sinclair stopped on the thin mountain trail to adjust the straps on her backpack. They weren't digging in, but it was heavy, and the weight of it was hurting her back. Michael did the same. The scent of pine needles hung in the early evening air. The sun slanted across the peaks, creating long evening shadows. It wasn't expected to snow yet, but the forecast predicted a cold front. They'd packed plenty of layers, some waterproof gear, and lots of food. They were prepared to stay up here for a while.

"Do you think Nadie, Milo, and Ava will be okay?" She started walking again, picking her way along the thin woodland trail.

"I thought Ava would be the problem, but she loves the idea of spending an extended vacation in Vancouver." He wasn't out of breath or fatigued in any way.

"What about her boyfriend, Caleb? Did she make a fuss about leaving him?"

"She knows the reason they were captured is

because she called him. I think that knowledge has helped her grow up and put things in perspective."

"Do you think Vancouver is the best choice?"

"I do. Everyone knows everyone in a small town, and a multi-race couple won't stand out in a big metropolis."

She had never considered Milo and Nadie a diverse couple. Just as she never thought about Michael as being Native American. She loved him because of who he was. All the other stuff didn't matter.

The forest gave way to a clearing, and her she-shed came into view. She'd chosen a flat piece of land next to a small stream. The cabin was built on a ten-foot-high platform to keep wildlife out. It was accessed by a ladder, which was hoisted up when she was in the house and was left lying on the ground when she was away.

"Wow, you thought of everything." Michael stared at the structure. "Is that a glass front door?"

"Yeah, David bitched about getting it up here, but it was worth it." She was always filled with a sense of pride whenever she visited. In every way that mattered, this was home. She'd designed it, built it, and decorated it. Her brother had helped her, but Michael was the only person she wanted to share it with.

She pointed to a cache that was about two hundred yards away. It was just a small hut and, like the living quarters, it was on stilts. "That's for food storage, and it's also my cooking area.

He nodded, smiling. "This place is awesome. What do you want to do, rest and then make dinner, or eat first?"

"I think we should eat first. Once I lie down, I might just stay there."

She started a campfire in the designated cooking area, opened a can of soup, and set it to heat over the grate. Michael explored the place, stored the food, stowed their gear in their quarters, and plugged in Marie's portable solar panel so they'd have power.

They ate their meal in silence around the fire. She had no idea what he was thinking, but she was a mess. So much had happened in such a short time. They'd gone from being friends to lovers. Although, if she was honest with herself, she'd never thought of him as being just a friend. It seemed as though she'd been in love with him forever and was only now coming to terms with that truth.

Once they were done washing their dishes, they retired to the she-shed. She collapsed onto the double bed.

He stretched beside her, yawned, and then said. "I like that you have a composting toilet and a sink."

"Me, too. I'm girly enough that indoor plumbing is important."

He rolled on his side to face her. "Listen, we

have to talk."

"Oh, God." She tensed, and her heart stilled. Those words were always followed by bad news.

He lay on his back, not looking at her, as he gazed through the window at the setting sun. "I called your boss at Child Seekers."

"You did what?" she screeched.

"I told her who I was, my history and qualifications, and that I would like to be your new partner when you go back to work."

"You called my boss?" Her mind was numb. She didn't know whether to be happy because he wanted to work with her or mad because they hadn't discussed it.

"I also said I'd like to be assigned to the Native American community to track down the missing women."

His announcement stunned the anger out of her. He'd been running from his heritage for years, and now he was finally being responsible. "You're taking Grandma Pelle's advice."

"Yes, it's time I grew up and used my experience to help my people. But if you don't want this, if you'd rather have a different partner and be employed abroad, just say. I'm not trying to ambush you. I just didn't want them to hire someone else and have you end up with another partner like Jake. That bastard told the Syndicate where and when to attack you and then staged the break in at your office to divert suspicion away from himself."

If there had been any trace of irritation left, it disappeared. He wasn't trying to take over her life; he just wanted to keep her safe. After everything that had happened, knowing someone she could trust was covering her back was a relief. As much as she hated to admit it, the ease with which Jake had drugged her had left her feeling vulnerable. For the first time, she hadn't looked forward to doing her job, but with Michael caring for her, she knew she'd be safe. "I like the sound of that, but I'm a linguist. If Child seekers needs me to work abroad, then I'll go." She was grateful he wanted to protect her, but she couldn't allow him to dictate her career. "And for future reference, life-changing decisions are things we should discuss together."

He smiled, revealing his dimple. "You mean like a real couple? Maybe we should discuss our relationship."

She sat, making the bed bounce. She'd really walked into that one. She stared down at him, expecting to see him gloat, but his mouth was pressed into a thin line and he wouldn't meet her gaze.

He punched his pillow a couple of times and then lay back down, finally making eye contact. "This...us...it can never be casual for me. I love you. I'm not going to pretend I don't, and I won't lie about it. I know I have issues. I block people out. I need to work on that. And I probably don't deserve another shot, but that's what I'm asking for."

He was putting his heart on the line, taking a risk, which was something she had been too cowardly to do. Burying her emotions, even from herself, was ridiculous because it didn't change how she felt. It just made her a fool. When she'd been kidnapped, she'd thought she'd never see him again, and now she'd been given a second chance. She couldn't throw it away. He was willing to try and make this—them—work, and that was all she could ask of him.

"I love you, too." A weight lifted off her chest. Declaring her feelings aloud was a liberating experience.

He frowned. "What about all that 'I don't do relationships' stuff?"

She smiled, straddled him, and buried her fingers in his short, thick hair. "I can make an exception just this once. Besides, we aren't in a relationship."

"We're not?"

"We're in love."

Sign up for Marlow's newsletter and you'll receive two Gathering Storm stories

You'll also be notified of sales, giveaways and new releases.
You can unsubscribe at any time.
https://www.subscribepage.com/marlowkelly